TO THE BONES

VALERIE NIEMAN

TO THE BONES

a novel

WEST VIRGINIA UNIVERSITY PRESS · MORGANTOWN 2019

ISBN:
Paper 978-1-946684-98-1
Ebook 978-1-946684-99-8

Library of Congress Cataloging-in-Publication Data
Names: Nieman, Valerie, 1955- author.
Title: To the bones / Valerie Nieman.
Description: First edition. | Morgantown : West Virginia University Press, 2019.
Identifiers: LCCN 2018040365 | ISBN 9781946684981 (pbk.)
Subjects: LCSH: West Virginia--Fiction. | GSAFD: Mystery fiction.
Classification: LCC PS3564.I355 T68 2019 | DDC 813/.54--dc23
LC record available at https://lccn.loc.gov/2018040365

Book and cover design by Than Saffel / WVU Press

An earlier version of Chapter 3 previously appeared in *Monkeybicycle* (2018).

For the readers, always.

For the writers who helped shape this book: Kevin Rippin, who got it started and saw it through; and Al Sirois, Shymala Dason, James Tate Hill, and Grace Marcus, who offered their wise insights.

For Fred Chappell, Sue Farlow, and Marjorie Hudson for constant support, and Abby Freeland, who believed in this book.

Horrible smell. Dark. Cold.

This is how it feels to be dead.

Darrick raised his head and immediately vomited. The nausea came in waves, at every motion of his battered head, echoed by his back, ribs, legs. If he was dead, and this was the afterlife, then it seriously sucked.

He breathed in through his mouth, but it didn't help much. The smell. He tried moving his left leg, numb and twisted under him, and was surprised when it responded. The pressure on his knee eased. He rolled over, put his hands down to push himself to all fours, and his fingers slid in something greasy and vile. If this was the afterlife, then it wasn't one he'd been prepared for, by catechism classes or college philosophy.

Dark. He shook with the cold and the dark.

Then I'm not dead.

He crawled, carefully anchoring his knees into the sloping ground, pausing whenever the nausea roiled his gut. Unsteady rocks shifted under his knees, and he heard a skittering sound.

The last thing he remembered, he had been driving. A two-lane road, the trees so close, an inky tunnel pierced by his headlights.

Maybe the car went off the road.

Maybe you're buried, his unpleasant thoughts mocked.

There was a faint lessening of the gloom ahead. He kept crawling, sticks rolling under his hand. Something chitinous and leggy moved across his fingers. He pulled his hand away, then put it back down. The thin gray light increased. He could see that, if not much else with his glasses gone.

And his shoes were gone, too, the toes of his socks dragging across the damp rocks.

He seemed to hear things breathing nearby. Waiting.

No one's coming back for you. Ever.

He crawled around a ragged corner and the light became a crack in the sky, a white intensity that squeezed shut his eyes and made the back of his head spasm in pain. He opened his eyes just enough to see a hazy field of rocks and debris. A dump. He picked up a large round object and brought it close to his weak eyes. A pair of empty eyeholes stared back. He flung the skull away, hearing it crack and roll to a stop, and he realized those rocks and sticks were bones and that he was among the dead.

He looked up at the light. It was quite far away. A ragged slit. The opening of a cavern? A mass grave? Had all these dead just stumbled down from the surface like mastodons marching into a tar pit?

Darrick crept forward until the space ended at a wall of crumbling rocks. He crawled back to what seemed to be the center of the space. He patted his pockets. Coat, cell phone, wallet, keys—gone. Medication gone. He began to weep. The easiest thing would be to lay back down and let the process continue, until he became bones as well. Just fall asleep.

Can't fall asleep. He could remember the infirmary nurse singing in a language he didn't understand. "You have a concussion, little *mausi*. If you sleep, you may die. I will tell you the story of the brave knight but you must stay awake for the whole story." All the night and the next day, the nurse had kept him from sleep.

I'm not dying here.

A gleam of something in the charnel caught his attention. He lifted it, but a chain held it to the skeleton. It was a locket, a heart-shaped locket. He let it slide back.

He had been driving. Late. Low on gas. The lights along the exit ramp ended and the trees closed in. For mile after mile.

He put his hands back into the muck and rot, and in a methodical way began to search for a way out. He crawled away from the locket until he came to a wall of sticky earth. Digging only brought down more dirt. He crawled back, turned left. The ground tilted downward—that was where he'd come from. A current of dank air rose from an even deeper place.

He made his way back. This time, he saw the flash of light on a lens. His glasses, one stem broken off. He settled them on his nose and felt infinitely reassured, for a moment, to be able to see—until he counted four skulls, and saw insects working in the flesh of a recent body. It was the one with the necklace. This time he yanked at the necklace once, twice, three times until it came free, the body settling back on a wave of carrion smell. He slid it in his pants pocket, proof of something, to someone—maybe to himself when he woke up to find no necklace, no bones, nothing but the rags of a dream.

Turn right.

This time, his progress ended at a rocky wall. He began to lever himself up, toward that ragged sky both close and distant, but when he grabbed hold of a rock, it pulled out and sent him sprawling backward. He needed something to anchor, something to climb with.

Darrick searched among the bones and found a femur. And another. He smashed them between stones until the knobby knee-ends broke off into splintered points. He jabbed them into the rotten rock and began to climb.

He emerged into an open area with a scattering of bare trees. Traces of snow clung to brown grass and fallen leaves crisp with frost. A thin, cold wind sliced through his damp shirt. *My new parka. Shit.* Though he turned around, slowly, he could see nothing beyond the hollow field draining toward that crack in the ground. The movement nauseated him, his head hammered, and his mouth tasted like a sewer. He retched again. Nothing came but acid water.

Darrick picked the downhill side of the declivity to climb. He staggered through the frozen leaves and fallen branches, his socks (soaked with mud and God-knows-what) chilling his feet. His injuries and the exertion to get out of the hole had triggered a recurrence of the episodic ataxia he'd had since childhood, causing his unsteady, lurching gait.

He reached the top of the hill and looked down into more trees, including a thick stand of pines. No houses to be seen, no smoke or sound of traffic. A shiny barbed-wire fence was strung just below the summit on metal fence posts set a regulation distance apart. He saw the blank back side of a sign. He lost a little blood and a good bit of dignity on the stretched wire in making his way to the other side.

KAVANAGH COAL AND LIMESTONE
PRIVATE PROPERTY
KEEP OUT!
PATROLLED BY ARMED SECURITY GUARDS

The fence extended in both directions, up and down the rugged hills, with signs at regular intervals.

Darrick heard water flowing. *A river down there, somewhere. And maybe a road.* He descended into the deep green enclosure of the pine woods, out the other side. The land began to flatten out. Signs of civilization appeared—a discarded washing machine, rusty barrels, then a dirt road. A thick smell of chemicals and rot tainted the air. As he angled toward the road, he heard the mutter of a stream over rocks, then saw the flash of water. Thirst caught him by the throat. He didn't care where that water came from, it was water. He saw some trailers but heard no sound, nothing but moving water and the shriek of a startled bird. It was some sort of camp, a scatter of travel trailers and a small store advertising bait and soft drinks. But no lights, no sounds. When he reached the road and saw the river, he knew why.

The river was filled bank to bank with orange glop, a cold, stinking lava that stuck to the bottom and the rocks. The remains of dead fish poked through the frozen ooze. He closed his eyes. When he looked again, the scene was the same. He didn't know anything much about West Virginia, a place he had occasionally crossed on the interstate, but this couldn't be normal. The sign touting RED WIGGLERS, CRAWLERS, CRICKETS, FATHEAD MINNIES was recently painted. He tried the door of the shack, peered through the Plexiglas window. He saw tanks, with rafts of small fish caught in a film of ice.

Darrick tried the doors on a couple of the trailers. At the third one, he forgot niceties, put his shoulder to the flimsy vinyl and pushed his way inside. A box of sugary breakfast cereal was still on the table. He tried the light switch, expecting—and getting—nothing, then the water taps. The hiss of nothing. He opened the tiny refrigerator and was slammed with the smell of abandoned food, but he knelt and poked through, finding two sodas, a juice box, and half a pint of cheap bourbon. He chugged the juice and one of the sodas. Then he staggered to the bed, got under the mildewed covers and pulled them as close as he could around his shaking frame.

He woke stiff, aching, hungry. His head pounded, and when he tried to raise it, the pillow came with it. He pulled it away from his head, his body rising involuntarily at the pain, and then, when he saw how it was matted with blood and skin and hair, threw it across the space.

The rags of a dream stuck to his thoughts, merged with what might have been memory. *Why had I gotten off the interstate there?* He'd missed the opportunity to get gas earlier, rejecting an off-brand place isolated on a hillside. With the needle dropping, he took an exit with no name, just a road number, and the logo for a convenience store. A long drive through black woods, a twisting road, one car, no houses. *Shouldn't there be banjoes?* Finally, the lights of the store. Gas, Groceries, Grill.

He drifted back to sleep.

All a dream, the whole thing, it had to be.

He had pumped gas and pulled his car up to the front, gone in to get something to eat. Two little tables. He ordered a grilled-cheese sandwich and a caffeine-free Coke. The woman behind the counter was cordial at first, smiling as she asked him with a nasal twang, did he want chips or fries? A sheriff's deputy came in, got coffee and didn't pay for it. He remembered that, how the deputy stood around, went out to his cruiser, and then came back. Something about how he looked at the woman.

"Ready," she called as she slapped the paper plate down on the counter, her tone surly, smile gone.

He remembered eating. The deputy was gone. He finished his chips, which were stale. The woman didn't look up from the bill as she gave him change. It wasn't a dream, or it was a dream that was also a memory. Darrick huddled under the blankets, revolted at the stink of decay and death, at the memory of the rock becoming a skull in his hand. He pushed and tugged at the darkness, trying to uncover what had happened.

The trailer was getting dark. He was hungry, therefore, he must be alive. Fighting his stiffness and pain, Darrick got up and scavenged for food. The cupboards had microwave popcorn, oatmeal, cans of Beanee Weenees and Vienna sausages.

Not dead yet, he thought, *but these things might kill me*. He popped the tops, one after the other, and devoured the little sausages in their greasy fluid, and the beans. He topped off his meal with Lucky Charms and the last soda. Although he considered the bourbon and the pain relief it might bring, alcohol would only make a bad situation worse.

It was getting dark, and colder. He searched around and found a pair of hunting boots and a ragged brown coat with an orange patch on the back. Both were too big, but three layers of somebody else's socks made the boots usable.

I need to report this. He kept thinking about the deputy, something that seemed wrong. He needed to call his office. *What day was it, anyway? Tuesday?* He'd been driving back from a field visit in Tennessee. Someone must have missed him by now.

He left the trailer, stood in the dirt road, wondering which direction to walk. Downstream, he guessed. He had a vague memory of reading that when you're lost, follow water. So he did. The stars had begun to show, but clouds were streaming in; the river looked normal as colors faded and its neon tint disappeared into gray. A sign warned NO DUM ING, the *p* having been covered by a splotch of white paint.

Across the river, a huge metal building loomed against the sky. On the side, a spotlight illuminated a vaguely Celtic-looking logo, a triangle of interwoven letters. KCL.

Darrick thought about the deputy and the waitress. He'd finished his meal. Remembered the lights of a car pulling up to the store. As he walked out, the waitress didn't say goodbye. The car that had pulled in was still running, next to his government sedan, the headlights blinding him. Then blackness.

The gravel road intersected with a paved highway. He could see the glow of lights to the left. To keep his balance, he planted his feet wide apart, leaning from one side to the other as he walked like a drunken sailor on the deck of a pitching boat. A car passed him but did not stop. *I wouldn't either.*

A few houses appeared, set close to the road, but their curtains were drawn. A dog barked wildly from inside one of them. A closed store, a long-closed barbershop with a faded FOR SALE sign askew in the window. Padlocked gates. No such thing as a public phone any more.

He saw a sign flicker to life: MOUNTAINEER SWEEPSTAKES!

Lourana opened the door to the sweepstakes parlor to check the skies. Robbie as he left had reminded her again about the winter storm. "We're under a warning come midnight. Close up and get yourself home—it's gonna be a bad one," he told her, not that she couldn't tell from the empty seat at every machine.

Lourana had her doubts. The last storm panic had brought but two inches of snow to Carbon County. Still, clouds were building out of the north. Lourana didn't like the look of them, heavy with snow off the Great Lakes.

Then she saw the man.

He was coming down the road from the fish camp, obviously shit-faced drunk, and with her luck, he'd become her problem. She wished she could lock the door and leave, but that would be the end of a job where she was hanging on by her toenails as it was. She fingered the pepper spray in the pocket of her smock, hoping he would just keep weaving his way toward town.

No such luck.

He might have been unsteady, but his path brought him right to her door. He pulled it open and stood there on the stoop.

She should have followed her gut. First, that coat didn't fit him at all right. Then the blood, my God, his head and neck all black with it on one side. Finally, the smell that wafted on the cold breeze made her gag despite her best efforts.

"You'd best be going right back out," she said, trying not to breathe.

"Please, help me." The man stood with his oversized boots wide apart. Thick glasses, probably broken from a face-plant on some roadhouse floor, were cocked sideways on his nose.

"I was attacked. Robbed. I need help."

He moved inside, the door shutting behind him. She backed up, balancing the pepper spray on her left palm.

Robbed? Where had he come from, with nothing down that way but the closed-up remnants of the fish camp? He didn't sound drunk, or crazy, though how could you tell? But the smell! Robbed or not, how did he come to smell like a deer lying dead on the side of the road for three summer days?

"Let me see your driver's license. Sweepstakes rules." That should send him on his way.

"I don't have it."

"Tell you what. I'll give you something to drink and you keep moving. You got to have a license to use the machines." Just Lourana's luck that not a soul was inside. Maybe it was time to call the owner.

He rubbed his disgusting hands up and down his stubbly face. "I know I stink. You've got no idea where I've been. I was thrown down a hole, left for dead. Please, just call the police for me."

She laughed harshly and handed him a bottle of water. "You don't call the police hereabouts. Ever."

Something seemed to click when she said that. His eyes got distant, then wary. "I'm from the government."

"And you're here to help us," she finished. She would have laughed again, but he looked so stricken.

"I'm an auditor. Federal auditor. I go through the accounts, make sure things are right, money doesn't get wasted."

"I know what an auditor is."

He leaned against the machine closest to the door, its screen strobing and flashing with the lure of quick riches, but he didn't sit down. "I was driving home. I stopped at a gas station. Off the interstate."

"The C-Mart?" It was one of those places where things happened, where people from out of town sometimes stumbled over the realities of Redbird, West Virginia.

"I don't know. I needed gas. There was a clerk, and a deputy." He squinted, as though he were trying to see something. "And someone else. I can't remember. When I walked out—that's all I remember until I woke up in a cave."

"We don't have caves hereabouts."

"It was underground."

"Probably a mine crack. Got those all over. Take out the coal and *whump*." She demonstrated, dropping her hand from high in the air to show what happened when the longwall chewed the insides out of the mountain.

He got a desperate look on his face, making her think again about that pepper spray. "There were bodies down there, ma'am. You have to believe me. I woke up with bones and rotting bodies and skulls. I crawled through them."

Lourana felt her chest tighten and made sure to keep that control she'd cultivated these many months. *Don't let on.*

"I wasn't the first person that went into that hole." The man chuckled grimly. "But I guess I might be the first to rise from it."

"Could you tell anything about them?"

"Some were just skeletons, but one was pretty recent. The body . . . " He looked at her and stopped. "No wallets or anything, that I saw. Not much for clothes. I guess they stripped them too. They took my coat and shoes. My wallet. Anything to show who I am, that I can . . . "

The man was gathering himself to say something more when a car turned into the parking lot.

"Come on." No time to regret this decision. She opened the door to the back, almost laughing at the strange expression he wore, somewhere between shock and relief. A little while ago, she'd been praying for one of the few regulars to show up. Now she wanted to keep this guy around long enough to learn what he'd stumbled onto. "Here's the bathroom. Lock the door." She grabbed a can of deodorizer and sprayed it all the way back out. When she opened the hall door, she nearly ran into Jersey, his hand reaching for the knob.

"I wondered where you was at," he said. "Whew! What died in here?"

"We might could have a rat somewhere." She busied herself signing him in.

"You best get Pete on that. Tell him to put some money in here 'stead of just hauling it out in buckets."

He took his accustomed station near the front windows, which were covered with tint to keep the inside dark like a genuine casino. As soon as he settled, the Rieser sisters and Curly came in, also usual customers on a weeknight. The machines began their electronic racketing as people poured real money into the virtual slots. After a while, Lourana announced that she had to "get supplies" and headed for the back, half-thinking the stranger would have disappeared as mysteriously as he had appeared.

She found him sitting on the commode in the single bathroom, hair plastered down and dripping like a wet rat. Water ran pink with blood from the mammoth gash across the side and back of his head. *Was that bone showing through?* It needed to be stitched up, but the clinic was closed and she didn't know anyone she could trust to do the job and keep quiet. The wound would draw together, that's what her pap always said, keep it clean and it'll draw together.

"I used all your paper towels."

"That's OK."

His borrowed coat was buttoned up tight and the garbage bag was full.

"I got rid of my shirt, but I can't do anything about the pants." He smiled self-consciously, showing nice, even teeth. "Still stinky?"

"I gotta get back," Lourana said, cutting him off. She felt nerves shuddering all through her. "Come along here. This is an exercise studio, yoga and such. You keep the lights out and you can rest safe. Here's peanuts and another drink. That's all I got. I'll be back at closing time."

"Thank you," was all he said before folding to the floor like a scarecrow off his pole.

She grabbed a case of Nabs and some coffee packets off the supply shelf, made a show of restocking, but no one much cared. They were too deep in their dreams of jackpots, of the reels clicking into place or the lines connecting simultaneously as everything came together across the screen.

Lourana didn't have much to do, any night, and usually spent it reading the Mountain EcoJustice website. Fracking. Mountaintop removal so they could keep the tonnage up while cutting employment. Invasive species. Global warming. And of course, acid mine drainage and the massive blowout, the most recent and maybe final insult to the beautiful Broad River that once flowed cool and inviting from the higher peaks down through the town.

The last diehard clocked off just before midnight, sullen at having made a pile and lost it all again. As she turned the key, Lourana could see that snow had started to whiten the parking lot. She shut the door blinds, switched off the signs. She left the main computer running at the snack counter. No one would notice she was here late, as she often stayed to read into the early hours.

In the back, she opened the door to the yoga studio. A wedge of light fell across the stranger curled on the carpet. With his face relaxed and busted glasses off, he wasn't bad looking. A little younger than she was, thirty, maybe thirty-five. Dark hair, a broad forehead and strong chin. Her mama would have said he was a stubborn sort because of that. She'd always been a believer in appearances, that what a person was on the inside couldn't help but show through on the surface.

"Hey, you there." She poked his shoulder. "Hey, wake up."

He didn't respond. She hoped he wasn't dead. Guilt ran through her— she'd been more concerned about keeping herself out of the Kavanaghs' way than helping him. No, that wasn't entirely true. What she cared about was Dreama, and the possibility this man might hold the key to finding her. She shook him harder. He drew in a quick breath and threw up his hand to shield his head.

"It's me."

"Me, who?" He rolled partway over and looked at her, blinking.

"The crazy woman who let you in here. What's your name, anyway?"

He sat up with some difficulty, put out his hand. "Darrick MacBrehon, lately of Brookland."

"Where's that?"

"Washington, DC."

"The government, right."

"Despite my untoward appearance, I am a solid citizen. I've never had more than a speeding ticket."

"Lourana Taylor." She felt awkward leaning down to him, shaking hands like at a business meeting. "One of those silly West Virginia names. From my pap and mama, Louis and Anna. Lourana."

Darrick scrambled to his feet, stood swaying for a moment before lurching after her, back to the sweepstakes parlor. "I don't think it's silly. Rather nice. You carry them with you forever, with those names."

That got her. Nobody anymore could punch through the wall that encased the emptiness inside, but this man just made a good dent in it. She was glad he could see only her back.

"You were telling me about the convenience store."

"I don't know what happened, but the people turned hostile all of a sudden."

"This town, it's a strange place," she said. "Things happen. People don't appear here, like you. They more disappear."

"You have a serial killer or something?"

"Maybe something," Lourana said. "The Kavanaghs. My pap worked for them. They wrung every drop of sweat out of him. Pap died because he was used up. Never called in sick a day. Just plain used up, like everything around here."

"I guess small towns are like that."

Damn. He had dismissed her family, her life, just like that.

"But why me? I don't know anyone here. I have to get to the police."

"You're listening but you ain't hearing. KCL owns the coal, the gas, the downtown, the trees, the land, anything worth grabbing, either outright or around the back ways. That means they own the people too." She didn't care if she sounded bitter. "Didn't you say there was a deputy there? Yeah? Cops, judges, politicians. The newspaper. Even the UMW. Anyone that has any kind of pull."

"Because of these . . . "

"Kavanaghs. They roost in their mansion, behind their iron gates, and no one even sees them anymore."

"Somebody sees them."

"I imagine their creatures see them, to get their orders."

"So you're saying I can't go to the police." Darrick started to turn his head but stopped, frozen with pain. He started to put his hand up but paused, his fingers hovering a few inches above the wound. She couldn't help looking, right down into that gash. *Yes, that was definitely bone. No wonder he staggers around.* Her throat worked to stop what wanted to come up from below.

"Then I'll start with my office. I'll call them."

"No phone here." She wasn't about to let him use her cell. "You could Skype."

"Where am I, anyway?"

"Redbird, West Virginia."

She could hear the phone ring and then a recording. Darrick turned to her, his pale eyes distorted behind those wrecked glasses, and whispered, "What day is it?"

"It's almost, it is, Thanksgiving."

He let out a sound like he'd been punched before leaving a brief message that he'd been delayed, car trouble. "I was driving back on Monday night. Really, it's Thursday? Nobody is getting this message any time soon."

"Don't you have someone else to call?"

"My landlord, I guess."

"God help us both, then, not to have a soul to call. I got nobody in these parts to know if I get safe home of a night or end up like you." It just came out, and now she regretted letting him know she was alone in the world.

"I'll send an email, at least." He signed into his office account, making a point of showing her that he was who he said he was, though that didn't impress her much. "But so far as getting out of here . . . "

"You don't have a phone, a license, even clothes. Much less a car. I don't think you're going too far anyways. But hey, we've got the internet. And I can fix you a coffee." As the words came out, Lourana wanted to slap herself. *Don't get involved. You're already in too deep.*

"Maybe tea," he said.

Darrick could feel his stomach growling; worse, he could hear it.

"You haven't had anything to eat," Lourana said reproachfully.

"I broke into a trailer. Stole some canned goods—Vienna sausages."

"That makes you an honorary Redbirdian, I'd say."

Another rumble. "Maybe you could order a pizza? I can pay you back as soon as I get out of here." He crossed his heart, as he had nothing else to offer in surety.

"You gotta be kidding. We got no Domino's." Lourana didn't mince words. She was a no-nonsense person, from her blue sweatshirt plain as prison garb to her no-name sneakers. "But what am I supposed to do with you, anyway? I can't leave you here for the cleaners to find."

"I can sleep in a garage, shed, porch, wherever. I don't want you to feel unsafe. But I don't want to be alone here." He'd fallen out of his life and was now a transient. Housebreaker. Bum. Homeless. He'd never felt so hapless, so lacking any control, at least as an adult. Her warnings about these Kavanaghs made what was probably a random robbery feel like a long-brooded plot on his life. He looked at her, wished he could read some emotion in her brown eyes, see some hint in how she held her mouth. *God, I hate to beg.*

"I'm home for a couple of days."

"Oh, the holiday! You have people coming over."

"Nope."

"If you can find a place, just for a day or two. You can lock me in, out, whatever."

"Oh, don't worry, I can take care of me." She pulled a can of pepper spray from her pocket and showed it to him.

They peered out at the early morning streets. It was snowing steadily and the roads were covered. Nothing moved. Streetlights marked out regular intervals into the sleeping town, at least as far as a curve that blocked a longer view. Lourana went out and started her beige miniwagon, an older Subaru, a billow of exhaust rising from it like a fluffy tail. He watched as she scraped the windows. She opened the passenger door and beckoned for him. He lumbered to the car, feeling exposed as a roach. As cold air hit his head wound, the raw flesh drew in and stabbed him with pain.

"The deer hunters are happy with this snow," she said as she returned from locking the front door. She moved fast; how he wished he could move like that. And she drove too fast, the tires spinning before she eased off the gas.

The road curved as it followed the arc of the river. The water looked black, snow falling into it like stars going out.

"What's going on with the river? The orange stuff?"

"Acid mine drainage. They had a blowout at Kavanagh No. 4."

They were in the downtown, a stretch of mostly two-story brick commercial buildings, an old courthouse, a newish city hall with small bands of windows breaking the concrete expanse. One building towered over the rest, a spotlight glowing on that same ornate monogram. KCL. Kavanagh Coal and Limestone.

"Acid?"

She made a left. "The coal hereabouts has a lot of sulfur in it. It's called that, high-sulfur steam coal. What keeps your lights on in DC. When water runs through the seam, it picks up the sulfur and turns into sulfuric acid."

"That's what the orange glop is?"

"Yep. A spill like this one, and this one is crazy big, just kills everything. The Broad River was one of the prettiest in the state, even if there was a little bit of acid drainage from some abandoned mines. Nothing like this. We had a swimming beach at the park, ruined now. And nobody's going to be fishing up at the camp anymore."

Darrick had done audits at the EPA and OSM, but it was all numbers, nothing that connected with this alien place where giant cracks opened in the ground and orange goo filled the rivers. He'd never imagined that ordinary rocks underfoot could leak that kind of vile pus.

Lourana started to hit the gas to beat a yellow light as it was turning red, then hit the brakes instead and slid to a stop. A white car pulled up beside them. It made Darrick turn his head. A white car with a light bar on the top. A memory flashed from the convenience store. A white car with a green seal on the door. A round-faced young cop. Like the one who was staring back at him.

The officer flung open the car door and leaped out with his gun coming to bear.

"Drive!" Darrick yelled.

"Stop right there!" The cop's face washed from red to pale, like he'd seen a ghost. Darrick watched him yank back the weapon's slide. He looked into his eyes and felt, no, heard, the man's fear, an intense clanging sound. A wave of pressure surged across him, promising to pull him down with its lightless undertow.

He pushed back. Hard.

The young cop's face seemed to swell. Like a pink balloon squashed in a child's hand, it bulged and relaxed unevenly. His eyes became huge. The gun slipped from his hand.

"Go! Go!" Darrick watched, unbelieving, as the man collapsed to the pavement. "Get out of here!"

Lourana seemed frozen. Her eyes flicked from him to the empty patrol car, the door wide open.

Darrick wanted to shake her but was afraid she'd scream. "That's the cop who tried to kill me. At the store. I remember."

She stared wildly at Darrick. "What happened? Where is he? Is he under the car? I can't drive over him."

"Just drive!" He expected the cop to get up any moment, even as he felt that dreadful pressure fade away.

Lourana slammed the shifter into park and got out, ran and slid around the car. Darrick opened his door and saw the man facedown between the cars. He looked smaller, as though he'd previously been filled with something other than his breath.

"He's dead?"

Darrick leaned out and put his hand on the side of the man's neck, the way they did in mystery shows. The warmth made him lift his fingers away, but then he put them back and waited. He couldn't feel any pulse or breath. "I think so."

Lourana backed up a step. "Did you do something to him?"

"I never touched him." His heart hammered. "You saw, I never touched him."

"But he's *dead*."

She retreated, and he thought she was gone, expected to see her running away up the street. Then she came around the back of the car and got in again. "We'd best go."

Darrick fervently agreed. Nothing good would come from sitting here beside a dead cop. He looked back as they pulled away, the dome light shining in the empty car, the man sprawled on the street and already his uniform was whitening. Their tire tracks followed them wherever they might go. He held one hand balled inside the other, as though that might stop whatever had just happened from happening again.

They drove in silence then. He had been counting the turns because he always did that automatically, and now because he might have to find his way back out on his own. Her knuckles were white, gripping the steering wheel, and he could see how she was checking on him from the corner of her eye.

What was that? What had he done? Hadn't he just tried to protect himself, blocking that mental blow?

The engine whined as the street climbed past houses, some with smoke going up from the chimneys; they passed an access road that curved steeply up to a Walmart plaza. Then it was just trees and farm fields and a lone house, everything turning white and tranquil as a Christmas card. Finally they pulled in at a small, dark house, gravel in the drive rattling under the tires. An American flag hung in frozen folds from its staff on the porch.

"Stay there."

Darrick didn't figure he was getting inside. He slumped back, gingerly resting the other side of his head against the headrest, and crossed his arms to retain what heat he could in that canvas coat. Maybe she was calling the cops. So be it. He was exhausted. No fight left in him, no energy to wander away into fields disappearing under snow. He'd actually started to nod off when she came back and opened the car door.

The cottage was bright with lights, now, a single overhead globe on the porch showing worn stone steps and wide-board floor. Inside, a small, cluttered kitchen and a living room with a recliner facing a large television set. Two closed doors that he suspected had not been closed before.

"Yeah, so I watch a lot of TV," she said. "Go on in there."

He went to the kitchen and sat in one of the two plastic chairs as she put down bowls and silverware and two mugs of water. The microwave dinged and she pulled out a bowl of stew that she set in the middle of the table beside a loaf of Sunbeam bread and a tub of margarine.

"Eat up before it gets cold." She ladled meat and vegetables into her bowl and then broke a slice of bread across it. He was too hungry to be polite, filling his bowl and then a second time.

"Who was he?" he asked quietly.

"Jimmy Cooper. A rent-a-cop." She took a drink. "Still, he was Jimmy, a shirttail relative. Not a bad kid, finished high school and no place to go but the Kavanaghs."

She scraped the bottom of her bowl and licked the spoon.

She's used to eating alone, Darrick realized, remembering his solitary meals bolted down from takeout boxes.

"It all came back when I saw him. His car was sitting next to mine as I came out of the store. I caught a glimpse of him right before something hit me. I guess he did, and dumped me down that hole." Darrick couldn't stop seeing the man's face swell, one side and then the other, and his eyes pop wide, his mouth pursing out like he was poised for a kiss. Then the air just went out of him.

"Why did he die?" she asked.

"He just—I don't know."

"That's not good enough. He's just a kid. You must have done something."

"I don't understand what happened." Her eyes met his, impassive. He realized that he had no idea what she might do. "I've never hurt anyone."

"Ever in your life?"

"All my life, I never fought back. I didn't fight back this time. But I could hear something. Hear his thoughts."

She scoffed. "So you're psychic."

"No, I could just hear how he was thinking. Not what he was thinking. His emotions, really. He was terrified, and that came over me as a loud sound, a sound like a loudspeaker blaring. Fear of me, but behind that was something else, big, that he was even more afraid of." Darrick tried to find analogies, some way of making sense of it all. "I could hear how his mind was working. He was consumed by fear. It was like a terrible wave that rolled out of him, across me, like it was going to smother me. I sort of pushed it back. I think that killed him."

She looked doubtful. "You pushed."

"I can't explain it. I mentally shoved his fear away from me."

"You just thought something at him and he croaked."

How his face swelled and distorted.

"And this is the first time this ever happened?"

He nodded, once, wincing as the gash in his head pulled. "I don't know where it came from."

"Maybe the clonk on the head did something to you." Lourana stared at him for a long moment. "Can you see inside of me?"

He didn't want to know, but even as he rejected the idea, his mind searched around her for anything like what had happened with the rent-a-cop. Jimmy. No sound, no sense of what she was feeling. A blankness, not of emptiness but of a carefully constructed barrier.

"I can't feel anything."

"That's because I won't let there be anything," she said. "No emotion. Nothing they can take from me."

* * *

She got up and cleared the table, rattling the glasses and bowls into the sink.

"What did they take?"

Lourana stood staring into the sink, the suds rising. Seemed like she spent too much of her life cleaning up messes. "What didn't they? Pap, like I told you, wore out from work. Then him dying took the heart out of Mama. My ex, his back ruined, addicted. But when Dreama disappeared, my little girl, that was the last straw. My little girl."

"I'm sorry."

She shook herself, refused the tears.

"It was so damned hard to get away. I thought we'd done it at last, my ex getting clean so he could get a job that wasn't tied up with the Kavanaghs, and we were out of here." She remembered looking out the back window of the car as they crossed the bridge, thinking, *Screw you, Redbird, that'll show you.* Her chest nearly caved in at the memory. "Three years later, Dreama graduates from South Charleston High School and damn if she don't run right back and take a job at KCL. I don't know what possessed her."

"Maybe it was home."

"What's home?" Lourana wished she could feel real anger, but what came out was flat and factual. "I was born in Redbird and I'll most likely die here, sooner than later, but it's not home like you want it to be. You don't want to be here unless you are from here, and if you're from here and you got any sense, you want to leave."

"They never found out what happened to your daughter?"

"The police said she probably run off with some man. Not that she wouldn't, maybe, she wasn't no plastic doll baby, but she would have let me know she was all right. That was what my family did—you went somewhere, you always called to let folks know you got there safe."

"Lourana, when I was in the hole. I found something. A necklace."

She turned from the sink. Soap dripped from her arms onto the floor.

"What did it look like?" What if it was Dreama's necklace, that single strand of gold beads she'd taken to wearing every day in the months before she disappeared? Lourana held her breath as he dug into his pants pocket and pulled out an antique silver locket, heart shaped, swinging from a dirty chain. She put out her hand. He dropped it into her palm as though it burned him. His face went white. "I'm sorry, I'm so sorry. If I said anything that pained you. About the bones."

She pushed on the catch and the heart sprang open. Inside, where there should be a picture of a boyfriend or a curl of baby hair, was nothing. *How sad.* "It's not hers, at least, not anything that I remember her having." The chain slid through her fingers and she dropped it on the counter next to the dish drainer.

Darrick looked as lost as she felt, but Lourana didn't let herself get pulled in, reminding herself that he was a guy with a strange story that couldn't be verified. And that he could, maybe, kill.

Or maybe Jimmy just stroked out.

"I don't know if I'm sorry that it's not hers, or relieved," he said.

"I guess that's somebody's daughter down there, even if it's not Dreama. I've tried to accept she might be dead, because I would have heard from her. Eighteen months gone."

Lourana emptied the sink, watched the dirty water gurgle down one drain, the rinse water down the other. She wiped down the counter and wrung out the dishrag. One of her wedding gifts, part of a hand-crocheted set she had treasured and kept put away for good, until there was no reason to save anything. The possibility of knowing what happened to Dreama had lifted her up and let her down hard. It could be she was down in that mine crack. Even if the necklace came off another body, maybe that activist who was missing, who's to say her girl was not lying there as well? Lourana would have to see for herself. See that mine crack for herself and she would know if her baby was there.

"Lourana. Mrs. Taylor."

She gave him a look. "Lourana will do. And Taylor is my own name. I took it back."

"I'm just—I shouldn't be here, but I don't have any place to go. And I'm a mess in your house."

"I guess I didn't notice the stink anymore, but yeah, I'd as soon you didn't wander the grave-dirt all over." She put on a bit of a smile to reassure him. "The bathroom is this way."

There was only the one bathroom, but Lourana had quickly stashed away her most personal items before she'd allowed him in the house.

"Clean yourself up." She put down some towels, ones already worn or stained. "I got no men's clothes for you to put on." She pointed to the chenille robe hanging behind the door.

He took a long time in the shower. When he emerged, Lourana almost laughed. The robe that brushed the floor on her didn't reach so far on him, but with the purple color and the belt and all, he looked like he was playing one of the three kings in a church pageant.

"Come and let me dress that wound." She had the first-aid kit open, ready—overdue, but she didn't tend to concern herself about others much these days. He sat in the kitchen chair and pulled the robe tight across his legs. She teased hair away from the wound, which was big and raw but no sign of infection. You could see the bone, quite clearly, and quite a lot of it, but she couldn't tell if there was a concussion or fracture or anything like that.

"In a way, you're like them," she said, as she cut back the matted hair with cuticle scissors and dabbed antiseptic from a packet, hoping it wasn't too expired. Best she could do.

"Heh?" It was half question and half yelp.

"The Kavanaghs. You look ordinary enough."

"I guess that's true."

"But so do they. They don't have horns and tails, but there's weird stories about how they got hold of everything hereabouts. About what they can do to those who get in their way. They've had a chokehold on this town since they dug the first hole into the ground. Let me just tell you that. Powerful men. And I saw you do something I can't explain and neither can you."

She knew the wound needed stitches but couldn't bring herself to get out the sewing kit and try. Instead, she laced some big butterfly bandages across the gap, making him jump each time she tried to fasten an end down. Finally, she fixed the bandages in place by wrapping gauze around his head, so he looked like the guy in the *Spirit of '76*.

"You can sleep in the recliner. I got no second bed. I'll be honest with you, I was going to take you to the hard road and let you figure out your own way out of Redbird, till you showed me that locket. That decided me, that you weren't making the whole thing up."

"I don't have the imagination to make up stuff like this. I can't thank you enough for—"

She held up her hand.

"I need to find out why this happened. Why me?"

"And why Dreama?" she added.

"There has to be a reason."

Lourana pulled off a piece of tape and secured the head wrapping. *No, there doesn't*, she thought. *Shit happens, as they say.*

THE VOICE OF THE MOUNTAIN

Two miles back in a slope mine, the longwall chews coal like teeth taking niblets from an ear of corn, light gleaming on the hydraulic haunches holding up the top. The cutter opens a methane pocket; the sensors taste it. More than 5 percent, less than 15 percent, and the power cuts off, the mine goes silent, the only sound the breath of the miners and their prayers that it is not 9.5 percent, the perfect number, the oxidation point when the mine blows itself out like a candle. The voice of the mountain is a deep groaning. You can hear it as the machinery whines to a stop, the complaint of Atlas under his burden, the mountain flexing its muscles.

—CBK

Darrick clicked the remote. Snow, snow, snow, the television screen echoing the view of blowing snow through the windows. "Is your cable out?"

Lourana turned from the refrigerator. "Cable? Hah! Try antenna."

"You're kidding."

"You can get public TV, NBC sometimes, CBS, and a religious channel. Knock yourself out. And yes, we do have cable in West Virginia, they
just won't bring it this far up the mountain for one house."

Darrick held up his hands. He didn't know how to respond to her
unfiltered statements.

He hit the button and a fuzzy picture rolled and stabilized. " . . . story,
authorities are leaving no stone unturned as they seek answers in the
death of a young security guard."

Lourana dropped something on the counter, a dull thud like a fist
into a body, and came in to watch.

"James Wayne Cooper, twenty-two, was employed by KCL Security.
He was a graduate of Carbon County High School and was engaged to
be married." A photo showed him in a black gown, somber faced and
gripping a diploma, an unfortunate pimple on his forehead right below
his tasseled cap. "His body was found on Center Street beside his patrol
vehicle." Video of a snow-covered street, the white car, police vehicles
all around it with their lights strobing red and blue through the falling
snow. A skinny cop crossed the screen, unrolling a line of yellow tape.

Cut to a shot of a crew-cut man behind a desk. "Sheriff, what do we
know?"

"We don't have a cause of death at this time, but his gun had been drawn; we know he was being threatened. Whoever did this will be found." The sheriff leaned toward the camera and scowled. "Jimmy was left on the street like a dog. We will find whoever did this and prosecute to the utmost. No one is getting out of Redbird, or Carbon County, until we find the perpetrator."

"Had the gun been fired?"

"No."

"Sheriff, Sheriff Zabrowski!" A high-pitched female voice from out of the camera shot. "Is this connected with the disappearance of Susan Tedesco?"

The sheriff looked down, moved his tiny set of US and West Virginia flags to the left.

"Susan Tedesco-Jones, with Appalfolk? She was here taking water samples—"

"—from the Broad River, yes, I know. We don't see a connection. We don't know that she's dead, just that we can't locate her."

"But—"

"Miss Person, you and the *Gazette* been beating that dead horse for too long. Them agitators come in from outside and then they're gone, on to the next thing."

"She's no outsider. She's from Mabscott," came that high-pitched voice again.

The sheriff cut his eyes to one side then returned to glaring into the camera. "We've got one of our own lying dead in the morgue now and we'll be focusing on that."

The news break cut away to a weather update—unexpectedly heavy snowfall, front stalled over the Appalachians, roads closed, expected to move through followed by bitter cold.

"Sealing off the town seems almost irrelevant," Darrick said, as the broadcast returned to the Thanksgiving Day parades. He clicked off.

"Snow, not ice. Four-wheel-drives can get out. My little Subaru will go about anywhere, until the snow gets too deep and packs up underneath."

"And how deep is that?"

"I believe it's about to be that deep." A little smile tried at the corner of her mouth, a space that looked like it was more accustomed to a grimace; still, her brown eyes remained flat. "The wind's started making drifts. We ain't going nowhere for a while. But they got things locked down, anyways, sounds like."

Lourana went back to making breakfast. Darrick nursed his tea. She'd looked at him when he refused coffee, but more than a hint of caffeine could bring on an attack of the staggers. She'd found a tea bag on the shelf; the cup it made was harsh and cheap and thin. He felt shitty about critiquing it when this woman had done so much already, put herself in danger. But it was bad. The breakfast, on the other hand, was delicious. Eggs done soft and slices of sage-heavy sausage fried hard. Darrick ate like a starving man, which he guessed he still was, devouring three-quarters of the sausage and a stack of toast. He would have to square things up when this was over.

"The woman they talked about, Susan something? When did she disappear?"

Lourana cocked her head to one side. "I think it's been a month, six weeks. She was up at the mouth of Laurel Fork taking water samples, last that her people heard from her. Supposedly, she was onto something and was planning an announcement, then she was just gone. They haven't found her car, nothing."

"I think she might be down there."

Lourana nodded. "That locket. Haven't been any other women to go missing."

"But there have been men."

"That's different. You take a college girl in a ponytail, people pay attention when they disappear. More'n some local girl. And sure more than a man, 'cause they run off troublemakers regular."

Darrick helped her clear away, and she ran scalding hot water to soak the dishes.

"I've always been a believer in *follow the money*. Always comes back to that. This is my pal," she said, patting the case of a geriatric Mac. "I get my news from outside of the local media. And I do my research."

"Anything new on Dreama?"

She made a small sound, noncommittal, but as the screen lit up, her face was already taking on that abstracted look of someone electronically engaged. The faces he saw at cubicles in his office, and in coffee shops and on the Metro. The face he himself wore most of the time.

"Damn!" Lourana slapped the desk and pushed the keyboard back. "The internet is down."

"At least we still have," and the lights flickered, "power."

Another flicker, and the house went dim and silent.

* * *

Lourana had picked up the coal scuttle when she realized that she did not want to go down there, leaving this man behind her. *Don't be para-noid,* she told herself, *he's got no reason to hurt you.* She had trusted his story—who could make up that graveyard smell?—but seeing Jimmy fall dead had left her shaken. *Who, or maybe what, was this guy?*

No good second guessing now. If she had to make a run for it, her car would probably make it down the hill. Might make it.

"Do you want me to get that?"

"Sure." She handed him the scuttle and opened the door to the cellar. "You'll see the bin. Just shovel it full."

It was some relief when he lumbered one step at a time down the narrow stairs. Lourana turned to the fireplace, starting the fire that she kept laid for when the lines went down. She could hear coal rattling against metal, a deeper echo of the rattling of branches against the side of the house. A bump and a yelp. The basement was hand-dug, and you had to watch your head or meet up with the floor joists.

He came up and set the scuttle down too hard, so that coal dust poofed up from it.

"I've never in my life seen coal burn," he said, watching the fire take hold. "I thought that skinny fireplace was just for show."

"Nope." She pushed a chunk closer to the main flame. "Everyone used to burn coal. You could dig it yourself. What you call drift mines, where you just see a seam cropping out of a sidehill, there for the taking. And sure easier than chopping wood."

"You grew up here?"

"This house? No. My family had a sort of farm. Run beef cattle and such. I just rent this." She laid the poker by her chair. "I couldn't abide living in some little hutch of an apartment over top of a store."

Darrick pulled a kitchen chair around by the fireside. He'd gone into the bathroom and unwrapped the gauze from his head, after she'd taken some care with that. The butterflies had decided to stick, sort of, but the wound was exposed. At least it was on the other side so that she didn't have to look straight into it.

It'll close up. Don't go soft and get yourself in dutch. Find out about Dreama. That's what is important.

"Well, looks like it's campfire story time." Darrick peered at her through his ruined glasses, the odd angle making his eyes appear to swim behind the lenses. "Tell me more about these Kavanaghs."

"The official history or the real one?"

"Both."

"Poor Irish when they come over."

"Starving in the Potato Famine. I've heard that old story."

"Well, maybe. Anyway, their luck turned. They took the right side in the Civil War—both times."

"Both times?"

"When the state was part of Virginia and then when it split off to join the Union. They was right there, one hand on the new constitution and the other on the contracts. Wasn't much here at first, but what there was, Kavanaghs got hold of it. The grist mill, the post office. They cut the trees, provided timbers for their own mines, built docks and barge companies and rail lines."

"Vertical integration."

"Whatever, it worked. KCL's been the only going employer in the county, except for government work."

"You said they own the county. Or is that just a saying?"

"Not all the surface, though they have plenty of that, developing the best of it and selling off whatever wasn't worth the trouble. But they kept the mineral rights, surface and deep, coal and gas. They've taken out about everything these mountains had to give, and now they've moved onto fracking."

"Sounds like classic capitalism." Darrick fingered the spot on his forehead where he must have connected with a beam. "But everyone's afraid of them, you say."

"Now we get off the authorized biography." Lourana got the last of the coffee before it went stone cold. "The Kavanaghs laid out this town. They reserved a big chunk of land overlooking the river for their mansion. Looks like a castle, with an iron fence all around, and landscaped by the guy that did Central Park."

"Olmstead."

She nodded. "Sunken gardens, fish ponds, a pool, all that. It's no legend that all of Redbird has been undermined except for their home and the square downtown where they built the courthouse and the KCL Building, with the company offices and the First Miners and Merchants Bank."

"Which they own."

"You catch on fast." Lourana sucked down the rest of her coffee. Even talking about the Kavanaghs made her nervous. "Nothing goes on here the Kavanaghs don't know about, which is why I think they're behind Dreama's disappearance. I can't prove it—yet."

"What about the state police?"

"No detachment here. The sheriff patrols the county."

"Power corrupts, absolute power corrupts . . ."

"*Absolutely.*" *Look surprised then. You might not think I have any smarts, but you would be wrong.* "The great-grandfather was a real heller. They called him Old Scratch, like the devil. The grandfather not much better. The current lords of the manor, a father and two sons, they're more corporate types. No one's seen the father for years—Patrick. The two sons are just about as reclusive, though you used to see a picture in the paper with one of them presenting a check or something. Not lately though. Eamon is the older, by about twenty years, the heir to the throne. The other one is Cormac."

A churning, ratcheting roar came toward the house, and she saw Darrick flinch. A snowplow barreled past, flinging up a wall of snow followed by the rattle of cinders hitting the pavement.

"Maybe they're all dead. Faked photos."

"Just out of sight. They like it that way, pulling the strings. The Kavanaghs have their creatures to do for them what they want done. Like they say, you may not see Satan but that don't mean he ain't real."

"Satan? Pretty strong language."

"Listen. We got people gone and no bodies to show, and not just these recent ones. The old folks said that Old Scratch could strip you right to the bone, kill you dead with a look. Sound familiar?"

Darrick flushed and looked away.

"A myth, maybe, but it's true another way. People walking around all but dead from their work. You sit downtown and watch for a while. Men with black lung on oxygen tanks, or broke up, missing legs, twisted and smashed." Lourana felt her hands shaking. *Too much coffee.* She noticed that Darrick wasn't drinking his tea. She wondered again what he'd done to get tossed down a mine crack. Poking the skunk—she might as well keep on.

"OK if I ask you some things? Like why you walk that way? Is it from getting conked on the head or that some kind of a birth defect?"

Darrick reached up and reset his glasses, touched his head, then gave an embarrassed laugh. "Been this way all my life. I was raised in a children's home up north. They told me I was left in the confessional booth by a young woman; whatever Father Ronan knew about me was sealed."

Lourana thought that seemed convenient to cover someone's tracks.

"I walked like this from my first steps. Episodic ataxia, genetic. That much I know, but that's all."

"I'm sorry. That was over the line, asking you that," Lourana said, but was secretly relieved to know that the lack of medical attention wasn't to blame.

Darrick breathed in and out, like he was steadying himself. "What bothers me is not knowing why. Why I was abandoned. Whether my parents had this. As a kid, I wanted to be a doctor, of course, so that I could find out, but between my bad eyes and my clumsiness . . . Along the way, I learned that numbers were friendly. They made sense."

"So you became an auditor."

"CPA first. When I became an auditor, it was kind of a kick, like being a detective, to see where someone tried to fudge things. The people who run things think they can fool everyone, but ultimately, the numbers won't lie."

The plow came through again, on the other side of the road. Lourana wondered if it was Yancey on this route. He often came in the sweepstakes after his shift. As crappy a job as hers was, the video parlor had cocooned her, provided her with something almost like family. As she considered Darrick's life, it began to seem more like family.

"Your story?"

She snapped back to the conversation. "My story. I grew up here and met Steve here, and we got married here. He worked the loading bays at the limestone quarry. He was up fixing something when it let loose and he fell, hurt his back. He wasn't like Pap, just suck it up. Instead, he got started on the oxy."

Darrick looked puzzled.

"Oxycontin."

"Yes."

"So he got addicted and it about killed him. About killed me, too, except I had Dreama to think of. Steve got clean, finally, with jail and church and NA and my boot in his ass. We got out of Carbon County and started over near Charleston."

She seemed to see herself, Steve, Dreama. Tiny faces, so far away, like looking in the wrong end of a telescope. Everything that was big and painful shrunken down to something she could cover with her thumb. She remembered how Dreama had been such a small baby. She wouldn't gain weight, a skinny girl who finally, magically, blossomed. Her junior year, she'd been the prom queen, in a royal blue gown like a Disney princess.

"He went back on the pills. Then the pills got hard to get, and more expensive, same old hillbilly hard-luck story. Then Dreama disappeared. Then the pills became heroin. Then I divorced him." Lourana hesitated on that, wondering if her ex was still clean, if he'd stayed down in Charlotte where he got a job through an old friend. *Enough.* "So I came back to find her."

They sat for a while, just listening to the wind. Lourana poked the fire and stood up.

"I don't expect the power to come back any time soon. We better eat up some of what's in the fridge."

They worked on assembling a lunch. Ham sandwiches, leftover macaroni salad, melting ice cream.

"Happy Thanksgiving," she said.

Darrick raised his jelly glass of milk. "Happy Thanksgiving."

The snow had pounded down till after dark, and squalls were still moving through, filling the air and then subsiding. The crews had been out non-stop on the main roads, which were slushy with salt and cinders. And the main roads all led to Walmart.

The parking lot was half-full and people stood huddled in a miserable line, waiting for midnight when the real festivities could begin. As eager as she was to get what she needed and head home before the promised bitter cold arrived to freeze it all solid, Lourana wasn't going to get into that mess. You could get crushed in the stampede for the Chinese televisions, ones with names that were almost like the brand names. She sat in the car and watched kids sliding around the parking lot, throwing snowballs, using the cars for cover. A pair of giant pickups with blades were pushing snow to the edges, opening more spaces.

She had left Darrick in her house, the power still out, sitting by the fire in that purple robe. *What the hell. He could be an axe murderer.* She laughed at herself for that. He didn't need any axe. One thing in his favor, he wasn't part of the local system. Plus, the big plus that kept her believing, maybe he could lead her to Dreama, horrible as that was to consider. Worth the hazard, though last night she'd wedged a chair under her doorknob just in case.

Her dashboard clock might have been stuck permanently on daylight saving time, but it was right on the button except for that one-hour difference. As *11:00* showed, the line began moving. She wrapped the scarf around her throat and trudged toward the entrance.

The doors opened with a blast of warm air and the smell of popcorn and overcooked hot dogs and cinnamon and the fake pine scent of car air fresheners. Instead of stooped senior citizens in their blue vests, the greeters were all big guys, bruisers who could handle the doorbuster rush if it turned ugly.

The crowd in front of her, thinned by the weather, quickly dispersed among the garish Christmas displays. Most were headed for the high-dollar sections. Lourana was not enticed by the rollback prices and bright colors.

She saw people from the sweepstakes parlor, recognized others who had been high school classmates. Some were glassy-eyed and jovial with the bargain hunt, distracted. Some just threw up a hand before turning grimly back to the task of providing Christmas cheer. A woman she used to work with at PTA bake sales pretended not to see her. She could imagine their thoughts like they were tethered on balloons overhead. *Sad, sure; first Steve, then Dreama, but Lourana just won't let it go, writing letters to the editor and pestering police and speaking at city council meetings.*

Maybe it was like cancer. They were afraid if you got too close, death would leap across and take one of their children.

Women's wear had sweatpants on sale, and she slowed down, thinking she just might, just might, but she could get them at the Word of God rummage sale for a couple bucks. In the men's department, people were stacking flannels in their buggies and tearing through a display of leather coats.

"I went by the sweepstakes but it wasn't open."

Lourana turned to face her accuser. "We're closed for the holiday, Helen. I had the sign up all week."

"Not everyone has family, the turkey and trimmings. You should know." Helen Decker looked like Mrs. Claus, round faced, with her white hair up in a bun, but the temper lines between her eyebrows and bracketing her mouth were not jolly.

"We'll be open on Monday, if the roads are."

"Monday! No way to make money," she sniffed, and Lourana wondered if she meant herself or the parlor owner. "We might none of us be here Monday anyway."

"Excuse me?"

Helen leaned as close as the pile in her cart would allow. "You've heard about the zombie?"

"Ex*cuse* me?" Lourana realized she had repeated herself and wondered if she was having an episode. The Christmas music repeated like that, the same song over and over, and she had an eerie feeling she was trapped inside that kind of loop.

"The living dead. Like in the shows? We got one right here, and if you see one then there's sure to be others."

Lourana tried not to giggle, thinking of roaches. She chewed on the inside of her lip so that a laugh didn't burst out.

"He was seen on Fish Camp Road, staggering along, all bloody. The Rodeheavers saw him, the whole carload of 'em. Eyewitnesses."

"Oh, Helen. Really." Lourana reached out and touched her arm. "Next thing you'll be saying there's UFOs."

"You go ahead and mock, but this is the real deal. Missy and Buster and their kids, they all saw him. Head bashed in, walking all stiff-like. They hightailed it out of there and called the police, but of course they laughed at 'em. Until poor Jimmy Cooper. That zombie killed Jimmy, sucked the blood right out of his body."

"That would be a vampire." Lourana couldn't help herself, but all the time her mind was racing about who might have seen Darrick. Nobody went down that road these days, no reason to, with the camp evacuated for "safety reasons."

"Well, maybe it's a vampire. But they don't come out in the daylight, do they?"

"Anyway, zombies eat brains."

Helen looked at her suspiciously. "Be careful. That thing would've come right by your parlor—God knows where he is now. And this weather! I'm gonna get my deals and get home. Got these new towels, and a comforter." She looked sharply at Lourana's cart, which held only men's clothing.

"For Steve," she explained, wishing she'd thrown some other stuff in the cart so the contents weren't so visible.

"Divorced how long and you're still doing for him?"

"We were married for eighteen years, Helen. That don't go away. And he's having it rough."

"Again."

"Again, yeah."

Helen shook her head and pushed off.

I wouldn't buy Steve a rope to hang himself, Lourana thought. *No, that's not true. Quite.*

She stuffed the underwear beneath the khakis and a pullover. He hadn't specified, but she had appraised Darrick for what he was, and that wasn't a buffalo plaid shirt and Wranglers. He'd been apologetic, again, about not having any money, but what could you do? She went back through the women's department and tossed a pair of sweatpants across the pile, then swung through the groceries for a few essentials. The milk was gone, like every time a storm come through, and the bread was down to a few squashed loaves. She grabbed one anyway, and with eggs and some peanut butter, they had enough to get by. Oh, and tea. Ugh. She had to search to find green tea.

She was in the toiletries, hand on a toothbrush, when Marco came around the end of the aisle.

"Hey, there," he said, smiling wide enough to bring a smile to her face as well. Marco was a genuinely decent sort, one of the few public servants who didn't have the stink of the Kavanaghs. It didn't hurt that he looked quite a bit like Ponch on *CHiPS*. He had the thick hair and the sparkling dark eyes, though his teeth weren't Hollywood perfect.

Lourana dropped the toothbrush in the cart. *He'll have to use one of my pink lady-razors, I'm not buying any more stuff for people to gawk at.*

"Heck of a night to do the shopping," she said.

"Yeah, but you gotta make the dollar stretch. I've done good so far, got both the kids the toys they been whining after." He tapped a gigantic pink box with a picture of a dollhouse on it.

"You're still with the cleaning service?"

He nodded, and looked away. A former deputy, Marco had been fired "at the will and pleasure of the sheriff." Everyone said it was a shame. He'd been fair with the top dogs and merciful to the under sort. He also didn't gossip, unlike Helen, who'd be telling everyone that Lourana was still head over heels for that no-good Steve Castile who put her through the wringer.

Lourana took a chance.

"I may have a lead on Dreama." She talked fast, before she lost her nerve. "You work the KCL offices, right? Could you let me in to see the mine maps?"

His gaze was sharp and unwavering, the kind that would make a felon decide it was better to give it up. "Why this all of a sudden?"

"I've gotten some information."

"Connected with the spill?"

"Maybe." Lourana thought it was just as well if he were a little misdirected.

"I'm off tonight but I'll be there tomorrow night, well, tonight, that is. Buffing the floors. If you can get there, I'll let you in the door around by the dumpsters."

"I'll get there."

"Make it eleven, right when I start. Around the back."

THE VOICE OF THE MOUNTAIN

Coal itself is not one thing. Coal brought up near Wilkes-Barre, anthracite, is like holding a chunk of obsidian, light reflecting blue from its planes like the flame it will produce. Cannel coal, coking coal—beautiful names! Lignite is brownish and crumbly, a pastry baked too long, and it breaks in the hands. Even the peat that the Irish cut with wooden spades and burn in their cottages is coal, as the seed in the womb is a baby though not yet become a baby. Here, we have bituminous coal, steam coal, best for generating power. The mountain is full of ancient forests, dinosaurs, and fish. You can shatter the coal and see them there, still alive; methane is their breath and the water that springs orange from the mine is their blood.

—CBK

When Lourana got home from Walmart, the lights were blazing at her cottage and the driveway was clear.

"I don't believe it," she said, dropping her packages on the kitchen table. Darrick stood there in her bathrobe, looking raggedy ass but smiling like a sixth grader who's just gotten an *A* in math.

"The shovel was by the door. Seemed like I could do something."

"In that?"

He must not realize the robe didn't offer much coverage. As her eyes slid away, his face went red and he tucked the flaps over and pulled the tie close. She kept her gaze safely elsewhere, but for a moment . . . *Haven't seen one of those for a few years.*

"No. I wore the dirty pants and the coat you'd put out back. I showered, trust me." His face crumpled with disgust.

"Not a wise idea to be outside, you think?"

"I kept an eye out for headlights."

"That's good. You know there's a zombie on the loose."

Darrick stared at her. She could almost see the gears rotating.

"Me."

"Yep. How many cars did you see when you walked in from the fish camp?"

"One." He lingered on that. "One car."

"At least it wasn't a parade. But the family in it, they've been telling all over town that they saw one of the walking dead headed for Redbird. I heard all about it."

"If I'd seen me, I might have thought the same thing." He laughed, but it was a tight, nervous sound.

Between the bloody wound on his head and the lurching walk, he did look like a zombie. She had thought he was a drunk, at first sight, but someone with more imagination—yeah, she could see it. The living dead. It was sort of a hoot until she remembered Jimmy Cooper.

"Here." She opened the sacks and took out clothes and toothbrush and necessities, piled them on his outstretched arms. "You can't go around looking like Merlin the Magician."

"Thank you again." He clutched the clothes to his chest. "I burned everything. In the burn barrel out back, OK?"

"Very OK." *Good thing I grabbed that fleece coat.* "Are you hungry?"

"I could eat."

So they did, after he put on the new clothes and presented them for approval. What meal it might have been at two in the morning was unclear.

"Thanks for the shoveling. I made it out OK, but it was a rough patch, and more snow on the way. When this stuff freezes it will be like a rock." She yawned, finished her milk, and pushed the bag of cookies away. "I feel like a zombie myself."

She went into her room and changed into pajamas, but this time when she locked the door, she did not put a chair under the doorknob.

*   *   *

She was wakened by the noise of car doors slamming, and Darrick rattling her door and whispering. "Police."

"Just a minute!" she yelled. "I'm not decent!" She looked out the window and saw a cop walking around to the back door. Darrick was crouched by the recliner when she came out. His face was rigid. "The cellar," she whispered, thinking fast. "The coal bin. There's a door at the back, to a chute. Crawl inside and close it."

"Ms. Taylor? You all right in there?"

"Just let me get my pants on. Crimony!"

Darrick scuttled away and down the stairs, more quietly than she thought he could. She turned on a game show to cover the sound of the metal hatch squealing open and shut, unlocked the front door to find a red-cheeked young deputy on her doorstep.

"We're doing a safety check. You know we got somebody dangerous on the loose."

"Isn't this where on the cop shows they ask for a warrant?" She gave him her best wish-I-was-twenty-again look.

He shuffled back and forth. "Yes, ma'am. We'd like to look around, for your safety."

She swung the door wide. "I'm just giving you a hard time. Come on in. Glad you're watching out for us. I gotta put on some coffee. I was out late, getting those doorbusters at Walmart, y'know?"

The deputy, a new one, but not a local kid, said that his wife had been there, too, and they about got their Christmas shopping done, how about for her? His name tag read *Anderson*.

She bustled around, filling the place with noise and activity. "I fell asleep in my recliner, watching one of those old horror movies. Silly thing but you get interested. I heard people talking about a zombie—a zombie in Redbird! Isn't that wild! They watched too many *X-Files*." She picked up the blanket that Darrick had used, folded it, reorganized the pillows, pushed the boots deeper under the chair. The coffee maker beeped. "Didn't crawl into bed till 4:30. What time is it now? You want a cup of coffee? I'll bet you're cold, jumping in and out of the car." The black fleece jacket and other items were still piled on the end table. Steve was gonna have to be her cover again.

"Yes, ma'am," Deputy Anderson got in. "And one for my partner."

She poured three big cups. "Where's he at?" At that moment, she heard snow being knocked off boots on her back stoop. She met him with the coffee. "Hey, Ben, I thought you had more seniority than this. Here you are rousting me out of my beauty sleep." Ben Upsher, "Big Ben" to everyone, grinned. When he was on evening shift, he did a lot of checking in at the sweepstakes parlor. Sometimes Lourana thought he might be trying to get something going, but he'd never come out and asked her.

"I see you cleared your driveway out," said Anderson. "Wish my old lady would do that."

* * *

It had taken all he had to go into that cellar the first time.

Now, in the dark, Darrick felt his way back down the stairs, crouching to avoid the low ceiling. This was a pit, the scraping-out of shelter by a primitive tribe. He forced himself forward, his bare feet recoiling from the dirt floor, because what was behind would be worse.

His hands found the sides of the wooden bin. He stepped over the threshold into a layer of coal chunks, his feet twisting as he stumbled to the back, to the small door he'd glimpsed and given no more thought. His hand touched rusty metal. He raised the door and pushed his way inside the chute. Face first. He kept his mouth closed, hoping not to cough on the coal dust stirred up. He levered himself forward on his elbows, the door like a blade cutting into the back of his legs, his knees splayed to find purchase. He heaved and wriggled and finally the door flopped shut behind him.

The chute was narrow as a coffin, and slanted up. He could see a little bit of light leaking around the door up there, but it had to be covered deep with snow.

So cold.

The gas furnace cycled on, and he imagined that roaring flame leaping across to the coal, the conflagration. When the furnace sighed off, he could hear conversations upstairs but could not tell what was live and what was television.

The metal was cold against his shins. No time for socks and shoes. He could feel things crawling on him. Imagined them, as it was far too cold for the many-legged to be moving. Enough light filtered around the door that he could see streaks of coal dust on the metal. It was like being in the mine crack again, as though these hours with Lourana had been a dream as he faded toward death on a carpet of bones.

Darrick's teeth chattered. Cold? Fear? *A man should say cold.* He knew it was both. He had gone from one hole to another, except now his escape depended not on his own initiative but upon a woman he barely knew.

She had no reason to hide him, every reason to turn him over. She was afraid of the local authorities, that much was clear. Her attitude did not conceal the terror beneath. Now that he was trapped, he could see with clear eyes that she would, inevitably, turn on him.

Why not? If Nicole could betray him, then why not this stranger? Love had not been enough for Nicole. Not all his devotion. Not the love that she swore she felt for him. They shared their desires for a home, a family, had discussed the number of children, their names, how they would school them. Then she went home to visit her folks, and everything changed. She had been sweet, sexy, empathetic—until she was not.

He could hear heavy footsteps, more conversation.

Lourana had no reason to protect him. She had sent him down here to a trap, with no escape. His soles ached as they pressed against the frame of the lower door but he could not move them and risk rattling metal on metal. His mind raced. Could he even get out if he had to? Had there been a catch on the outside of the lower door? He couldn't remember. What if she was taken away? What if she left? He would freeze to death in this metal box. His heart thumped alarmingly. He stretched one arm toward the upper door but could not reach it, not without making noise.

The first rule he had ever learned: don't make noise.

You didn't make a sound when they put you in the isolation room. The quieter you were, the quicker you got out.

The isolation room had been a kind of closet. No light, no chair. A standing coffin. The children's home had many kids with behaviors. Acting out, they called it. Darrick had behaviors that the staff did not like. He walked strangely, not always, but whenever he was stressed, which was often—but because it was intermittent, some thought he chose when to stagger. He saw unclearly. Often in those days he spoke with difficulty, slowly—now it only seemed that he was deliberate with his words, but then they saw it as mocking. *The authorities.*

One afternoon he had been slow to respond to the call for dinner. He was engaged in something, a book, a project, crucial then but forgotten now. He talked back to the dorm supervisor and was put in isolation. Something happened. The hour turned into hours, the common area got quiet, the light that seeped under the door disappeared. He stood in his bare cell, abandoned. Sometime in the evening, his bladder released.

They realized he was gone at bed check. It was the janitor who found him, alerted by the pool of urine outside the door. He was paraded, shaking and wet, down the hall, past dorm rooms where laughing faces turned to follow his passage.

"You cannot be flouting the authority," said the nurse as she helped him clean up, took his temperature because of his shuddering. They said she had come from overseas, from the Communists. "What they say, you must do, or it will not go well with you."

That was when he had started to learn.

He heard the click and return as the string was pulled on the light, the crunch of boots on the stairs, the creak of old wood.

"What's down here?"

"The furnace."

The older one, taking the lead, was calm. Darrick could feel his caution, a steady vibration, but no fear. The second one, however, must have been thinking about zombies, because his mind pulsed and roared. He poured his focus into the gun under his hand. It was half out of the holster. It was a heavy thing, a safe anchor in a whirling vacuum.

Darrick reached out, tentative. A wave of fear surged across him and he followed it back, his thoughts encountering the younger one's mind, and then he was moving around inside his head. There was pressure, answering pressure, and he felt the young deputy tremble.

"Watch the overhead," he heard Lourana say, sounding so assured and assuring.

He withdrew from the deputy but could still feel the rawness of his emotion, as well as the sturdy equanimity of the other man. He saw a fragment of light move into the chute as they stood between the coal bin and the furnace, pointing their flashlights into the corners.

Be quiet.

The younger man was first to go back up. His fear had not lessened, but it ebbed the farther away he got, until at the top of the stairs, Darrick could feel only a shadow of that dark wave.

Now he was aware again of his shins freezing against the metal, of the tension in all his body. He heard nothing from upstairs and began to think the worst. She had gone with them, or they were gathering forces for an assault, or preparing to fire down the chute from the outside. He could hear the television blasting laughter, but no other sounds. A door shut, on the television, or maybe for real. He waited.

Soft steps on the stairs. "It's OK now."

He let his feet relax against the lower door, and it gave way, opening, and he slid down the chute and out on his knees in the coal. He could see Lourana's feet in rundown slippers, halfway down the stairs. Gracelessly, he got to his feet and emerged from the bin, blackened and shivering.

"Look at you," she said, clicking her tongue as she headed back up. "Nice new clothes and all."

"It's terrible," he croaked, "to be in the dark."

She turned to him in the kitchen, her face solemn.

"I didn't think how it would bother you. But there wasn't any other place to go. My closets are full."

"But you don't get shopping channels," he said, trying to be light, and failing.

"No. I'm a bit of a hoarder." Her mouth moved down ruefully at one corner.

"Why did they come here?"

"They've got an all-hands search to find whoever killed Jimmy. They're looking for a stranger because of that crazy zombie story. They're working the roads that have been plowed. The crews come off the highway to run this road past me and one more house and turn around."

"They don't know who I am."

She shook her head. "Someone must know who you are, right? Because they got your wallet."

"And my car. Somewhere."

"I'd bet Lake Dunwoody. Here." She threw the robe at him. "You'll have to be Merlin again for a while so I can wash that stuff."

He stripped off the fouled new clothes in the bathroom, looked in the mirror to see a blackened face, his eyes staring. He found a dark washcloth and scrubbed his face and hands and feet. He breathed in and out, deeply, several times. By the time he came out, he was walking better and felt he was back in equilibrium.

"When you asked me to get the coal, I thought it would be outside," he explained. "When you opened that cellar door I nearly panicked. I have a phobia about dark, closed-in places."

"After the mine crack, I can understand that."

Darrick kept any further explanation to himself.

"You know, back in the old days, they used to pay boys a few cents a day to work the doors inside the mine," Lourana said. "They called them nippers. Little nippers. Just sitting there alone, opening a door when they heard the rumble of the wheels."

He shuddered.

"Some of them might have been eight years old, nine. I guess it was better than being a breaker, sorting coal with their bare hands. Whole families went down, back then—when the Monongah mine blew up, they said 362 died, but it was way more than that. The men all took their kids down to help load."

Darrick was ashamed of his panic. It was one thing to be afraid as a child, but he should be able to overcome that as an adult. He imagined himself, that boy he had been, down in a mine, in the dark, alone, straining to hear the sound of something that connected him to the world above.

He sat on the other chair while she curled in the recliner, waiting on breakfast, on whatever the next step was. Outside, the snow had eased off, but the world was white and alien. Here he sat in a woman's bathrobe, without any of the accoutrements of a normal life, his life. He imagined his neighborhood this morning, people out walking their dogs and going to Starbucks, picking up the *Post* and sharing the headlines, their voices approving or indignant. This was like being stranded on a desert island. He didn't have any control over his own life right now, and that was a lousy feeling, one he'd worked very hard not to experience again.

Lourana got up and started clashing things around in the kitchen, with a running commentary as she did. "It's a special life, mining. Nothing romantic about it, but it takes something special to do it. You have to grow up with it, always an ear cocked for the whistle that says something's gone wrong. When a miner's wife kisses him goodbye in the morning and hands him his dinner bucket, she can't know if he'll be walking back through the door that night."

"I guess you have faith."

She snorted. "That's for selling newspapers. Any disaster, look at how they depict the families praying and calling on Jesus and all that stuff. Not saying some ain't religious, but most are like my pap. He always said when your time's up, it's up."

"He was a miner?"

"And his brothers, his father. The Taylors been mining as long as they've been here. UMW the whole way, and the union got us good contracts that always kept that new pickup in the driveway."

"But not your husband."

"The jobs went away. Longwall didn't need so many men as conventional mining, then the seams started tailing off, and demand's dropped. They're blowing the tops off whole mountains south of us and hauling them away with draglines. We got more schoolteachers than miners these days."

She shuffled in with a mug of tea for him and a box of muffins. "I wouldn't have minded a bit if Steve went underground. You gotta be fatalistic about it or go crazy. Any little thing might do it—the roof is bad, the bolt don't set right. A methane pocket, a spark. Miners are all beholden, to the guys on their shift, to the fire bosses, to the company, to the damn mountain."

"I guess it's like the army," Darrick offered. "You look out for your unit. Your buddies."

"What if you got no buddies? No one has your back?" Lourana's impenetrable eyes seemed to soften, and her face became vulnerable for just a second before the gates closed again.

Darrick was fascinated by the change. Was this who she really was, when she dropped her guard? *Leave it alone.* He quickly took a bite of muffin. "Good," he said, "Blueberry."

"Walmart." Lourana sat straight and slipped back into her pugnacious self. "Eat up. We got someplace to go tonight."

Consider the crossing lines on a graph of coal production and employment. In 1924, it took 116,000 men to mine 150 million tons of coal in West Virginia. In 1957, it took 67,000. In 2006, just 20,000. But now both lines descend together.

—CBK

"You gotta be able to see." Lourana was bent over the kitchen table, where his broken glasses and a pair of sunglasses lay dismembered on the yellow tablecloth.

"Any particular reason?" It was fascinating to watch her large hands (and they were large, capable) manipulating the tiniest of screwdrivers to remove the screw from the temple and then marry the frames.

"We're going to look at some maps."

"Maps?"

She ignored him and continued to work. The screw fell out. She jiggled it back into place, turned the screwdriver, but the sizes were off and it wouldn't hold.

"Plan B," she said, holding up a roll of electrical tape.

It had been dark for hours. His time sense was all askew. What day was this? Still Friday. It had been Friday this morning when he cowered in the coal chute, Friday as they napped on and off to the murmur of the television, exhausted by the encounter with the authorities, Friday as the sun went down and the shadows reached out long and blue across the snow.

Lourana ripped a thin strip of tape from the roll and gently bonded the stem to the frame. When he put them on, Darrick was visited by a memory of broken glasses when he was a kid. Frames held together with tape at the bridge of his nose after he fell, or was tripped. It was an eternity until the state provided new ones; meanwhile, the kids at school had their expected fun.

"Will they hold?"

"I think so." He rocked them gently on his ears until they seemed stable. "Thank you."

"It was hard to look at you with them sitting lopsided like that."

"Hard to look at me anyway."

She didn't answer his attempt at humor, instead carefully inserting the screwdriver back in its place in a small tool kit, replacing it in a drawer. *She might be a hoarder, but she's a neat one.* She dusted off her hands as though she'd been splitting wood, and looked at him appraisingly. "I have to ask. When you were in the basement, did that happen again? Like with Jimmy?"

"It could have." Darrick felt he had to be careful, parse his words. "I could hear—feel—no, it was more like hear. The young one was afraid. Emotion. Pounding, loud, dissonant. Now the older one, I could not hear him as much, maybe because he was so calm. But the young one's fear came over me, the same way, the blare of his thoughts."

"Blare?"

"Noise, but not random. Just too full of notes, like someone who doesn't know how to play a piano bashing on the keys." It was a flimsy description, but he was no poet. "The sound comes in waves, until it becomes crushing, and I push back against it. Smother it. I have to."

"So you pushed back?"

"I started to, but I stopped." Which wasn't entirely true, but close. She seemed to need reassurance that he wasn't out of control. A deranged zombie killer.

By the time they left, the moon was high and the snow reflected its cold light. Darrick looked around as they left, taking in the weight of the forest just above the cottage, the lights thinly scattered below.

The snow had frozen hard, leaving washboards and icy ruts. They slithered down the hill into the town that hugged the black curve of the mutilated river. They circled the old courthouse, its pale dome brilliantly lit, topped by a statue of a robed woman. Blindfold, scales, and sword like all the others across America, Justice with no sense of irony about who and what was actually weighting those scales.

Lourana made a second circle, peering down side streets. All sorts of cloak-and-dagger. The town was dead, empty of people but also empty of businesses, the windows with FOR LEASE signs in the corner or covered with the remains of patriotic murals. An IRON CITY BEER sign flickered in the window of a bar below the street level. It appeared to be the only place open.

Lourana pulled behind the KCL Building and backed into a space near the dumpsters. He saw her check the time before they climbed onto the loading dock and she knocked on a gray metal door.

* * *

Marco opened the door to Lourana's sharp knock, eleven right on the dot, but he pulled back at seeing not one but two figures dark against the snow.

"What?"

"A friend," Lourana said. "Let us in."

Fuck, he thought, *this was a mistake.*

Marco didn't allow them entry so much as Lourana bulled her way past him, the stranger in tow. He shut the door behind them and they faced each other in the unheated receiving room, breath puffing around their faces under the dim fluorescent bulbs.

"Who's this? A new boyfriend?" Marco sized him up with a glance. *He'd have me on reach, but that's it. I could take him, easy.* "I thought you were wanting to find out something about Dreama."

"I told you, I wanted to see the mine maps."

"And how does that connect with Dreama? And him?" He knew how harsh his voice was, but was surprised to see bafflement move briefly across her face and disappear, an unguarded moment swallowed by her usual flat expression. *How could she think this was OK? She already cost me one job.* "I'm asking again—who is this?" The guy looked nervous, kept backing toward the door like he might bolt. The longer Marco looked at him, the less he thought, *easy.* There was something weird there, that creep-up-the-back feeling when you know that hostile eyes are on you, or the darkness of a room that is occupied by someone breathing, waiting.

"This is Darrick. He's on our side."

"Which side is that?"

"Whatever side isn't the Kavanaghs, right? He was attacked out at the convenience store the other night. Left for dead. Might could be that's what happened to Dreama."

Marco shook his head. "Maybe he just pissed somebody off. I don't know. That's his problem. I'm not sticking my neck out for anyone but you." He jerked his thumb at the door. "You can wait outside, dude."

Lourana put her hand on his arm. "Please. He's hip deep in this too." Her eyes were full of shared history. Marco remembered in high school, how she was always involved in Pep Club and things like that, helping out, anything that was about other people getting attention but not her. He could have gone for her, but Beth got him first. She was wearing his ring when Lourana got involved with Steve, and then it was too late. Over the years, he'd had run-ins with her ex, had read him the riot act and more than once thought about showing him the county line at the business end of the 12-gauge he carried in the trunk. *But you didn't, did you, fuckhead? Too little, too late.*

He watched the guy keep sidling awkwardly away until he found a certain distance and kind of stayed there. Was he looking for an angle to attack? When Marco moved a step toward him, the stranger backed up, and again Lourana stopped him.

"Tell him, Darrick."

He had his back to the door, now, with his hand on the doorknob. "I've gotten on the wrong side of the Kavanaghs as well."

"How?"

"I was attacked. When I woke up, I was down in a cave—"

"Mine crack," sighed Lourana.

"—surrounded by bones and skulls. I wasn't supposed to get out of that hole. I guess they thought this would be enough."

The guy turned away and slowly bent his head so that the light could reach. An ugly wound showed, with wholly inadequate butterfly bandages trying to hold the flesh together but allowing a view right down to the white of his skull.

Marco began to laugh. "Christ on a crutch, *you're* the zombie! You're the fucking walking dead! Hot *damn*, Lourana, you sure can pick 'em."

She cut her eyes at him, like, *enough said.*

"That's why we want a look at the mine maps. We need to find that mine crack, because maybe . . . "

"Dreama is down there," Marco completed.

"And a bunch of other people," said Darrick.

Marco couldn't stop himself from staring, wondering if the zombie stuff was just crazy talk, or something more. This guy gave off strange vibes. His eyes didn't seem to track just right, but that wasn't it. He kept having to re-evaluate that first gut impression.

"How many?" he asked.

"Four at least. I counted skulls where I could see, but the hole falls off to a deeper level at one end. Who knows what's down there?"

"Four." Marco started tallying up the missing, incidents back when he was still on the force. Talk in the squad room that silenced when he came in. That motorcyclist, Black Dog. And there was that loudmouth Peters from Poplar Bank over near Charleston, spouting off about how they were never gonna frack his family farm, he was gonna go all anarchist on KCL.

"One was a woman."

He looked at this Darrick character. "How do you know?"

"I found a necklace."

Marco remembered the environmentalist who had disappeared, pretty thing from West Virginia University in her L.L. Bean boots and her backpack full of water-testing kits. The rest of the Appalfolk crew had scattered when she dropped out of sight. He wondered how wide and how deep this went, if it reached beyond the boundaries of Carbon County.

"Who knows you're here? And maybe more important, who knows you're walking around when you're supposed to be dead?"

"I don't think anyone, on the first count."

"No one?"

"Not yet. My office is closed."

Jesus, his office?

"The Rodeheavers saw you. They're the ones started the fool talk about the walking dead," Lourana said, hands on her hips. "Now, we all introduced proper? Time's wasting."

The First Miners and Merchants Bank occupied the ground floor of the KCL Building, boasting a lobby of marble and gilt, with teller cages to the right ranked like sentries before the enormous vault. The broad desks of midlevel bank employees filled the space to the left, while executives were out of sight on the mezzanine. At the back of the echoing space, murals flanked an elevator bank, with miners and coal trains on one side, a gleaming city of stores and factories on the other. Marco had quickly learned to hate every lavish inch of the ornamentation—carved wood that had to be dusted, mirrors that always were finger marked, pendant bowl lights where at least one bulb was always burned out, crevices where leaves blew in and clustered like dead bugs in a spiderweb.

"Classy joint," said Darrick.

He didn't know where this guy was from, but Marco caught the whiff of condescension. *Yeah, I'm sure this is hayseed city for you.* As Darrick started to move, he pulled him back. "Cameras pointed at the elevators."

"Oh."

They retreated to the rear stairs, where nobody went other than cleaners and maintenance men, their movements not worthy of recording. "Sixth floor. Hope you're up for it." He'd seen how this character moved, like he had some kind of palsy. The stairs were metal and they made a helluva racket, especially those clogs on Lourana, but there was no one around to hear. "I still don't get why you're not getting the hell out of Dodge, back to . . . "

"Washington."

Figures. "I'll drive you out, tomorrow or the next day," Marco added aloud.

Darrick stopped on the landing. He looked back, like maybe he was planning to leave right this minute.

"Well?"

"I don't want to leave here until I know what has happened to me."

"Unless you're FBI, this situation is way above all our pay grades," said Marco. "Remember, you're an outsider."

"But I'm the one who woke up in that hole. I can't just walk away and go back to my old life, as though everything would be like it was before."

"I said, you're an outsider. You don't have a clue what that means. You should lay low and get out. Let someone else deal with the bones."

Lourana held up her hands. "Debating society is closed for tonight."

The sixth floor was the KCL mining operations center. An electronic lock sealed the outer door. Marco keyed in the code, letting them into a long hallway of identical offices. "It's on the left," he said, counting the doors. Another electronic lock and they were in the map room. It smelled of wood and lemon oil, leather, musty paper. Computers sat silent on desks and antique surveyor's tools were locked in tall glass cabinets.

Lourana had coordinates and quickly pulled the printed maps. "This should be the quadrangle. Here's the mine tipple," she said, talking to herself, "and here's Bailey's Fish Camp." She looked up at Darrick, her eyes gleaming in the one light over the big desk. "How did you get down to the road?"

"When I came out of the crack, I was standing at the bottom of a kind of bowl. Like an amphitheater. I walked out on the low side, which was toward the river."

"He was headed south," Marco said, pointing at the curved line of the river.

"I had to cross a fence. There was a stream on my right."

"Yeah." Lourana traced a boundary line with her finger. "You were on Kavanagh property when you came up. The fence marks the surface area they own, though the deep mine extends all around, back the other way and then right under the river and on the other side."

"My uncle worked that section, years ago," Marco said. "Bad roof. They had falls no matter how many bolts they punched into that slate." *He left two fingers and his lungs down there.*

She examined a place where the lines looped. "I'd say that's the bowl you're talking about."

"When did you learn to read topo?" asked Marco.

"I've taught myself a whole lot of things." He watched as she took a pad and pen from her pocket and began noting down coordinates. She'd put on some pounds and earned some wrinkles, but as she bent close to the maps with her smartphone and a little notebook, her hair pulled back and gleaming in the light from overhead, she could have been across the lab table from him back in chemistry class.

"Why don't you just look this up on the internet?" asked Darrick.

Marco answered. "Can't. Active mines are not public record."

"And I quote: 'Maps of currently permitted operations are considered confidential until the mine permit is closed out.' Proprietary information." Lourana made a face. "That covers a lot of sins. The main production is from longwall on the other side of the river, but they're still pulling pillars in sections that were long ago mined out with continuous miners."

She went back to the files and pulled out another map. "What are they doing underground at No. 4?" she mused. Marco knew the real conversation was going on inside her; they were just listening in.

He kept an eye on Darrick as he moved to the other side of the map table. The way he walked, he probably had a concussion if not worse. Must have been a tire iron, gun, something serious to open him up like that. A couple of inches one way or the other, where the skull is thinner or where the skull joins to the spine, and he wouldn't have been walking around at all.

Darrick ran his hand over the polished table. "So Dreama worked here?"

"On this floor," Marco answered. "She left at five, a normal day, but never got back to her apartment."

"The Kavanaghs?"

"Smart money would say yes, but there wasn't any reason. We never found the car, any trace of her. Not an ATM withdrawal, not a toll road hit. Just evaporated, like others who've gone missing."

"Maybe the authorities don't look very hard in these cases."

"By that you would mean me. I was lead investigator. I went everywhere legal and some places that weren't." Marco felt a little surge of pleasure to see Darrick recoil from this slapdown, physically shrink away from him as Lourana glanced up from her work to catch the whole thing.

But Darrick wasn't quite done. "I understand most of the people around here are Kavanagh's—what do you call them? Creatures."

"Some. Not most. You can tell. There's something about the ones that are, ones that made that deal with Knockaulin House. The rest of us just live our lives and pay the bills. The economy ain't such that you can get out easy, leastwise if you have a mortgage upside down on a fucking house you couldn't sell if you tried."

"What the hell?" They turned to see Lourana stabbing her finger at the map. "Right here. The map shows a pattern of boreholes from No. 4. Recent boreholes, from the date on this map."

Marco looked over her shoulder, at the circles and slanting lines that indicated the bores. "But why would they do that?"

"They could lead into the Bella Jean. Dumping the untreated water from No. 4 over into the old workings." She was flipping maps, taking photos one after the other.

"But it's No. 4 that blew out, not the seal on the Bella Jean," Marco argued.

"Yeah. You're right," Lourana muttered. "It don't make sense."

Marco tried to see the mine through those neat lines and numbers. He could estimate how many klicks to a sniper, but couldn't visualize this underground world he'd made damn sure was not going to be his life. "Tell you what, I think we should go up there tomorrow and take a look."

"You want to get that involved?" Darrick said.

Marco might have said a lot of things, including *yeah, because of Lourana*, but he flipped his cleaning service badge and said, "This isn't the uniform I should be wearing. I was top deputy until I got too deep into Dreama's case. There's something with the Kavanaghs, I know that much—the more I dug, the more pushback I got. Went from detective to patrol, day shift to midnight. I went in for my shift on a Tuesday night and the sheriff met me at the door. Done."

"But they can't do that!" Darrick protested.

"Yes, they can. Maybe not in Washington, but the sheriff's office isn't civil service. I'll tell you, it grinds me every time I collect that KCL paycheck. You understand, I got a family depending on me." Marco thought of his wife, the kids growing up bright as new pennies, and counted his blessings even if he couldn't give them the kind of life he wanted. Lourana didn't have anyone but a messed-up ex and now this guy glommed onto her, who said he had no one to call, no one to care if he'd died in the hole. *Must be a hell of a way to live.*

Darrick once knew a woman who was terrified to cross the expanse of concrete termed a *plaza* by the anonymous architect who had created the equally anonymous office block where they worked. She'd park in the back, close to a retaining wall, and keep her hand on the brick as she scurried for the rear door, hunched over as if a terrible bird were about to descend from the sky and pluck her up. Agoraphobia. He'd never understood it before.

It was one thing to go out under the cover of darkness, like last night, driving into a dead town. But daylight would come soon, revealing everything.

I feel like a cockroach when the light is turned on.

The stabbing agony that had accompanied every fractional turn of his head and speared his brain at a sudden light or sound had subsided to an unrelenting, twisting pain, as though that blade now was reaming its way into his brain. If it weren't for that, and the feel of the wound under his fingers (gingerly, delicately) then he would think it was a dream. Things like this didn't happen, at least to people he knew. Maybe it hadn't happened to him, either; he was caught in a baroque nightmare that would release him eventually. Not that he was prone to such. But as he watched Lourana pull on yellow hunting boots that she laced up over cheap sweatpants, he knew it was no dream. She looked at him quizzically as he sat glued to the kitchen chair, unwilling to finish putting on the socks and boots that once were worn by someone he didn't know.

"We need to get going. Gotta be there at sunup."

He bent over (pain swelling) and finished the job, stood and put on the black coat she'd bought for him. It was a size too big, but he wasn't complaining. Lourana handed him a pair of bright orange gloves and a hunting hat the same shade that he stuffed in his pocket. She wore one of those goofy woolen hats with the strings that hung down on each side of her face, along with a camo coat that had orange patches pinned to the back and front. She looked more like an escapee than he did.

The sky was hard and black and strewn with more stars than he thought existed. With the snow-covered ground and smoke rising straight from the chimneys below, it could have been a postcard, except that as you got closer, you saw the buildings were ratty and the river oozed like the residue of a fire in a traffic-cone factory. It was a Saturday morning on a four-day holiday weekend, and if you had a job, you weren't going to it.

Darrick slid lower in the seat as they drove into town, the streetlights starting to click off one by one as the sky lightened. Maybe it was that grayish sausage gravy and biscuits she had fed him for breakfast, but his stomach was sour and turbulent. Or maybe it was the sight of the KCL logo everywhere, like a triangular brand burned into the town, and the name emblazoned on signs. Kavanagh Federal Credit Union. Kavanagh Boulevard, a new road sweeping along this side of the river between rows of young trees standing with their arms up, frail as refugees. Two bridges arched across the water, one concrete and the other a rickety metal span, and he'd bet at least one had "the name." Below the blank backs of stores on the opposite side, a band of grass and trees had been installed. A pier stuck out over the water with an ornate pavilion on the end. It looked like something from the 1890s, with metalwork legs and a cupola that might have been copper aged to verdigris over many years.

"What's that?"

She glanced left. "Kavanagh Park."

He grimaced.

"All that area used to be the old waterfront businesses—a cement plant, metal recycling facility, bulk materials dock."

"Nice things to have in the center of your town."

"Yeah, agreed. No one could ever get rid of them 'cause they were grandfathered in, though the EPA shut down the cement plant for air pollution. Then a few years ago, the Kavanaghs—actually the younger one, Cormac—bought what they didn't already own and tore it all down, turned the rail line into a bike trail, and gifted the park to the city."

"Guilt."

"I'd suspect a tax write-off."

He stared at the orange-hued banks, the languid streamers of pollution drifting through patches of discolored ice.

"That stuff, what do you call it?"

"AMD. Yellowboy."

"Does this always happen when you mine coal?"

"It can, if they don't do it right, but this blowout isn't like anything anyone's ever seen."

"Can anything live in there?"

"Like that? The pH that low? Not even a carp."

They passed the sweepstakes parlor, the parking lot unplowed but marked by a few sets of tracks. Hopefuls, perhaps, who thought just maybe it would be open. Now they were bumping down the road he had walked. It was familiar, but under the snow it had a skewed reality like everything else here, half in a dream world. The sheet-metal walls of the mine building were streaked with rust and ice, glittering where snowmelt had run down and then frozen. Like before, the fish camp was deserted, a ghost town created by toxic water. He saw a striped cat bound across the road and disappear into the overgrowth. Someone had spray-painted *Zombie Apocalypse* on the wall of a building—had that been there before and he didn't see it as he turned toward the lights of the town? More likely it was one of those kids in that car, blank faces turned toward him, who had returned to leave this warning.

A white pickup truck with a cap on the back was pulled off the road by the bait store, a KCL pass hanging from the rearview mirror. The back window was raised, showing the inverted silhouette of a leaping buck. Marco came around the truck wearing an orange coat and orange coveralls. A coil of rope was slung over one shoulder, a rifle on the other. He carried a second gun that he pointedly handed to Lourana.

That's OK, Darrick thought. *I have no intention of carrying a gun.*

"That all your orange?"

He showed Marco the gloves and hat.

"Legal. Barely. Put them on."

And you're wearing enough for both of us, Darrick thought. He tried stretching the hat over his head, but that wasn't happening, so he stuck it in the collar of his coat.

The emotional noise from Marco, which at their first meeting had been a dissonant mass of dark and braying instruments, a dozen amateur orchestras attempting Stravinsky in a junkyard, had lessened to a tolerable roar. Somehow the jagged edges were less jagged. Still, it was a complex blend of rage, shame, sexual desire, and desperation. Darrick learned that he could follow the threads into the mass, keeping track the way you could keep several things in your mind at once, an old song and something nagging to be done on your desk and the angle of the jaw when that actress turned her head in the TV show you watched last night, all the time you were driving or eating.

"Let's head up." Marco gestured him forward.

He felt less than comfortable walking with an armed man at his back, but still, it was good to get some distance from Marco. Lourana trudged beside him, seemingly unbothered, though her impenetrable emotional core would not allow him to know if that was the case. She cradled her weapon in her arms. Darrick wondered if she knew how to use it.

The snow was crusted over from daytime thaw and nighttime cold, covering thick layers of fallen leaves that concealed tangles of branches or dips in the ground. Darrick fell, and fell again. He tried to keep his balance by setting his feet down carefully, which made his gait even more exaggerated. He tripped on a vine and pitched forward, losing his glasses, which necessitated a clumsy search in the snow. Marco did not conceal his irritation. He walked up to the glasses, pushing them forward with the toe of his boot. Shots echoed, none close. Darrick felt like a hunted deer himself.

Lourana had her phone on compass. She kept orienting their path to the topo map, tracking the degrees of elevation and the visible landmarks. "We're headed back from the main entry here for the old mine. Does this look right?" she asked him.

"It all looks different in the snow."

Marco made a dismissive noise.

"You must have been pretty much out of it," Lourana said, glancing back at their companion.

"It was like a dream."

"Maybe it was," sniped Marco.

Darrick felt less and less sure as they made their way up the mountain. Dead leaves hung in clumps from the branches, brown and leathery, unable to let go. Pines made dark belts across the woods, the ground bare under their pendulous branches. Were those the pines he had walked through? It was like a fairy-tale forest, and not the good kind. He'd never been one for the outdoors. When the activity fair was held each fall in the gym, he'd always avoided the Scouts and opted for chess club. Never harvested the odd burn or scrape that other kids showed off like badges from their scrimmages and campouts. He couldn't name the bird or animal that issued a rattling call from the woods, or those hectoring notes like a child accusing, "He-he-he-he!" Otherwise, there was so little sound that he wondered if the coal pollution had killed off the birds too. They crossed no other human tracks, though Marco would sometimes bend to read the hieroglyphics left by animals.

They came to the border fence: beware, Kavanagh property. Darrick remembered crossing it, but the distances seemed off, as though they had come farther up than he had come down. But the fence must be the one he'd sighted along, the briers and scrub trees even looking somewhat familiar. Finally, they crested the rise, and could look down into a natural bowl in the land, and at its center, a ragged black scar.

For a moment, they stood and just caught their breath.

"That's it," he said.

Lourana traced her finger along the map. "Makes sense. We're above the Bella Jean workings, abandoned decades ago."

"Somebody comes here. You can see the tracks." Marco air-sketched the double line of indentations under the snow, shadows of the path made by a truck or ATV from the mine crack up the far side of the bowl and over.

Lourana checked her map. "The closest road that way would be Sawmill Run."

As they walked down the slope, Darrick could detect the scent of decay, getting stronger as they approached, but neither of the others said anything. Marco found an adequate tree and fastened the rope to it, the line already fitted with some kind of clips at its ends. He scaled the loops over to another tree, ran the rope around it, and rigged the end around his waist. He went to the lip of the hole and tested the edge.

"Why do you think you ended up here?" Marco focused on Darrick, and in this strong sunlight he could see the deputy's eyes were not black but dark brown. Much darker than Lourana's. There was a bitter sadness in them, but also an assurance. He seemed to be at home doing this work and the activity quelled some of his emotional storm.

"I have no idea. Can't you smell the bodies?"

Marco shrugged. "Probably deer carcasses. Let's see what we see. If what you say is true, then it might answer a lot of questions around here."

Marco tested his rig and had Darrick take up the slack. "You wanna give me rope *slowly*, OK? Belay me. Let the tree bear the weight." Darrick nodded. He stood where he was told and set his feet firmly, relieved that he did not have to descend into the darkness blooming with the smell of death.

"I still think the best thing you could do is let me haul your ass out of Carbon County, right now," Marco offered, one more time.

"I can't run." *How can I run away from this homicidal monster I've become?*

Marco's head was just about to go under when he fixed him with a heavy-duty stare. "Whatever happened, you're not safe here. But I'm more worried about Lourana." Marco turned on a small flashlight and held it in his teeth as he disappeared.

You don't know when your time will come, when you'll be summoned to do your part. That's what Father Ronan told me, toward the end when not much that he said made sense. And so what if I never go back to my condo and IKEA furniture and that one painting I loved enough to pay real money for?

The rope bit into the soft bark of the tree; the dead weight was greater than Darrick expected. Even with the pivot he found himself slipping. He sank his oversized boots into the ground and tightened his grip.

"Smells like hell." Marco's voice came muffled. "Keep giving me rope."

Darrick let the rope slide through his clownish gloves. He had a moment of fear that Marco's weight would pull him over, that he would find himself back among the bones. He settled his shoulders and felt the muscles move along his back. His wound howled at the strain, and then the rope went slack.

"Fuck. Fuck me! Bones everywhere."

Darrick felt a whoosh of relief. He glanced at Lourana, and realized from her open-mouthed expression that she hadn't quite believed his story.

"I'm going to look around." The rope began to pay out slowly, pacing the dull thud and occasional crack of his footsteps. Darrick remembered that pavement of bones and rot, the miasmic flow of damp air from unseen depths.

"Be careful at the far end, it drops off," he called.

"Gotcha. I see three, four. I count five skulls." Flashes of bluish-white light as he took pictures with his cell phone. After a while, he called, "Take up the slack and start pulling me out. Careful."

Darrick and Lourana both put their weight to the rope and inched Marco to the surface. He floundered at the soft edge and slipped back, then got his torso over and levered himself onto the trampled ground.

"God help us." Marco stood up, scrubbing his boots vigorously into the snow. "Didn't think I'd ever see such in my home place."

"Guess I'm not loony then." Darrick waited for them to say something, to affirm his rightness. Instead, they were silent, seeming to assess him. "Right?"

"Yeah, right," Marco said. "You weren't lying."

"We'll hold off on declaring your sanity," Lourana said, with a little conspiratorial grin that took him by surprise.

"My question is, how the hell did you get out of there? Fly?"

Darrick felt the edge of accusation under Marco's question. "I found two long bones. Leg bones. I jammed them into the wall." He thrust one hand and then the other. "I climbed. It took a while."

Marco whistled, low. "I know desperation gives people the ability to do things. Damn."

"So what's the plan?" Lourana glanced up at the sun, a reminder that time was getting on.

"I got some pictures and tried not to do any more damage down there. I'll put together the information I have on the missing people—I started keeping copies of my files at home. Come Monday morning, I'll be in Charleston. I've got a buddy I can trust at the Bureau of Criminal Investigations. He'll move quickly."

"And I'll get in touch with my office in Washington."

"Maybe the FBI?" added Lourana.

"Damn straight," said Marco. "Bring the black helicopters if you can get 'em."

They headed for the truck in silence, like three people who didn't know each other who are uneasy to find themselves accidentally too close together on the same sidewalk. Darrick fell back, letting them choose the path so that he could walk at a pace he found manageable.

They'd just stashed the rope in the back when a dark green Jeep pulled up, bumper to bumper with Marco's truck. "Fucking game warden," he spat. A lanky man got out, settling his Smokey Bear hat on his gray crew cut as he did. "That's old Hovatter. Great. He's a hard-ass."

Darrick eased away from Marco. The renewed turmoil in his thoughts was painful, a lacing of envy there now as he looked at the DNR officer in his crisp uniform, along with the simmering anger and frustration.

"You folks wouldna been hunting up on the KCL land, would you?" His face was leathery as an old saddle, and deep-set eyes were made sepulchral by the olive drab hat.

"No," said Marco, slamming down the back window on the cap. "Just over behind the fish camp, below the pines. Good to see you, Lyle."

The game warden nodded, once, but kept looking at the three sets of tracks in the snow.

Inflexible. Unyielding. This was a man who'd set out on a course and hewed to it. Darrick was surprised, again, not just by the hammering on his mind but at the tonal differences of people's emotions.

"Hunting licenses, please."

Marco produced his. "I'm the only one hunting. They're just driving for me."

Lourana nodded.

"I see two rifles. That's two hunters, in my book."

"I don't even know how to use it," she protested.

"Then you got no business with it. You gotta have a license if you're going to carry a gun." He looked hard at Darrick, "I ain't heard a thing from you, son. I don't believe I know you."

"I'm a friend of Lourana's."

"That rifle, I'm thinking, is most like to be your gun, and she's covering for you. Let's see your identification."

Darrick could see his body slamming down on the bone pile. Maybe with company. Maybe without.

"Lyle, you know me," Marco put in, an edge of desperation on his words. "I'm after a deer to fill the freezer. I'm not working proper, you know. They're just out for the walk. For Chrissake, do they look like hunters, either of 'em?"

"I'm doing my job."

"Don't you have bigger fish to fry?" Marco had had his rifle slung when the Jeep pulled up, but it now rested lightly in his hands. The DNR man's eyes had caught that as well, and he set his hand to his pistol.

Darrick moved back, again, saw the game warden's eyes flick his way.

"Look at the fucking river," Marco accused. "Why aren't you writing a citation on the Kavanaghs for that? How many tons of dead fish they got piled up at the Youngsville Lock and Dam?"

"That'll be enough of that. Whatever happened on the river will be taken care of in its good time."

"Yeah. Sixth of never." Marco had settled into a sort of loose half crouch. The escalation was pounding Darrick from two sides, the game warden roused now, his professionalism challenged. And with that, a familiar drone of fear, that same vibrating deep note sounding through too many people in this town.

"The Kavanaghs will make it right. Don't they take care of Redbird? You say you ain't working but you draw your paycheck from KCL—look there, right on your mirror. You owe your job to them, and here you are gunning on company ground, knowing it's not safe up there."

"You're right about that," Lourana put in.

"Now I'm going to say this once. You put your rifles on the ground, and we'll take care of this like civilized folk."

"And end up dead." Marco closed his mouth on the rest of what he might have said.

Hovatter looked at him and smiled.

"I see where your footprints go. I can follow them right to the fence and over, sure thing. There's places you ain't supposed to go. There's things you ain't supposed to be seeing."

Darrick's heart fell. Hovatter knew exactly what was in that crack in the earth. Whatever mental arrangements he'd made to square that with himself, they were long fixed.

"Marco, Lourana, we'll be going downtown. And you, buddy, don't think I've forgot about you." He swung his attention to Darrick.

The emotional crosscurrents pounding between Marco and the warden overwhelmed him. Darrick bent, crushed by the rage and fear and anger and pride, a turbulent surf that seemed to rise, merge, become one great raging mass.

He didn't want to hurt anyone, not Lourana nor Marco, not even Hovatter, but a howling black spiral was closing down around him. He had to breathe.

He pushed *out*.

Leave me alone. Leave me alone!

At first he just shoved blindly at the mental pressure, feeling both men recede, but Marco, *I don't want to hurt Marco*, so he groped through the cacophony and parted Marco's wild angry confusion from the game warden's implacable hostility. Marco was bent double, his head moving, a pool of vomit spreading across the snow. He *turned* his attention away from him and toward the warden, like an antenna coming around to focus.

There was no mistaking what happened, there under the blue sky and the bright sun reflecting off the snow, everything sharp and visible as it had not been under the streetlights when Jimmy died.

The game warden had pulled his gun, but it had fallen from his grip near where he lay sprawled on his back. His weather-beaten face was deforming, swelling on one side and then the other, going red and then livid white, as though pressure inside was trying to find some way out. His throat flexed and rippled. One eye sank and the other bulged out, continuing to emerge until it popped from its socket and lay, dangling from its nerve, on his quivering cheek.

Darrick tried to pull back, to release him, but it was too late. His body collapsed like an emptied balloon. His bladder and bowels emptied and the smell of fresh mortality rose with the steam into the clear, impossibly bright air.

Darrick slid to his knees, drained, head in his hands. *What am I?* He heard a cold steel slither, the sound of a gun being readied that he knew from a hundred detective shows but never in real life.

"You're the one killed Jimmy."

Marco had the rifle trained on him with the ease of someone who knew exactly how to use it on a man, and had before. His face was impassive, weirdly like Lourana's, and Darrick was startled to realize that, along with Marco's rage and revulsion, he could now hear something from Lourana as well, a faint sense of disgust and empathy.

"I don't understand how it happens. I don't control it. Jimmy pulled a gun on us." *I am a monster.*

"You're not doing that to me." Marco's voice shook, but the gun was steady.

"Marco, wait." Lourana tried to put her hand on his arm but he flung her off.

"Best thing I could do for this . . . *thing*, and everyone, is put him out his misery." Marco looked down the barrel of his rifle. "I knew Jimmy. Worked with him. You know we waded through the floods last year, hanging on to each other, to carry an old woman off her porch. And you killed him like that? Like what I felt in my head? Maybe you killed all of them down the mine crack."

"You can't believe that." Darrick started to stand up but Marco gestured with the rifle and he sank back.

"There's not much I won't believe, not after two tours in Iraq. People will do about goddamn anything to each other."

"Why would he bring you up here, then?" Lourana looked back and forth between them.

"Maybe to kill us. Who the hell knows? He's a freak, Lourana, some kind of freak, and you're just lucky I'm here to protect you."

"Marco. Listen to me." Lourana put her hand on the rifle and pressed it aside until it was pointed just past Darrick's shoulder. "Look at me. Now he could have killed me a thousand times over, if he'd a mind to. In the sweepstakes. At my house. Anytime."

Marco's thoughts tumbled and pressed darkly on Darrick; he tried to avoid them, to curl into himself like a snail in its shell, stop hearing what he could not help hearing and most of all, to not react.

"Marco, I didn't try to kill your friend. It wasn't deliberate. I don't know what happens. I am terrified of myself. Something has happened to me."

"What? When?"

Darrick saw the rifle come to bear again. He bent his head forward, showing the wound. "This. When this happened. Down under the ground among the bones."

"So stop it."

Darrick looked past the rifle's cold eye, trying to reach Marco whose gaze was just as black and unreadable. "I never meant to hurt Jimmy. It's worse this time, that I did know what would happen. I'll admit, I intended to hurt the warden. Not kill him, but I had to stop him. To save us."

Marco didn't move, either to pull the trigger or not.

"I might as well be a zombie. I know."

"I felt it, felt you pressing on me," Marco said, with a kind of terrible fascination. "You could have killed me."

"But he didn't," said Lourana, her voice was soft, persuasive.

"I figured out how to turn away. Whatever this is, I don't understand it but I'm learning to control it. I could feel you, all of you, and I turned away and focused on the warden. But as God is my witness, I wish I hadn't killed the man."

The rifle barrel moved down, slowly, until it was pointed again at the ground.

Darrick let out a breath that he seemed to have been holding forever. "You were in the military."

"Marines."

"I never was. Maybe you had to kill someone . . . "

"Yeah." He bit off the word. "The first time's hard. But so's the second."

"Because then you know."

Marco, nodding, ejected the round, put the safety on, slung the rifle. Darrick clambered to his feet.

"We need to get out of here. Now." Marco looked around as though trying to decide where to go. "He radioed in, I know that much. Even if he didn't describe my truck, which he likely did, somebody is going to show up when he doesn't report back in."

"We have a plan. Let's stick to it," Lourana said.

"We're all in this together now," Darrick said.

"If we can protect ourselves from you," Marco replied, showing how fragile that truce was.

The sun shone down cheerily on their little group, three misfits standing around a cooling body.

THE VOICE OF THE MOUNTAIN

Coal is the fat in the belly of the earth, the rich black distillation of the sun. Some places it runs thin, and we call it low coal, so that men lie prone in coffin machines in order to fillet it out of the stony flesh. High coal, a man can stand up.

But never is coal just one thing. Slate layers through it like tendons or cartilage, brittle stuff to be stripped out. When the slate dump with coal still breathing in it gets big enough, the coal remembers what it is meant to do and it burns. Even the slate is transformed, like a new Adam, and becomes red dog that they spread on the roads.

—CBK

10

The drive home was silent. What do you say to a man who seems like the most inoffensive, wounded creature, yet who's killed two men stone dead—armed men, no less—right in front of your eyes? Without even touching them? It's like seeing a neighbor's beagle tear the throat out of a Rottweiler.

I ought not to have been surprised, but I was, she thought. *Things look different in the day than they do in the dark of night.*

She had him lie down in the back seat, lest anyone see a man in her car and start adding one and one to get two. Things were going to get tight, real quick, soon as Hovatter's body was discovered. Lourana had argued for setting him up in the driver's seat of his Jeep, like he'd had a stroke or something, but Marco nixed that. No leaving evidence on the body. No one had touched him, or his vehicle, so there was nothing but some tire tracks and footprints melting beyond identification in the sun.

Darrick said not a word as they arrived home. She pulled the car up close and hustled him inside. He flopped down in her recliner, just like that. *I guess as he's sleeping in it, he thinks it's his now.* Still, Lourana considered it presumptuous. She pulled around a chair from the kitchen and turned on the TV to fill up the empty space.

"I'm starved," she said, after the third commercial for fast food. "You look like you could use something."

Not a word. He just moved his hand a little, yes or no, you couldn't say.

"Well, I'm eating, and you can, or not." She started to fix a fried egg sandwich with cheese, because it had been a hard morning and she wasn't pretending to be anyone's supermodel anytime soon. She set out the hot sauce and got the pan heating, pulled a bag of potato chips out of the cupboard. "Last chance," she called as she began breaking eggs.

No response. She stuck her head around the corner. "You look done in. Maybe a shot of liquor?"

"Not a good idea." He looked back at her, his pale eyes large and intense behind the thick lenses, and she had an uncomfortable feeling that he was trying to worm his way inside her mind again. She went back to the stove and turned down the heat on the smoking pan.

"I am drained," she heard him say at last, "but I couldn't eat a thing. You have tea?"

"I do now." She got her eggs sizzling and put a cup of water to heat in the microwave for him while she pulled down the can of Maxwell House to make a pot for herself. She thought about the pint of Jim Beam she kept in the cupboard. Thought twice.

She waited for the drip to finish, then took her coffee and her sandwich on a paper towel, along with that sick-looking tea.

"Thank you."

"It's little enough."

He shook his head. "I mean today."

"We're either gonna stick together or we're all going down."

"You could have just turned me over. You and Marco." He waited, as though expecting her to say something, but Lourana didn't know what it was he wanted from her. She had her reasons.

She set down her sandwich, picked up the remote and flipped around until she came to the Alabama game in progress. "Hope you ain't a War Eagle." She could feel him staring at her over his cup. "Auburn? College football? Never mind. Anyways, I'm mostly a Marshall fan, but they don't make national TV much."

"Is that where you went to school?"

"Not hardly. Not hardly." Lourana remembered the kids who went off to WVU, Wesleyan, Marshall, a handful from the whole county—too many of them came back, with or without their degrees. No one in her family had ever gone to college, ever needed to back when the mines were running three shifts. "I just like the team, and I like Alabama, no particular reason. What's your team?"

"My college didn't have football."

"Must have been pretty small."

"St. Bonaventure. Raised Catholic, you get tracked that way."

Lourana would not have pegged him as a Catholic, but she didn't say so. Marco was one, too, but not so's you could tell.

"I liked it, actually. Small school, and the Franciscans are—well, Franciscan. But no football. They had basketball and I still enjoy that."

Alabama was rolling, the score ticking up. Noise, at least it was noise. The hours crept by, like the chains dragging up and down the field, measuring things off by inches. Lourana wondered how outlaws managed, always laying low somewhere, hiding in a box canyon or lone cabin, living on beans and jerky. No wonder they were ready to shoot the first person who showed up. Snow was melting off the roof, dripping past the windows in the bright, cold sunshine. Occasionally came the tinkle of an icicle dropping.

"News break! Another Carbon County law-enforcement officer has been found dead."

She turned up the sound a little.

"Officer Lyle Hovatter, a thirty-three-year veteran of the Division of Natural Resources, was found dead beside his patrol vehicle a short time ago on Fish Camp Road." The camera panned across the area, showing yellow police tape, the usual. Now the reporter, a startled-looking young woman gripping the microphone. "Police are tight-lipped about the cause of death. We are expecting a statement from Sheriff Zabrowski. Meanwhile, local residents are fearful." Cut to a man in a Caterpillar ball cap. "Don Rodeheaver says he's encountered a man who may be a suspect."

Rodeheaver looked straight into the camera, his eyes squinting against the sun that highlighted a rusty hunting-season beard. "I saw him first thing. Right close by. Staggering up the road, me and the wife both saw him. Now we got two officers dead from this zombie and who knows where it's gonna stop?"

Cut to the reporter, who was nodding agreement. "With this latest death, the unsolved death of James Cooper and the continuing investigation into the disappearance of an environmental activist, the pressure certainly is on local authorities." A pair of photos flashed up, that same graduation shot and one of a blond woman holding a protest sign. "We'll have more updates as information is released. This is Tiffany Smith, reporting live from Redbird."

The sound exploded into the middle of a Doritos commercial.

Lourana got up and went to the kitchen, poured another cup of coffee to settle her nerves. She stared out the back window at the woods for a long time, then opened the cupboard door and added that splash. The kick of the alcohol vaporizing in the black coffee put everything into sharper focus. *Why didn't I call the police while he was sleeping and been done with it? Or after Jimmy, for sure. A woman with any sense would have. I don't have the sense God grants to little apples.*

She heard the recliner squall as he got up, heard his heavy, uneven footsteps. Could he smell the liquor?

"I think I should go," he said to her back.

"How's that?" Had he squirrelled into her thoughts?

"I thought you might drive me somewhere. Or Marco. Or I'll walk."

"I imagine the county's even more sealed off, with finding Hovatter. You try walking the roads and they'll have you inside an hour. Cross-country, no way. Where you were is not the only mine crack in these hills. You'll end up worse than you started." *Talked myself right back into it.* She turned to face him. "Anyway, we're all in this now. Me and Marco, we were already on the radar before you showed up. Might as well be hung for a wolf as a sheep."

He half-smiled. "I thought that was hung for a sheep as a goat."

"Now that makes no sense at all."

"I'd rather not hang, either way."

The television blared. She reached up in the cupboard, brought out the Jim Beam and held it up. "Let's drink to that."

Darrick put up his hand. "Truly, I can't, or shouldn't. Alcohol, caffeine, it all makes the ataxia worse. And as I'm without my medication, it's bad anyway." He held up his teacup and offered a toast. "Here's to finding Dreama."

Lourana took a big gulp of her doctored coffee to stop the sudden rush of tears, coughed, and blamed the bourbon.

"You keep turning over rocks, maybe you find a key," he said.

"You keep turning over rocks, could be all you find is a nest of rattlers." Lourana could feel the liquor in her stomach, that nervy excitement taking her back to a time she didn't want to revisit. No point in dancing around. "I need to know how do you do it."

He looked like he was in pain. "I did not mean to kill Jimmy."

"But you did mean to kill Hovatter."

He turned away and she heard a low, "Yes."

"Can you control it? Whatever it is? What if it just breaks loose and kills everyone around you? How close did you come to killing Marco, killing me?" Lourana didn't say the worst that was on her mind: *What makes you any different from the Kavanaghs?*

"It's not some kind of death ray," he flashed back, his eyes glittering in defiance. "I think it's a defense mechanism."

"From violence?"

"From fear, anger. Strong emotion."

She waited. *First one to speak loses.* Either he was staying or he was going, but she needed answers. Like on repeat, her memory kept going to the warden's face, swelling and contorting, his head soft as a balloon, his eyes staring in terror. A chair under the door handle was nowise enough.

"I was the kid who got pushed around, OK?" He spoke slowly, finding some kind of footing as he went. "Whenever I was under stress, or had to exert myself, or was startled, I'd have an attack. I was alone, didn't have any brothers or anyone to stand with me."

"You never found out about your family?"

"The kids said I was found in a basket, left by the stork. Along with orphans, the home took in kids removed from their parents because of abuse or neglect. I always envied them. Even if your parents were nightmares, at least you have a name."

"But you have a name."

"Whose? Old Father Ronan found me, and then baptized me and gave me this name, but never would say why. Then a five-hundred-year flood wiped out the children's home records. I have a copy of my birth certificate from the state archives in Albany. Male child. Mother unknown, father unknown."

Lourana couldn't imagine having not a single person to anchor you on the earth. Her heart ached for the child, and for the mother who had to give him up. What had happened to her? How could she not think of her baby, every day the rest of her life? Not that she herself had much family to cling to anymore, parents gone too young, one distant brother, but she did have some uncles and cousins and great-aunts scattered around, and graveyards where you could stare at the name on the stone and wonder about lying under that grass someday yourself.

Darrick moved to the kitchen sink and looked out the window, past the thready curtain of melting snow, into the pine trees that pushed their way right to the edge of her little yard. She spent a lot of time doing the same herself, knowing that no one was going to come riding out of that dark forest and change things. You grow up, learn to be realistic.

"As a kid, I used to look at people, wonder. I'd see someone with gray eyes, and maybe that was my mother. I sat behind a guy on a train one time, who had the same cowlick that I have, one the barber always complains about, and I wanted to ask him if he had any lost relatives. A few years ago, when they started offering DNA tests, I bought the full package. They say people are always surprised to find African or Asian blood. Me, I got a map of the Celtic world, and my male lineage shows an unbroken line all the way back in Ireland."

"You probably got relatives around here then. Lots of Scotch-Irish."

"That would be something, wouldn't it?" He turned around and she smiled to put him at ease a little.

"So, that's the story," he said, with a crisp, summing-up tone. "I grew up, played by the rules. I walked away instead of confronting a mean kid or a nasty supervisor. But when Jimmy pulled that gun, something came out of me in response. It wasn't the gun, it was his fear. I couldn't breathe. It was like standing near a jet engine. Noise. Pressure. It's all-encompassing. I couldn't do anything but push back."

"The same with Hovatter?"

"Not exactly." He seemed to be sorting out the words. "It was still emotion, but it was not just fear. The same kind of fear as Jimmy, or it felt that way, but mixed with pride, professional pride, and arrogance. The effect was the same though. The gun, the emotion—I had to do something."

"But what about me? And Marco?"

"You're shut down, you know that. Marco is different too. So much rage. When Hovatter was threatening us, I was getting pressure from Marco, too, but I learned how to tell them apart."

"Apparently it worked." Lourana could feel her chest tightening with dread. "But Darrick, are you in control or not? How can you stop from just flailing around?"

"I'm learning. One thing I know. When that kind of emotion comes at me, I just try to get some distance. The effect falls off pretty quickly. I could hear the young deputy when he was in the basement here, and he was afraid, but it wasn't intolerable. Marco, he's a boiling pot, so much emotion, but I can back away from him and not get overwhelmed."

Lourana remembered him retreating in the bank, his body twisted as though something was hitting him. "And none of this ever happened before?"

He looked exasperated now. "Listen. I have my job. I get excellent performance reviews and a raise every year. I have a nice apartment. I ride the Metro and eat lunch at the same place every day, and I never, never, could hear people's emotions until this." He jabbed at his head. "Before this, my life was neat and tidy."

Lourana thought of Steve, of how things were always at loose ends with him. Nothing tidy about their lives, from that moment outside the gym when he first showed her how to roll a joint. The rocks starting rolling then, like someone skidding down a mountain trail and the whole thing cuts loose.

Darrick went and sat down at the table, settled his face into his hands. The uneven slump of his shoulders looked so much like Steve's when he was in the dumps, unable to see a way out. She went over and put an arm around him, gingerly, felt him withdraw and then ease at the unexpected touch.

"I'm sorry this has happened to you."

He sat back a little, leaning into her arm. His back was warm against her. She could see the gleam of unshed tears and his hair fell across his temple almost like Steve's used to. She bent toward him, not meaning to.

He pushed away from her, screeching the chair across the linoleum, and she pulled back as well, startled at how they had fallen toward each other.

"No," he said. "Please."

"I'm sorry." Lourana's cheeks warmed. "I felt . . . "

"Pity? No thanks."

"No."

"Whatever it is, I don't want to hurt you." He began to walk with his awkward, lurching gait, back and forth across the little kitchen floor.

"But I'm not angry, or afraid."

"I don't know what will happen, don't you understand? I don't know. If you come at me with your feelings and I get overwhelmed? Even pity or compassion? Will it be more than I can handle?"

"But you were trying to get inside of me earlier."

"I was testing. That was wrong."

"It scared me."

"Me too." He stopped pacing but tension was still evident in his hunched shoulders. "I don't feel anything much from you. I think you won't hurt me, and you have certainly been kind, but it's different with you, like there's a shell."

"I've built that shell, thank you, and it's served me well. Keeping the inside and outside each in their own space. I can't let myself have feelings anymore and do my work for Dreama."

"There's something you're closing in. Not nothing. More like—a bomb. Something you can't let out so you squeeze it inside until it can't escape."

"And if it escapes?"

"Maybe you're just as dangerous as I am."

They stood there, then, and Lourana could feel herself shaking and wondered if Darrick was as well. Two strangers without a connection except loneliness, and that was strong as anything.

The television roared.

"I care about you, Darrick," she said at last. "I don't want to hurt you, but I sure as hell can't afford to get hurt."

11

"It appears I've multiplied."

Darrick folded back the Sunday edition of the Carbon County *Gazette* (flimsy paper, narrow format) and showed it to Lourana, who was standing at the counter, buttering toast and stacking it on a plate. Darrick didn't comment, but he hated other people touching his food, especially buttering his toast. There was a real pleasure in swiping off a pat of butter and troweling it across the hot surface, deciding just how much to use, then eating the toast still hot and crisp and unfingered.

Hovatter's death was splashed across the top of the paper, a headline running the whole six columns in end-of-the-world type. LAWMAN FOUND DEAD! A smaller headline under it, AUTHORITIES DO NOT RULE OUT MORE THAN ONE KILLER.

"You don't get much excitement here."

"We don't get two people dead on the street in three days, not hardly."

Darrick unfolded it and started to read aloud. "The discovery of the body of respected game warden Lyle Hovatter is the latest in a series of unexplained incidents that has Carbon County on edge. Deputies and city police are wearing the bulletproof vests bought last year by a Lions Club fundraiser, and the shotguns that used to be stowed in the trunk are now within reach."

He grabbed a piece of toast and took a big crunchy bite, refusing to let his phobia have its way. "The Lions Club? I didn't know they were still around."

"Still around." She was sorting through the advertising circulars from Walmart, Dollar Store, CVS, and this week there was a Red Plum circular with good grocery coupons. As Darrick continued to read aloud, Lourana remembered her father doing that on Sundays, long before her mother's macular degeneration closed in. He'd clear his throat twice, a signal, and then begin to read a story, slowly, enunciating the words, adding commentary. He didn't realize how exasperated that made her mother, who'd confess it later to Lourana. She wanted to read it for herself while she still could.

That intimacy, to share the paper over the breakfast table, made her uneasy now. Last night's near miss had sent her shaking to bed, and into dreams where Steve, a younger Steve with that dimple in his chin, stood on the other side of a mirror-smooth river and beckoned for her to swim across to him, but every time she tried, the water turned into orange goo and she sank.

Keep your guard up, girl, she told herself. *You crack and it'll be all she wrote.*

"Listen to this. The initial sighting of a strange man on Fish Camp Road, described by the Rodeheaver family as a *zombie*, has been followed by sightings elsewhere in Redbird and environs. 'We cannot substantiate any of these reports,' Sheriff Zabrowski told the *Gazette*. 'We are investigating each and every one, because unlikely as it seems, we do have someone in our midst who has the desire to kill officers of the law, and the ability to do it.'"

"What's the deal with multiplying?"

He continued to read bits from the story, people reporting that the walking dead were seen on the road or among their cattle in the barnyard or staggering along the river, headed west. Sometimes one, sometimes two or three together.

Darrick couldn't imagine anyone had seen him, except that family in the car—what was their name? Stoneheaver? So all these reports were pure fiction, stemming from either panic or a desire to get some kind of attention. "The stranger, or strangers, are always said to be male, and considerably larger than average." Darrick dropped the paper, held his arms out stiffly in a traditional zombie pose. "Do I look bigger this way?"

She almost choked on her coffee. "That's sick."

Darrick heard the shock in her voice. He dropped his pose, retrieved the paper, and hid behind it.

It was sick, she was right. He'd killed two men. His insides twisted at the memory. What possessed him to try to make a joke about the kind of horror he could inflict, intentional or not?

"Could you share a piece of the paper?" There was an edge now.

"Oh, sorry." He handed over the second section, Sports, without raising his eyes. He scanned the rest of the front page and inside, looking for other news happening in Carbon County, but it didn't look like there was much to report. A wreck that sent two people to the regional medical center. A report on the school board arguing over the amenities for a gym at the new high school, and a story on a town council taking a firm stand against vandalism. A zombie was the only news worth a headline.

"Oh for crying out loud!" The paper crackled as Lourana snapped her finger against it. "No wonder people think we're all ignorant snake-handlers around here!"

"What?"

"Letters to the editor. This brush-arbor preacher from up at Elk Shoals has started a movement, claiming the reports of the zombie are really a sign that the dead are being raised, the rapture, end of the world."

"People are scared. I guess I'd be scared myself."

"'A coalition of churches is planning a prayer vigil this afternoon, to pray for the Christian dead and for protection of the faithful as we enter the end-times.'" She scoffed. "They're going to gather on the pier at Kavanagh Park and pray the zombies into heaven, I guess."

It was too close to the stereotypes, that was for sure. Darrick remembered an old movie, *Night of the Hunter*, and how scared he'd been seeing it as a kid, that demented preacher, not to mention bad TV movies about moonshiners and crazy people back in the hills. Darrick thought that the idea of people praying for the apocalypse was about as scary as a zombie killer, and made about as much sense. He was saved from having to formulate a reply that didn't sound too sarcastic by the burbling of Lourana's cell phone.

He tried not to listen, burying himself in the "Daily Log" of police activity. Minor thefts, vandalism, fender benders. The woman caller was insistent—he could hear her high voice that left little space for reply—and Lourana went from repeating a flat *no* to a sort of *yes* as she kept talking. "OK. OK. Walmart in twenty-five minutes."

She clicked off and tossed the phone down. "I didn't expect that."

"Who was it?"

"That newspaper reporter, Zadie Person. She started some time back and has been covering the spill and the rumors about what the Kavanaghs are planning to do with a big chunk of land. Now she wants to talk with me about Dreama." He could see the hope, how her eyes shone while her face stayed impassive.

"Here?" Darrick didn't want to admit the fear of having someone else know about him. It was bad enough with Marco, who seemed to be on their side but who was hotheaded and unpredictable.

"She was headed this way, she said, but I'm not having her nosing around, don't worry yourself. I'm going to go down to the store and meet her. It seemed like a plan."

"She's this reporter?" He showed Lourana the article, pushed off the front pages by the homicide and the zombies and the end of days. It was a two-page spread on the acid spill in the river, but the photos of the orange glop were muted by being in black-and-white. Quotes from the state officials, mine workers, environmentalists. Charts and maps. She probably put in days of work on it, just to see it buried next to a state news roundup.

"That's her." Lourana was gathering up her pocketbook and coat and keys. "She's good, too good for this fish-wrap."

Darrick studied the capsule explanation of acid mine drainage. "Deep mining often intersects the water table, so water is constantly present in the mines and must be pumped out. Traditionally, when mining ceased, so did the pumping, and the mine flooded. That's the first step in the creation of AMD." So far, so good. "The iron and other metal sulfides that occur in the coal seams, such as pyrite or fool's gold, with the addition of air and water begin to create acid. Bacteria, especially those called acidophiles, accelerate the process. When the pH of the water is raised past three, iron begins to precipitate out."

The story went to the next page, where there was an accompanying interview with G. Edward Walsh, director of mining operations at Kavanagh Coal and Limestone. He was pictured in front of a gigantic hill of coal, an obvious publicity shot from his white shirt and clean, clean hands holding a spotless clipboard.

"I wouldn't trust my sister with this guy," Darrick said, examining his soft jawline and hard-set lips.

"Dreama used to work for him." Lourana looked distracted, like she was seeing something far away or far in the past. "Keep locked up here. I won't be long."

THE VOICE OF THE MOUNTAIN

Old Padraig followed the coal under the mountains. His son Domnall, my great-grandfather, is the one people called Old Scratch, because he was a hard man and he let nothing get in the way of his empire. No wandering tramp or union organizer or gypsy peddler troubled Carbon County. Old Scratch understood the coal, and loved it, and took us from mules to electric cutting machines. He would go down into his own mines, the men quiet as they saw that the Kavanagh rode beside them. He gloried at the sight of coal coming off the face, watching the mine become greater and greater by reducing the mountain from the inside.

—CBK

A big old black Caprice from the days when Chevrolets still ruled the roads rolled up beside the displays of inflatable Santas and snow globes. Lourana leaned out, her hand tentative in the air. The passenger door came open with a creak.

"Get in."

The high voice was familiar from the phone, but as Lourana settled onto the faded red velour seat, she was surprised to see the body to which it was attached. Zadie Person was a heavy-set woman with light brown skin and freckles that sprayed across her round face. She simmered with energy, a body that seemed to want to be *doing* something physical, planting an orchard or erecting a skyscraper, but was instead stuck behind a keyboard. She was also a good bit older than Lourana anticipated, not a fresh-out-of-college somebody.

"Not what you expected?"

Lourana knew she'd been caught out. Did this woman have some kind of weird powers too? "I thought you might be . . . "

"Younger, skinnier? Paler for sure? Yeah, I'm used to that. The voice doesn't fit." Zadie laughed, a silvery tinkling laugh. "I'm used to the double takes, like, who is this?"

Lourana relaxed, realizing that she'd given nothing away.

They wheeled out of the parking lot and twisted down side streets until they were in the shadow of the Fourth Avenue Bridge. Its arches spanned a wooded cleft, linking the downtown with Northside and shading a damp, dark expanse of concrete where nobody needed nor wanted to park.

"I was reading your article today, on the blowout."

Zadie flashed a toothy smile at her. "Thanks, that means a lot. I worked hard on that package, hoping it might get picked up nationally. Not that you could tell from where it was played."

"Didn't seem like you got a lot of answers."

"Not for lack of trying. I don't think anyone's got the answers." She backed up close to the bank, until the rank overgrowth of honeysuckle almost covered the car. "I'm no dummy about science. Lots of journalism school grads are, but I got my first degree in biochemistry before I decided a lab wasn't where I wanted to spend the rest of my life."

That explains her age then.

"I've studied AMD, but nothing like this. The Water Resources guys try to put a spin on it, but they're baffled too. Any mine drainage is nasty stuff, kills off the stream life and burns your skin if you go wading into it. But this blowout is worse, *way* worse. It's like the acidification process is being repeatedly intensified. Huge spikes in hydrogen. The pH is all over, sometimes going to the end of the charts."

"It's the worst I've ever seen, at least from the color in the river."

"Iron hydroxides. You could strain them out of the water for paint pigments." She shook her head. "But you didn't come here to listen to me rattle on about yellowboy. I've just had the spill so much in my mind."

Lourana couldn't hold back any longer. "You found out something about my Dreama?" She'd been jittering the whole time, inside, waiting to learn why this reporter wanted to talk with her.

"Maybe. I'm trying to figure that out." Zadie turned a bit more in her seat, so that Lourana could face her full on. "I'm coming in late on this, so I need you to tell me exactly what happened when she disappeared."

"I couldn't tell you, exactly to the minute." Lourana felt a kind of shame at that. *As a mother, I should have been able to feel it.* "I was living in Charleston still. Early June. I spoke with her on the phone on the eighth. That morning. I called her the next evening and never got an answer. Kept calling, that night, the next morning. Then I left out and come down here, thinking she'd just forgotten to charge her phone, or turned it off."

"And she was gone."

She nodded. "I told all this to the police."

"I've read the reports, but I'd rather hear it straight from you. What was she like when you talked?"

"Dreama sounded fine that morning. Nothing new, except she was happy about a new pair of boots she'd bought online and they fit really well. We talked every day, just for a few minutes."

"Nothing new at her job?"

"No, not that I recall. She was happy with her work, her pay."

"Something had changed, even if she didn't say so. This is what I've learned. She'd been the secretary to the operations manager, right?"

Lourana nodded.

"A couple of months before she disappeared, back in March, she changed jobs and became the personal assistant to the younger Kavanagh brother."

Lourana felt something drop inside her, felt the solid ground shift under her feet. "I didn't know that." Dreama had always told her everything that happened in her life, her crushes and disappointments, worries about grades, victories on the softball diamond, how scared she was of her driving instructor who liked to put them into spins and skids.

"I don't know that she told anyone. It was just happenstance that I ran into Cormac's former assistant, when she came in to the newspaper. She wouldn't say much, but I could tell she was angry or hurt or both. She had sold her house and was moving out of state, to Georgia, supposedly to be with her son, but there was something more. I'd say she was let go, pretty summarily."

"Did she have anything to say about Dreama?"

"No, she wouldn't talk about it. They probably sweetened the pot, gave her cash to go quietly. But I heard roundabout from someone who knew Ed Walsh that he was looking for a new secretary all of a sudden, because his had been kicked upstairs."

Lourana couldn't fathom why Dreama wouldn't have told her this. It was a nice promotion, something to brag about. Personal assistant, even if it was for a Kavanagh. She thought back to that March, April, and not a word, just the daily rattle about shopping and her apartment and Redbird gossip. But a chat over the phone wasn't the same as face-to-face, and Dreama had not been home again after visiting at Easter.

I could have told something was up if I'd seen her, but I was too damned stiff-necked to come to Redbird.

"Tell me again what you found when you went to look for her."

Lourana could remember walking up the sidewalk at Dreama's apartment complex, thinking what a perfect day it was. Blue sky, white clouds, birds flying back and forth to their nests and singing like to break their hearts. And she had gone past Dreama's empty parking space, up the stairs to 2-A, and rung the bell.

"I could hear the doorbell ringing, but nothing else. I got out my key and unlocked the door and went in. You know how you just know—*gone*? Like when someone dies, one minute they are there and the next, not? That was the way it was." She saw compassion in Zadie's eyes, how she bent closer. "I walked all the way through. Everything looked normal. She'd had coffee and cereal that morning. Her cup and bowl and spoon were in the dish drainer. She was always like that, neat." Lourana caught hold of herself. *Don't crack.*

"Did you see anything out of place?"

She shook her head. The memory cut into her, that blue cup and bowl, upside down, and one spoon in the silverware holder.

"Anything new?"

"I checked everything. Her refrigerator had fresh food in it. Her clothes were in the closet. Her new boots . . . were standing in the closet." She bit the inside of her mouth until she tasted blood, until the shaking stopped.

"I'm sorry to put you through this again. Vulture reporter, I know, but I am trying to help."

She noticed that Zadie had a little notepad in her lap, and pen, but she had not taken any notes. Nothing to report.

"I felt there was a link somewhere—the spill, then the Appalfolk woman disappearing while she was sampling the water, in my mind they went hand in hand. But Dreama? And these two officers dead? My theories just went bust, so I'm going back to the start. To the Kavanaghs."

"Good place to start," Lourana said.

"I know they have their mitts on everything hereabouts. I've dug through enough deed books. It's like the Old West or something, land barons. Always a step or two ahead of the game, snapping up land before the interstate came through, stripping a mountain flat just in time for a prison the state wanted to build."

Lourana wondered how long it had taken her to figure out something anyone in Redbird could have told her right off.

"But the spook tales? That you can't go into Knockaulin House and come out the same? That they can strip the flesh off you? Nah, that's crazy talk." Zadie yanked at a sliding bra strap. "Too much power, people will start talking that kind of stuff. The Kavanaghs want to be the lords of Carbon County, and they are, but I don't see any reason why they'd kill the officers. That doesn't make sense."

"Maybe it's the zombie," Lourana said, just to see what the reaction would be.

Zadie let out another burst of tinkling laughter. "You saw the paper today? Do you *believe* that crap? I'm surprised someone hasn't gotten filled full of buckshot, just walking down the road in the evening and some nutcase thinks it's one of the dead like on TV."

"Yeah, it's crazy."

"And now they're going to pray about it. Not sure if they want to pray them away, or pray that the rest of the dead start rising. At least I wasn't assigned to cover that circus; the editor's a deacon in his church and wants to be there himself and make a show."

They sat for a moment and watched the meltwater coming off the bridge. Years of dribbling had left white tracks down the concrete, maybe road salt, maybe something leaching out of the structure itself. Lourana wondered if she should tell this reporter about the mine crack, the bodies. But smart and dedicated as she seemed to be, her story had to go through the editor, and he was another one who stank of being a Kavanagh creature. *Not really a smell,* she thought. *Like maybe if you had better senses you could smell it, or see it, but somehow you just know, the way dogs can sense cancer.*

Zadie asked a few more questions, but it was clear she found the interview had been a bust. She stashed her notebook into her purse.

As she let Lourana out at the plaza, Zadie tucked a slip of paper into her hand. "Sorry I don't have any business cards. My home and work numbers. Call me if anything happens, if you remember something." She squeezed Lourana's fingers before letting them go.

Lourana went to her car and sat there for a while. She liked this reporter, who spoke like a little girl but had such a strong grip. It made her feel bad that she had kept something back, but Zadie might not be all she seemed. Lourana had a bad habit of trusting people based on how she felt about them, and sometimes that worked out and sometimes it didn't.

I've got the zombie living in my house, hows about that?

She should have turned left out of the parking lot and headed home, but she turned down into town. Sunday morning and everything closed, of course. The streets and small parking lots were fairly busy around the big old churches—First Baptist, First Methodist, St. Andrew's Presbyterian decorated with restrained garlands of greens—but on the edge of the downtown, where the nondenominational church had erected its arena-like sanctuary, the parking lots would be overflowing. She circled the courthouse block, the important buildings standing on ground that had never been undermined, ancient layers of coal solid under the things the Kavanaghs valued. Her pap, though, he said that wasn't entirely true, that an old doghole mine went under Knockaulin House, one supposedly dug by the family when it first arrived. Preserved like the first dollar framed on the wall of a shop.

She headed back, taking Casselman Avenue up to High Street. The time and temperature clock on the insurance agency was on the fritz again. Downtown buildings gave way to a broad avenue with young oak trees doing their best to replace the great elms that had died branch by branch from a disease in their veins. Just after the intersection for the new bridge, the street began to rise, going up the gentle hill that was crowned by the Kavanagh estate.

It was a different country there, that's what people said. The gray stone mansion topped an eminence that looked over town and the river and the hollowed-out, stripped-off stubs of mountains rolling away beyond. A black cast-iron fence kept in the lush growth of rhododendrons and specimen trees. The front gate onto the High Street sidewalk was always closed and locked—only on the side street, where a wide electric gate gave entrance for cars, could a person cross the borders.

Once she herself had crossed over, to make a personal plea to the Kavanaghs to help find Dreama.

That morning, she had parked on Goudy Street, on the other side of the property from the gate, so that she could walk along the boundaries. Between the trees, you could see an ornamental garden and a huge fountain with rearing horses pawing the water and air. The great house rose for three stories, with turrets on the corners, banks of chimneys, and row after row of upstairs windows with little diamond panes that sparkled in the sunlight. She had walked around the back, peering at the groomed gardens, empty of people. Had there ever been parties there, with music and lights and young people awhirl with life?

The air is different at Knockaulin House, people said. Some said that you'd die if you spurned the Kavanaghs' invitation, while others said if you go there then you can't leave, can't even properly die, lingering like that French chef who was still working at ninety until a fiery accident sent him to the hospital. He faded but clung to life, always pleading to be allowed back in his kitchen, until when he died he was nothing but yellowed skin stretched over bones. *Spook tales.*

She had been escorted to a kind of waiting room by a man slick as silk, so light on his feet you couldn't hear his steps. A butler, a genuine butler, English accent and everything. "The Misters Kavanagh will see you in the library, when they have assembled," he said, and withdrew. That was the word, like they used in mysteries, *withdrew*, leaving her stranded in a place that felt too much like a funeral parlor.

Dreama had been gone a month then. Gone without a trace.

The butler returned in a little while, time enough that she'd circled the room and looked at the paintings of sheep and castles, Coal Association awards, curlicue family trees that claimed kin back to Adam. He led her to a massive pair of wooden doors, which he opened and then stepped back, announcing, "Mrs. Castile to see you."

"That's Ms. Taylor, please." She walked past him, hearing her heels crack against the glassy floor, toward three men gathered around a carved table. *They'll remember I was here.* Behind them was the giant mouth of a fireplace that could hold entire tree trunks; above it hung an antique map, "The High Kings of Ireland."

"Welcome to Knockaulin House, Ms. Taylor. We are so sorry to meet you under these circumstances. I am Patrick Kavanagh." The voice was deep but soft, as though a commanding shout had been squeezed down by age or perhaps could no longer escape the old man's massive body. He half-reclined in an armchair big enough for two people, but even with the extra space, his shoulders and thighs struggled for more.

Lourana realized she was trembling. The butler had disappeared without offering her a seat, and there was no chair on this side of the table. She was like a worker "called on the carpet," as her pap would have said, and she trembled at facing the men whose mines had eaten up his life. But they weren't going to intimidate her. She put on her Sunday manners and spoke directly to the father. "Mr. Patrick, I'm here about Dreama, my daughter. She worked for your company and she's missing."

He seemed to wait for her to add *sir*, but she would not.

"We were all shocked by her disappearance. I'm Eamon, by the way, and this is my brother Cormac." Eamon was a big man, too, standing just to one side of his father. But he was not soft. He was like a slab peeled off one of his mountains, six foot six if he was an inch, with curly dark red hair and a voice that sounded like coal being chuted into a gondola car.

Cormac, who had been lounging near the dark fireplace, stepped forward and offered her his hand. He was much younger than Eamon, and did not look like either his brother or his father. Cormac was a slight man with sandy hair falling over a high forehead, a sensual mouth, and hazel eyes. His hand was warm and soft, a hand that had known no hard work ever, but still there was a feeling of restrained power in his grip.

"We remember your father's good service to us," whispered Patrick. "Certainly, if there was something we could do to help . . . "

You don't even know his name. It was Louis. But she wasn't there to settle old scores. "Is there anything that could help the police? Did something happen at work that day?" she asked. "It doesn't add up. It just doesn't add up."

"Ms. Taylor, we have already dealt with the police on this matter. They have looked at our security tapes and reviewed our computer logs and interviewed our employees. I'm not sure what else you think we might do," rumbled Eamon.

She looked to the old man, who might have been asleep. She looked to Cormac, but the younger brother had returned to the fireplace, staring contemplatively into a small, leather-covered book he had pulled from the bookshelves that lined three sides of the room. It was Eamon she'd have to deal with.

"I just thought—you have so many resources . . ."

"Are you asking if we will put up a reward? Yes, we can do that," said Eamon dismissively.

Lourana felt her face get hot. "I didn't come here to beg for your money. I'm asking for your help, because there's not one thing happens in Carbon County that you don't know about." She saw the sudden glitter of the old man's eyes under those heavy lids.

"Are you implying that the company, that we, had something to do with your daughter's disappearance?" Eamon seemed to grow wider, swelling in her sight, and Lourana felt like the air was being sucked out of the room.

"No, I'm just saying what everyone knows." She could feel her desperation rising. "You have your security men and all. Can't you find out anything?"

Eamon raised his hand and she felt an immediate menace. Her body did, anyway, a weird sensation that her mind could not recognize as anything more than a gentle wave, as though he were shooing away a fly.

"Might we have Bill put one of his men on it?" Cormac had stepped forward. "It would ease her mind."

And Lourana *felt* eased, felt the tension drain from the room. The younger brother had a stillness about him, the feel of some dark place like a deep pool under trees.

"Thank you," she said, only to him, and he smiled just a little.

"Yes. And we will put up a reward," said Patrick, rousing to sit straight in his chair, resuming command. "It was a grave omission not to have done that already, and we owe Ms. Taylor a debt for bringing us to ourselves."

"Thank you," she said again, not sure how to proceed, but the butler was immediately at her elbow, guiding her out, and before she knew it, she had found herself back at her car and the great house behind her as impregnable as before.

Now Lourana wondered how she had gotten up the courage to call and ask for that interview.

Fog had obscured the windows of the car while she drifted in memory. She started the engine and put the defrosters on to clear it.

To know now that Dreama had been working for Cormac before she disappeared! Lourana had believed he was sympathetic, but now she realized that he knew much more about Dreama and had chosen not to tell her anything. For all she knew, her daughter had been right there in that house then, if she was still alive. Somewhere in those dozens of rooms. Maybe it was only the news she'd gotten from Zadie, but now she believed that she had felt something, as she asked the Kavanaghs' help in that gloomy library, some trace of her.

Lourana put the car into gear and headed home. The only answer she'd gotten was one that troubled her even more.

13

Marco found that he was humming along to the band's drum-thumping version of the "Battle Hymn of the Republic," a tune he'd always associated with Civil War reenactments more than church. "Mine eyes have seen the glory of the coming of the Lord. He is trampling out the vintage where the grapes of wrath are stored." It didn't seem to square with that Hollywood blockbuster version of the Second Coming that was being peddled. "Sifting out the hearts of men before his judgment seat."

He swung his arm to the left, plastic baton pointing the way to additional parking. His orange vest crackled every time he moved. It wasn't a real job; still, Marco felt good about being back in uniform, even if it was reserve police officer's drag and an assignment on traffic duty. A little more cash would be welcome for the holiday kitty.

Already it was beginning to chill down. It would be dark by five and the temperature that had risen out of the single digits would plunge when the sun went down. The sky was cloudless. No question there would be black ice as meltwater clamped onto the pavement, with a night of accidents to follow. Beth, and the kids too, he supposed, were happy that he no longer raced to accident calls in the icy night, but he wanted to be back behind the wheel, waiting for the radio to crackle to life, to do something more vital than dust the woodwork at the KCL Building. Where he'd be later, and where he'd reluctantly agreed to let Lourana have another look in the files. The answers weren't in those files; they would come out of that mine crack. The photos on his phone would launch an investigation that even the Kavanaghs couldn't quash. He danced a little interior dance of excitement at being back in it.

People were still streaming across Riverside Drive from the IGA parking lot on the other side, and down the hillside streets where they'd been directed to park when everything filled up near the event. The pier was packed from the shore to the bandstand at the end, where the Redbird Community Band was backing a mixed choir and a podium was set up for the pastors to rouse the crowd over the imminent arrival of the rapture.

Like most people, Marco had gotten accustomed to the smells that wafted from the ruined river. Right after the spill, you could hardly breathe for the stench of dead fish. Now that was mixed with the smell of iron filings and struck matches. The Pentecostals might be looking up for the rapture, but hell seemed a whole lot closer to hand. The river sludged along, greasy orange under plates of stained ice, yellowboy glopped on the banks like some kind of demonic pudding.

The band was laboring its way through a tune he didn't recognize, but people were swaying, hands in the air, singing along. He didn't much care for these maudlin gospel songs. Marco saw few faces from his parish among the crowd, but he did recognize some from arrests and traffic stops.

"The *Lord* of *hosts* will come trailing clouds of glory, Amen, and the righteous will be *raised* incorruptible." The preacher shook a huge, floppy Bible in one hand and gripped the microphone in the other. "Signs have been manifested among us. As it was *written*, the *angels* poured out their bowls of wrath into the deeps, and all the creatures of the water died. And the third angel poured out his bowl into the *river*, yes the *river*, and the streams and sources of the water, which turned into *blood*."

People raised their hands and swayed back and forth. Some shouted "Amen" or "Jesus" or "Gather your flock oh Lord." The crowd pressed together and pushed toward the riverbank and the pier.

The whole thing gave him the willies, looking at the fouled river, thinking about what lay at the bottom of a mine crack. He imagined the rotting bodies rising from the dark, flesh coming back on the bones, eyes returning to the sockets of the skulls.

Marco felt a tap on his shoulder and jumped.

"Can I park there?" The woman, looking frazzled from her wiry gray hair to her off-kilter scarf, waved toward her car parked in the emergency lane. He just shook his head. She scurried off to find another spot.

This prayer vigil had turned into a big event, blowing up from when it was first launched Friday on social media and Christian radio. Plenty of church buses lined along Riverside showed that folks had come early, carried right from morning services to the river. Television stations were there from Charleston, their logoed vans parked along the street with antennas bristling from the tops. The newspaper, not to be outdone, had strung a big banner across the street, THE GAZETTE SUPPORTS RED-BIRD, the same one they had used for an Iraq War veterans tribute and a school supplies drive. The city high school had set up a stand within extension-cord distance of the back of the pharmacy, offering coffee and hot chocolate for a donation to the Boosters fund.

The preacher finished his rant and stepped away from the pulpit, mopping the sweat from his bald head, then pulling a Mountaineers stocking cap from his back pocket to protect it from the cold.

A trumpet solo, a few rising notes. A young woman in a long, white dress (she had to be freezing) stepped forward and began singing: "When the trumpet of the Lord shall sound, and time shall be no more, and the morning breaks, eternal, bright and fair . . . " A metallic squeal, like brakes on an old truck. She paused. Maybe it was her microphone? She tapped it, then held it out, as though someone would come fix it.

The band leader turned, looked at her, then pointed his baton at his players to gather them again. "When the saved of earth shall gather over on the other shore, and the roll is called up yonder, I'll be there." The squealing sound descended an octave, became a groan, something howling at the pressure being exerted against it. The girl set her microphone down slowly on the podium, as though it was hurt or might hurt her.

Marco saw the pier move and thought it was an illusion, some trick of the light. He blinked to clear his head.

The pier shuddered. The crowd began to mill, pressing forward as those on the pier began to move toward the shore. Then the whole structure shifted to the right, twisted abruptly and tipped up on one side, down on the other. It happened fast yet seemed like slow motion, the ping of rivets parting, screech of metal scraping against metal, and the people fell and slid, screaming men and women and instruments all moving in a tangled mass toward the river.

The choir fell in a flurry of satin, blue and black and red.

People caught on the shifting deck clawed to stay there, desperately scrabbling with their heels and elbows but slipping under the ornamental railing or out through the gaps where it had been torn away. The shrieking seemed mostly to come from those who had escaped the collapse, late-comers who had been standing where the pier was grounded on the bank.

The pier rotated on its remaining legs, the erratic motion throwing new souls into the water who thought they had been spared. "Emily!" A child in a pink pageant dress and patent-leather shoes glided toward the edge, her mother clutching after her, then went over the side. A city police officer caught the mother and slung her to safety, then jumped after the girl.

Those on land had fallen to their knees and were praying.

Lot of fucking good that does.

Something clicked, a memory of a rescue on thin ice, and Marco dropped his baton and ran. "Make a chain! Make a chain!" he yelled, grabbing a man's hand and anchoring himself behind a pole. The chain began forming spontaneously, one by one the human links extending down the tottering pier to those still clinging to its tilted surface. Survivors pulled themselves hand over hand along the uneven chain of men until others caught their arms and pulled them onto solid ground.

Marco felt the weight of all those people on his aching arms. He flexed his shoulders, made a tighter grip on the wrist of a black man who had leaped to anchor beside him. He realized it was Austin, who used to sell illegal liquor out of a house on Lemuel Street. Maybe still did. They were captive to the tug and sway as people made their way up the chain, pulled and pushed along. He had an unobstructed view of the river but wished he didn't, as he watched that police officer—a new man, one he didn't know—trying to hold up the girl in pink. He raised her above the slurry of ice and yellowboy and bottom mud kicked up by the collapse. His face was red, and his hands. Marco realized, as his kicks got weaker and his arms slowly let the child descend, that this was not from the cold water nor exertion. He was being burned alive by the acid in the river.

The girl howled as the caustic water ate into her tender skin. The police officer thrust his body partway out of the water and threw her toward the bank before himself going under. She flew like a rag doll, tumbling into the shallows face first.

Marco could see victims flailing in the contaminated river, their skin turning from pink to red, then horribly white until it sloughed away to show the meat beneath. A couple of people made it to shore, lying exhausted on the icy muck like trash fish pulled from the river and left to die.

The pier continued to rotate on its precarious supports. A tuba, caught against the railing, popped free and slid down to a gap and then over the side. A man dangling by a foot twisted in a support stanchion stared after it as it fell. It bobbed brightly on the water, headed for the lock and dam three miles away.

The TV stations continued filming, but the festival atmosphere was gone. Horrified voice-overs seemed to whisper against the lessening screams, as those who were to be saved were saved, and those who were lost gave up their struggles in the water. The newspaper photographer was running back and forth, camera pressed to his face, whipped by the shouts of the editor who had just walked off the pier when it went down. Everywhere, cell phones were being raised to record the disaster.

The fire department came screaming up Riverside with ropes and ladders, the men in their black turnout gear relieving the exhausted members of the human chain. A boat arrived from the sheriff's patrol, zooming to where a few people still thrashed weakly, pulling them in and racing to shore where the ambulances had backed down to the boat ramp to load patients, frozen and burned raw at the same time. Their eyes were ruined, milky globes in raw, red sockets.

Sunset. Reddish light spilled across the scene. Marco, who had slid down next to the pole where he had anchored the chain, could hear the old rhyme running through his head, *red sky at night sailors' delight*. This red light, streaming through the buildings and casting long shadows, reminded him only of nights on duty at fatal wrecks, the lights on his cruiser cycling across the destruction.

Then he heard someone singing.

The girl in the white dress, now with someone's coat draped across her shoulders, was standing near where the pier met the bank. She had been saved, somehow, had not slid to her death. Without a microphone, without affectation, with tears streaming down her cheeks, she was singing.

Abide with me, fast falls the eventide.
The darkness deepens; Lord, with me abide.
When other helpers fail and comforts flee.
Help of the helpless, oh, abide with me.

The rescue boats—three now, a bass boat and pontoon having joined the search—were making their way along the bank, collecting bodies that were slow to drift away in the thickened water. Floodlights worked their way back and forth across the river. The slight cast of mist over the water now looked sickeningly like smoke from the burning of those bodies.

The last hellish beams of the sun snuffed out.

Marco was scalded by the memory of the way he'd mocked these people just a few minutes before. He didn't know if he wanted to cry or even was able.

As they drove down into town, they could see floodlights trained on the twisted remains of the pier, throwing grotesque shadows across the river where small boats moved back and forth, their wakes glaring white as they churned up the polluted water. Red and blue lights strobed from emergency vehicles parked on the bank, sending waves of color across a crowd still encircling the scene, huddled, dark, motionless.

One of her customers had called Lourana to cry the news, Darrick hearing the horror even from across the room. He'd watched Lourana's face sag for just a second before the impassive mask was restored. *What did it cost her, to keep that kind of control?*

Others called, the cell phone each time offering its bouncy melody like a mad counterpoint to the reports of death and destruction. On the television, the movie they'd been watching was paused, an actor he didn't know caught with his mouth wide open as though responding to the news. After Lourana told him what had happened, they'd turned off the movie, eaten a cold sandwich in near silence, waited on the clock.

When the door opened at the KCL Building, Marco nearly dragged them inside, slamming the door and hurrying them down the corridor to the stairs.

"You know about the pier?"

They nodded.

"I was there. Working traffic. I saw it." Marco crossed himself. "The sound, the metal sound. It gave way all at once."

Marco's emotions would have been a sledgehammer if Darrick hadn't moved himself a good way down the hall. From that vantage, he could watch Marco explaining it all to Lourana, his hands and body tilted forward as though he were fighting an unseen opponent. His face knotted and relaxed, mirroring that internal struggle. He looked up, stared at Darrick for a long moment. Lourana drew his attention back by moving between them. She was trying to talk him down, the way a mother would calm a panicked teenager. He saw her hands resting lightly on Marco's forearms and how she leaned toward him, and Darrick was surprised at the jolt of protectiveness he felt.

She should be careful.

Whatever influence she had, it was working. Marco eased back to a straighter posture, his hands unclenched.

"How many did they save?" Darrick asked, edging closer.

Marco glared at him, his eyes wet with unshed tears. "Saved? We got some off the pier. No one who went into the water. I saw an officer try to save a little girl. He died. She died. I helped carry his body up from the river. Dead. They all died."

"Was it the cold, or the acid?" Lourana was steering them toward the stairs.

"Burned. The acid burned their skin off." He clenched his eyes as though that would stop the memory. "Raw."

They started up, the metal stairs clanging underfoot. "One of my customers called and told me the acid in the river ate away the steel supports for the pier," she said.

"How could it be that strong?" Darrick said to her back. "That's like battery acid, or something."

Lourana glanced back at him. "Exactly. How did the mine drainage get to be like that in the first place?"

Darrick could scarcely keep up with her, while Marco was moving slowly, pausing to sweep the area behind them. Jittery.

In the map room, Lourana showed no hesitation in pulling the records. She spread the map of the Kavanagh No. 4 Mine across the table and took another map from her purse, unfolded it and laid them side by side.

"We looked at all this before," Marco complained.

"I didn't have this old map." Lourana leaned close to the faded outlines. "I needed to see how the Bella Jean looked when it shut down."

Darrick was puzzled, remembering the previous lesson. "But how did you get that?"

"MSHA offices at Mont Chateau. Bella Jean is an abandoned mine, though KCL bought right up to it so they could take whatever coal remained around the edges of No. 4 and No. 9. Unlike active mines, the maps of abandoned mines *are* public record."

"Yeah, yeah. Since Hominy Falls," Marco broke in, then looking at Darrick, added, "Miners cut into some forgotten workings that were full of water."

"How can you forget about a mine?"

"Easy. There's nearly seventy thousand of them," Lourana answered, but her voice seemed far away.

He went silent as he tried to get his mind around that. Seventy thousand old mines, tunneling under the Appalachians in every direction. The solid-looking mountains more like anthills that a solid kick would collapse. He remembered Lourana's graphic demonstration of the land falling in on itself and a tilted house she'd pointed out along the road, condemned, sliding into a cavity.

"I don't know why this is important," Marco said. "We've got all the evidence we need. Soon's I get done my shift here I'm headed for Charleston. I'm going to be planted on the BCI doorstep at 9 a.m. with my typed statement and photos." He smiled grimly. "All hell is about to break loose on Carbon County."

"Hasn't it already?" muttered Darrick. *How much misery could one place absorb? Disappearances, murders, mine disasters, people dying in a river that might have boiled right out of hell. Why don't people just leave?*

Lourana leaned across the maps, her fingers (bare of rings or nail polish) moving along the straight-edged lines and topo curves like she was reading a Ouija board instead of tracing out the cartography of a dirty, dangerous place where men put their lives at risk to make a living.

"The boreholes—here," she said, tapping the map. "A whole array of them. Pumping the water out of Kavanagh No. 4 into the Bella Jean, like I thought. That way, they don't have to pay to treat it."

"And they can do that?" Darrick was incredulous.

"It's not unheard of. Smart engineers figure where they can shave a corner or two. Costs a lot to treat acid water, maybe a whole lot more when the stuff is this bad."

"But somebody's responsible."

Lourana just looked at him.

Marco went to the door and stood to one side, listening.

"Something wrong?"

"No." He looked at the frosted glass. "Nothing. I'd be best pleased if we'd get done and get out of here."

"Wait a minute." Lourana bent close to the map, reading the fine print. "We're looking at it the wrong way!" Her voice rose and she began to make long strokes across the map of the Bella Jean and then the other one. "Right here. Right in front of us! The boreholes weren't put there to move the mine water into the Bella Jean, *but the other way around!*"

"Huh?" Marco scoffed. "That's nuts. You're reading it wrong."

"Says you! Look at the old map when Bella Jean was closed and this new one—look at those bores. That's no accident. They're running between Kavanagh's mine and the Bella Jean, just the way it looks. But check the gradient and flow. They're pulling water *out* of the abandoned mine and *into* theirs."

"But why?" Darrick couldn't understand any of this, but it seemed counterintuitive for sure.

"Let's think this through. Kavanagh No. 4 has been idled, the seam about played out and the coal markets being so depressed and all."

"They're laying down a lot of money to keep the mine from flooding, and treat the water," Marco put in.

"Shifting the Bella Jean water—and there's gotta be a shit-ton of bad water there—that just overwhelmed the system." Lourana's voice trembled with horror. "They *created* the blowout."

"Then they're murderers," Marco said.

The word hung in the air.

"Murderers many times over," Darrick said. "Don't forget about the mine crack." No one was going to mention Dreama.

Marco raised his hands, palms out. "But why? Sooner or later someone will figure it out, Natural Resources or the EPA or someone. And when they do, the fines, the costs of the cleanup, it'll put them into bankruptcy."

"And that gains what? For who?" Lourana's excitement had subsided as the solution became suddenly murky.

Darrick thought of the stories he'd been reading about fracking, people opposed to fracking because it hurts the water. *If the water's bad anyway* ... "Maybe it's so they'll allow fracking," he said.

"There's already fracking all over," Marco scoffed. "People love fracking because it's all we got going on around here. We're fucking ground zero of the Marcellus Shale."

"Marcellus millionaires, we call them," Lourana said. "Those that hung onto the gas rights somehow, but like you'd expect, most of the millions are going to the Kavanaghs. Darrick, I'll show you when we go up the hill—the old farmhouse on the left with the McMansion behind it, and right there's the fracking pad. Built with the quick money. That's what he's talking about. But nothing about this would have any impact on fracking anyway. The Kavanaghs have permits on all their old workings." Lourana rolled up her map and snapped the rubber bands around it, replaced the No. 4 Mine map in its cabinet. "It makes no sense," she said. "I don't know what to think."

"What about your reporter friend?" Darrick asked.

"Lot of talk around, something the Kavanaghs were planning. They've been moving surface rights around, she told me, buying up properties, but nobody can find out why. Rumors are that they're planning a big splash, some major development."

"I heard tell a college, one they can name after themselves, like Carnegie Mellon," Marco said as he turned out the lights and locked the door behind them.

The hallway air was still and close, thick with the presence of power. The assumed right to own, to reshape the world to their ends, using men to extract coal and turn it into gold. Darrick felt a tremor take hold and he had to put out a hand to steady himself. It felt like he would fall straight down. It didn't add up—the attack on him, the blowout, the power of the Kavanaghs over these people, the pier sliding Christians to their death as they prayed for divine help. This was not the world he recognized. That world was sane and orderly, a place of numbers and deadlines. In that place, power certainly existed, and authority ruled, but stayed within the boundaries. Most of the time.

Keep your head down, mausi, *and all will be well. Keep your head down until the time is right for you.*

He wondered if he really ever found the strength to crawl out of that hole, or if all this was the delirium of a sick child, or a dying man.

"Let's shake a leg, gimpy," Marco said, with a toothy grin that must have disarmed a lot of girls. Beneath the surface, Darrick could feel Marco's emotional turmoil, changing and bubbling, his anger and insecurity already familiar but now agitated by a scalding blast of shame.

"Surprisingly, I've managed to take care of myself all my life," he shot back, but kept moving down the stairs, putting space between them as he wondered what had brought on this latest storm.

"Yeah? Maybe. But can you take care of Lourana?"

"Wait a dang minute! I take care of myself just fine, thank you."

"What the lady said," Darrick seconded.

Marco came down the stairs ready for a fight, his shoulders up and head lowered. Darrick stumbled to maintain the space between them.

"Marco!" Lourana caught him by the elbow.

He shrugged loose, but she wouldn't be so easily denied, pounding her fists on his shoulders until he turned to face her. "Marco, don't." She was a step above him, so that they stood eye to eye. Darrick, seeing all this from below, felt like he was in a movie scene, the echoing stairwell, Lourana and Marco frozen in the harsh light.

He's not going to intimidate her—or me. Darrick began to climb the stairs, wondering if Marco had lost his mind.

"Lourana . . ."

She glanced over Marco's shoulder at him, gave the slightest movement of her head that could have been yes, or no.

"Marco, pay attention to me. We don't need the testosterone, at least not at the moment," she said, making it light. "I am a fully liberated woman and don't need either one of you being my keeper."

Whatever she had done, it broke the fever. Marco's body relaxed; his head sank. Darrick felt only ashes where the emotional rage had been.

"I swear, I never seen two boys get so swole up with themselves," Lourana said, breaking loose from the stare-off with Marco and pulling Darrick with her as she headed for the back door. "We got what we come for. Call it a win."

Marco shooed them off with both hands. "Go on, get out of here. I got work to do and a bitch of a drive in the morning."

As they turned the corner of the landing, his voice followed them, "Count on me, Lourana—we're gonna bring Dreama home."

| | | | | | | | **THE VOICE OF THE MOUNTAIN** | | | | | | | |

The world demands power and electricity demands coal, eats it like plants eat sunlight. You cannot cast blame because we must devour the mountains' heart.

Death is in life and life in death, the coal is in the mountain and in the people, in their lungs and tattooed into their skin.

—CBK

Marco was heaving the last of the night's bagged trash into the dumpster when a sheriff's department cruiser rounded the corner and pulled between him and the back door. The tinted window eased down and he was greeted by Sheriff Zabrowski's usual tough-guy scowl, made ghastly by the garish sodium vapor light from the street.

"DeLucca!"

"Good morning, sheriff." He lofted a bale of shredded paper from the bank. "Out early?"

"Well, it's about to be a busy day." A 10-45 call burst from the radio and the sheriff reached to turn it down. "I heard about you, good work over at the pier."

Marco felt the twist of shame, a stab in his vitals. "I only did what anyone would."

"You were thinking, anyways. Nobody had any idea the acid could do such. Them poor folks. Leastways they was right with the Lord when they went to meet him."

Marco pulled the lid down and shook the frost and the rust from his hands. He wondered who had been talking him up. He tried not to get his hopes raised, but it was hard not to think there was some reason Zabrowski had pulled in here tonight. "I'm about done here." He waited for a response, got none, though the sheriff looked at him closely. "This temporary work—it's OK, but I hope to be getting back to law enforcement."

The sheriff didn't rise to the bait.

Marco saw another cruiser pull up, and that fucker Prichard got out. He was a Kavanagh creature if ever there was one, and directly the reason Marco had lost his deputy post. Now he was the shift commander at night, which sure seemed to be his natural time.

"Well, it was a helluva thing, that pier going down," the sheriff said. It was all so casual, but those airy castles Marco had started to build evaporated when he saw that the strap was unsnapped on Prichard's sidearm, and a second deputy watched closely from the passenger seat. "The Misters Kavanagh would like to talk with you."

He didn't think it was about a medal for his efforts at the river, but there was no point to arguing, much less running. They had him boxed in between the loading-dock area and the street. He could try to make it back inside the building, but there was no outrunning a bullet.

"My truck . . . "

"We'll bring that along directly."

Prichard held out his hand, his startlingly blue eyes like those of a husky waiting for a piece of meat to drop. Marco dug in his pocket, found the keys, and set them in Prichard's outstretched hand.

"Your cell," Prichard said.

He pulled that out, too, and laid it atop the keys.

"And I recall you having a pistol—every right to it, with your service and all—but we have to ask for it now," the sheriff said.

"It's in the truck glove box. Locked. The kids."

The other deputy was that kid Anderson, a flunky from the get-go. He opened the door for Marco to get in the back of the car. The cage smelled of bodies and body fluids, piss and vomit and blood, the smell of the desperate that was impossible to get out of the upholstery. *Fuck me.*

The sheriff pulled out and they followed, then Anderson driving his truck. He looked at the back of Prichard's head, the black hair cut close, his neck freshly shaven and starting to break out where his collar rubbed. *From up on Chestnut Ridge—one of those families supposed to be descended from lost Spaniards or Turks, but more likely Scots-Irish intermarried with blacks or Native Americans. It was surprising that he'd gone for deputy.* Marco had answered calls up there, but not many, as they mostly kept to themselves, handling their own business.

He wished he had whatever juju this Darrick character had. He sent his thought-waves against the back of Prichard's skull, like he imagined Darrick must. He remembered Hovatter lying there, his head swelling on one side and then the other, his eyes panicked like an animal that's been run over and can't crawl itself off the road. *Concentrate.* He kept thinking hard, grinding his teeth with the effort, but nothing happened. Prichard drove on, with not so much as a pimple burst for all his effort.

The east was beginning to take on some color. He thought about mornings on a still pond, a Jitterbug gurgling and the hole in the water when a largemouth rose to suck it in. Thought about a dawn patrol in Iraq when they'd been startled to shooting and then to laughter by a wandering camel. Thought about a lot of things, but mostly about Beth and the kids. If he'd just gone along and gotten along. If he'd stayed out of this mess with Lourana and that staggering fool. If he'd jumped in the river last night, like he'd been trained to do, he'd be a hero today. A dead hero, face in the newspaper. Instead, he would just end up in the mine crack. *Dead either way.*

At least they weren't likely to find the files, which he'd tucked deep underneath the bed liner before reloading the bags of cat litter that he carried in the winter for traction and to help out neighbors when they got stuck. Lourana knew where the papers were, if she could find his truck. His photos were also in the cloud—if they ever were to be retrieved. They'd kept the lid on so tight, out of natural caution. The bits of hope he was trying to light were just wet matches in a rainstorm.

As they approached the mansion, the outlines of the many-peaked roof, chimneys, and turrets showed like cutouts against the brightening sky. Marco looked back, but his truck was no longer following. *Fuck me.*

People said that old man Kavanagh, the one who founded KCL and was buried up in Pleasant Grove under a monument hauled all the way from Ireland, could tear the skin off you just by looking. It was only an expression, made bigger by fear of losing a job, a house, everything. His own daddy used to say, *I'll skin you alive, boy, if you do that again,* but it wasn't real. Now he'd seen it for real, acid eating the skin from those people as they howled in pain. He'd seen the raw pulp of their flesh exposed, the boiled eyes. The Kavanaghs could do a lot of things, or more like cause them to be done (he saw the bottom of the mine crack again), but no human could have made that river of acid.

The sheriff got out and rang the bell. No one came for a long time—*nobody home, might as well leave*—but finally a man in a monkey suit opened the door and nodded. Then Prichard let Marco out of the car and, bracketed by the sheriff and shift commander, he was delivered to what he assumed was a butler. The sheriff sent Prichard away and waited to be escorted in with his prisoner, but the butler dismissed him with a crisp "thank you" and closed the door, a hushed *thunk* of heavy bronze latches locking into bronze. Seeing the sheriff dismissed like a child sent off to his room troubled Marco as much as anything.

Marco followed the butler through echoing halls. The air was warm, almost too warm, but there was no sense of human life. No smells of cooking or perfume or smoke. Just the blowing of dry air from a hidden furnace, moving thin white panels between heavy draperies. He tried to glance into side rooms, but every one of the dark wooden doors was closed and, he had a feeling, locked. He wondered how old this butler was. He could have been forty or seventy, slender as the mannequins in Caplan's front window but with not a hint of tension in his posture, unafraid that Marco would attack him from behind or try to escape or hide himself in the house. Marco kept walking but he moved a little up on the balls of his feet, staying ready.

For what, he had no clue, but he had to admit a burn of curiosity. No one had much more than glimpsed the Kavanaghs for years, at least anyone who was talking. The father used to make ceremonial appearances, but he must have gotten too old for ribbon-cuttings and such. His sons did not participate anymore, either, sending their director of mines or some other functionary to do the honors.

The interior hallway opened into a large room shafted with light from the rising sun. A round table was set for breakfast, with silver pots on silver trays, crystal pitchers glowing bright with juice, and silver domes over platters of food.

"Mr. DeLucca, sirs."

"Thank you, Brodie," husked the old man, a deep voice gone soft. His enormous bulk occupied a massive wheelchair like a rolling throne. What remained of his hair was white and long, curling on the collar of his soft jacket. "Please find out what our guest would like."

The butler pulled out a chair for him on the near side of the table, a curvy antique thing with yellow striped cushions. Marco sat down but did not pull himself forward. A place had been set for him, right down to the napkin peaked on the plate.

"I'm fine, nothing."

Patrick Kavanagh was flanked by another huge man to his right, and a slender man to his left. Sons. They would be Eamon, the big one, and Cormac. He sort of remembered the faces. Eamon still held a teacup, a white and delicate thing lost in his hands, which he set carefully back on its saucer and placed on the table. "We are early risers in this house and expected you might join us for breakfast."

This is surreal, Marco thought as he watched the butler remove the covers from fancy eggs, sliced tomatoes quivering red and fresh as out of the garden in August, and perfect ranks of bacon and quartered toast. Brodie served the father, then approaching Marco's side with his tongs in hand.

"Just coffee," he said, unable to see himself chewing on bacon as the Kavanaghs debated his fate.

The butler inclined his head, then went about wordlessly filling the plates of Eamon (a lot of everything) and the younger son (toast only). He returned to fill their cups.

Marco spread his napkin across his lap. It was adorned with a walking lion, and he realized that must be a coat of arms, as a similar lion marched above a pair of crescent moons on a shield carved into the fireplace.

"You are admiring our family leopard," Cormac said. His words came smooth as glass, no hint of Appalachia. *Bred out, or educated out?*

Marco couldn't understand what leopard he was talking about.

"We are an ancient family. A royal one. That beast is considered a leopard, on a coat of arms, because a lion must be rampant to be called such," whispered the father. "Standing on its hind legs."

Cormac lifted his hands curved one above the other like claws, to emphasize what *rampant* meant. His lips were full and red, like one of the painted cherubs on the altar at St. Barbara's Church.

"Our symbol is called a *leopard lioné*, a lion that is walking and looking about him, the way that leopards do," rumbled Eamon. "They are not spotted like the leopards we think of today. It is all about their movement. Lion or leopard, it means the same in heraldry. Valor and strength."

"Though the leopard is considered to mark an element of rashness," added Cormac. He flinched when Eamon stared at him, and slowly dropped his hands to his lap.

Marco kept waiting to wake up. Beth would roll over soon and shake him out of his dream. He had to be kicking and thrashing in his sleep, the way he did when things were bothering him. *Come on, honey, get me out of here. Blow bubble kisses on my back till I'm roused.* He watched the butler circulate, taking away dishes. He pulled out a tiny brush and swept crumbs from the tablecloth into a small dustpan. *What the fuck?* Finally, at a glance from the old man, he backed out of the double doors across the room and shut them behind him.

The Kavanaghs sat back in their chairs, digesting their breakfast with the air of men whose lives ran along well-laid tracks. He almost expected them to light up big cigars or something. The yellow cheeriness of the windowed room and the rising sun glowed around them, so that their dark suits seemed darker and their somber faces were highlighted. They had no need to scowl like the sheriff, or strut and threaten. You could feel the power that emanated from them. They were who they were and did not need anyone's approval.

"We have something to discuss," said Eamon. It seemed almost as an afterthought, as though they'd come together to discuss family crests and lineage, and had just remembered that other thing. "Your truck was seen at Bailey's Fish Camp."

Hovatter had called it in.

"I was hunting."

Eamon nodded. "Did you get your deer?

"No, I bounced two does and a forkhorn, but didn't get a shot."

"But you did make a kill." The old man's voice was a thin shadow of Eamon's, but when he spoke, both sons automatically turned to him. "Why did you kill Hovatter?"

Marco hoped his face didn't show the shock he was feeling. *The Kavanaghs don't know what had happened, the all-powerful Kavanaghs. Someone was killing and it was not of their doing.*

"Hovatter? I never saw him. Went out early and headed in early."

"So your truck was parked there that morning, right where he was found dead, and that is mere coincidence," accused Eamon.

Marco thought the best he could do was brazen it out. "Seems like. Hovatter had a way about him. He pushed people, you know, nailed them over trifling stuff. Maybe he just pushed the wrong guy."

"You were that guy." Eamon became brusquer. "I find it hard to believe, Marco, that with your training and experience, you would do something with so little thought for the repercussions."

Marco stared back, stone-faced. *They don't know about Darrick. I hope that means they don't know about Lourana either.*

"And Jimmy Cooper?" Eamon continued.

"I was hard at work when that happened. Never left the building until I took the trash out. You can check the door logs. When I came out, the city units were wrapping up the scene."

"And then you went home to your family."

"Yes, my family." Marco's heart did a flip, sensing the threat under those words. He stared right back at the big man, knowing he was telling the absolute truth about Jimmy, and hoping that the truth served to cover the earlier lie. They must be afraid, no matter how they sat so easily in their chairs, like a magazine layout of rich people relaxing in their mansion.

Only Eamon's hands betrayed any unease, fidgeting with a fork he had taken off the table. "We know you've continued to nose around some old cases. We thought when you were fired as a deputy, you'd get the message."

"What is that?"

"Leave it be. Dreama's case."

"I'm not on the force any longer. I'm sure someone's still working on it, so maybe you need to ask the sheriff about that. Funny thing. When young women disappear, they don't just drop off the face of the earth and get forgotten."

"As though men do?" said Cormac. There was a slyness to the younger brother. A fox among the lions, or a visitor from another time, glowing with the elegance of a different world.

Marco thought again of the mine crack. The disgust he had felt while down there, the horror, but also a familiarity at the sight of bodies strewn around like trash. The alleyways of Fallujah. The way bodies so quickly lost their humanity and became heaps of rags, and then dust, dust.

"Lourana has not given up, and we know that you have been helping her efforts. It is only out of Dreama's intervention that we have not acted," said Eamon.

"Intervention?" Marco came to attention. "What does that mean?"

"It means that Lourana is protected, like your wife and children," he growled. "They are safe and heedless, today."

The bottom just kept dropping out. *I promised to take care of Beth. I stood at that altar and said the vows I should have said to Lourana.* Was she being collected by one of the Kavanagh creatures right now? And Dreama? Alive? Where was she? *The kids. Beth and the kids.*

"I go to work for you five nights a week, Mr. Kavanagh," he said to the old man, who seemed to have fallen asleep, so he turned to Eamon. "I'm a good worker now, and I was a good deputy then. Whatever is going on with these deaths, I'm not the one responsible. So let me get back to my family." He stopped, because he could hear the tremble. *Michael, just starting to turn from a little boy into a man. Amy.* The Kavanaghs stared back at him. He remembered a museum in Pittsburgh, a field trip when he was Michael's age, and the logs of petrified wood. Wood that was stone. You could get as much warmth from those logs as from these men. And as much milk of human kindness as you'd expect to drop from the marble breasts that had made him blush in the museum galleries.

"Please. Sirs." He held himself erect but inside he was crawling.

One of the double doors opened. Dreama came in and settled in the chair next to Cormac, who glanced at her and smiled before turning back to the family business.

"Dreama! You—your mother," Marco stammered. "You're all right."

"Things are not what they seem, Marco. When you lack information, sometimes it's a poor idea to be taking action," said Cormac. He laid his hand over Dreama's and as she smiled, the same dimple that marked her father's chin appeared on hers.

"You will be our guest for a little while. No outside contact, you understand," said Eamon.

He felt pressure on his arm. The interview was over. The butler had come in noiselessly and was moving him toward the door, but not the one he'd come in by.

16

Lourana snapped on the television while the coffee was brewing.

"Hope Pete got the lot cleared," she said, clicking toward the news but pausing to watch a favorite *Cheers* scene. "Some of the older women get peeved if there's the least bit of ice. Gonna break a hip, they say."

"And that's your 'Right-Away Weather' for a Monday morning." The camera switched from the local weather back to the national program.

"Long a fixture of the tabloid covers, international psychic Miss Huldah has catapulted back to prominence on her prediction last month of a fatal disaster." The balding anchor held up the front page of an issue that also featured a story on the "monster engineering" of Halloween candy. The headline said, "Great catastrophe of Christian lives predicted! Miss Huldah says it will happen where the river runs wide."

"Oh, crimony," Lourana said.

"The pier collapse on the Broad River in West Virginia, a disaster that took the lives of fourteen people at a prayer vigil Sunday and injured dozens more, has fulfilled that prophecy, Miss Huldah claims. She says that more is yet to be revealed."

A clip of the disaster scene was followed by one of Miss Huldah, her eyes heavily made up behind huge glasses.

"I have been receiving messages about the great dangers facing the people of this region. The river has been tainted from an unknown source . . ."

"Not so unknown," Lourana growled.

" . . . and the townsfolk are menaced by uncanny creatures, awoken from the dead. Travel is difficult for me these days, but my supporters have urged me to undertake this journey, so that I might bring light into the darkness."

Darrick stared at the television. "I guess I should be feeling tingly, or something, now that a psychic's coming to town."

"Just like Santa Claus." Lourana filled the cups, stirred creamer into hers, and carried them into the living room. "It's gonna be a circus here, with the national media and all."

"Maybe it's a good thing. Maybe someone will pay attention to what's going on."

"Just wait till Marco gets the BCI up to that mine crack. That'll clean blow the top off things. Not even the Kavanaghs can seal everything off this time." Lourana realized that was a bit of bravado, remembering all the local mine incidents that never seemed to make the news. Nothing as bad as Upper Big Branch, but one here or there, those two boys killed pulling pillars. It all seemed to stay inside the borders of Carbon County. Just like Vegas. To say nothing of the mine safety violations that were bargained down or assessed a tiny fine—but then, that was the whole industry, wasn't it?

She tried to estimate where Marco would be right now. If he left at seven, like he said he would, then he should be halfway to Charleston. Maybe he'd stop for breakfast. She thought about him grabbing a pack of mini doughnuts and a to-go cup of coffee at a gas station along the way, splashing his face with cold water, hitting the road again. He'd not let grass grow under his feet this morning.

The Dodge commercial had quit blaring and now the screen was filled with the image of a glossy young woman wearing a network logo jacket, the town spread out behind her. She'd found her way up to Indian Hill. Behind her, you could see the twisted wreckage of the pier, with all the activity around that, and the orange river and downtown. On the opposite side, on a knob long ago flattened by strip mining, the parking lots spread out around Walmart and the strip of little stores. Lourana imagined she might could see her house, a speck at the edge of the woods.

She caught bits of what the reporter was saying, "removal of the pier ... investigation ... memorial service." Her thoughts were all on what was going to happen when Marco made his contact, when a trustworthy cop took a look at those photographs. Once that was done, she'd fill in Zadie on the whole story about the mine crack, the necklace that might prove what had happened to her missing source, the boreholes. All of it. Even Darrick? That was a tough call.

She watched him get up from the recliner, which he had made his own, and moved to the kitchen to dunk another tea bag. He moved almost normally. Stressful things made the lurching come on, he'd explained, but therapy and medication had kept it under control until all this.

It was strange to have a man in the house, those half-remembered sounds and smells. Whiskers in the sink. She flashed on a memory of Steve, lean hipped, long legged, a mover, for sure. It was at senior prom, him in that formal getup with a carnation on his lapel. He could use his body, no doubt, but not his mind. Stuck here in Redbird until it ruined him. She remembered the orchid-colored dress she had worn that night, the fabric shimmery and tight across her chest and hips. *Wasn't so bad looking myself then either.*

"It's toast for breakfast, this morning," she said, shaking herself out of the past. "I'm fresh out of most everything, food-wise, so I'll stop by the store after work."

"That's fine." Darrick nodded, but his eyes were on the TV. *What a weird feeling it must be to be him.*

She was untwisting the tie on the bread when her landline rang, a strange, jangly sound, almost antique. No one much used that number— she only kept paying AT&T for the internet.

"Hello?"

"Lourana?" A woman, shaky and breathless. "This is Beth. Beth DeLucca. I didn't know who to call."

"What's wrong, Beth?"

"Marco never came home last night." There was an edge of accusation to her voice. Lourana wondered how much he'd told her about the reason for his trip, and was starting to reassure Beth when she went on,

"I know he was going to Charleston this morning, something serious with the state police that he couldn't tell me about yet, but he promised to stop by the house to look at Michael's history project and drive him in. He didn't."

"That's not Marco."

"For sure. You know how he is. If he says he's going to do something, he does it, come hell or high water. Michael was so disappointed. I took him to school. When I came back by the bank, I looked for Marco's truck, but it wasn't there either."

"He's not picking up his cell?"

Beth didn't answer. Lourana could hear sniffling.

"Maybe there's no coverage where he is. Dead zones all over the place on that road. Let's not borrow trouble, OK?"

"You sound just like my mama." The phone was muffled but she could hear Beth honking and sniffing. "Marco said you were involved in all this, so I guess it's about Dreama, but I don't understand why he wouldn't tell me."

"Beth, he's trying to protect you." Lourana stared at the back of Darrick's head, the gash gaping at her horribly now that the butterflies had let go. She was ashamed all over again that she'd let the snow stop her from getting help for him—well, that and fear. A tangle of all their fears. Now it most like didn't matter.

"You'll let me know if you hear something?"

"Of course. And you do the same, Beth."

She went into the living room, clicked off the TV (which had cycled back to the psychic), and faced Darrick.

"Marco may be missing."

"Missing? How?" His eyes were wide, and she watched him begin those repetitive movements, touching his glasses, his face, like he was reassuring himself that he was still in his body.

"That was Beth, his wife. He never came home this morning, after promising his boy. She went looking for his truck and it's gone, and he's not answering his phone."

"He said he was heading straight out. When would he get there?"

"It's 8:15 now. He would be there around nine, if he didn't stop along the way. Say 9:15."

Darrick looked stricken, mirroring the way she felt. If he was just broken down somewhere, that was something to hold onto. But she had a bad feeling that it was more than that, a deep, gut-sick feeling that Marco was in the wrong hands.

"I gotta get going and open the sweepstakes. Sit tight. Maybe it's nothing."

"What if it's not?"

"Then we'll deal with it."

Lourana put on her coat and slipped her feet into the fur-lined clogs that felt so good in this weather. Small comforts. She left Darrick slumped in the recliner, like an old man who wasn't expecting anything but bad news.

THE VOICE OF THE MOUNTAIN

An abecedarian: adit, brattice, cribbing, dragline, entry, face, gob, haulageway, inby, jackrock, kerf, lamp, man-trip, nip, overburden, pyrite, robbed-out, self-rescuer, tipple, upcast, void, white damp, yinzer. I could think of no word for Q, except the quest for the mountain's root, or Z, unless zap, the sound of the electricity as it leaps from the wire to the flesh.

—CBK

17

"What's that I smell?" Lourana asked as she plopped the grocery bags on the counter.

Darrick glanced at the clock and opened the oven door. "Hope you don't mind that I rummaged around in your kitchen." He pulled the pan from the oven and set it on the unsteady burners of the stove top.

"My God," she said. "That's one beautiful cobbler."

She was putting things into the refrigerator which, like the cupboards, he had found pretty bare. *How much did a person make running a sweepstakes parlor anyway?*

"It's a kind of miracle, I'd say, given what's here. I don't bake much. Where did you learn to cook?"

"The children's home made sure to send us into the world prepared." *They expected we'd always be like we were, without family.* "Anyway, it was something to keep busy. No word from Marco?"

She shook her head.

He thought she looked tired, maybe because she'd dispensed with makeup. He was used to seeing the women around the DC offices, always pulled together. She was wearing one of her usual sweatshirts, a shapeless thing with a pink bear on the front that mostly concealed what appeared to be a good body. Or maybe she really was tired, worn out from sitting all day in that cinder-block room with the outside blocked from view, the machines flashing and shrieking.

"I called my office this morning." She gave him a look that veered between surprise and worry. "I logged on and used my Skype account and not your phone, OK? I don't think Sheriff Doohickey has the savvy to be tracing that. I told them I was sick, which isn't far from true."

"Maybe we need to go ahead on our own, call the FBI or something."

"And tell them what? There's a hole in the ground full of bones? What am I supposed to say about the two men who are dead because I looked at them funny?"

"They don't know you did that."

"I think that's a little naive, Lourana. As soon as they know I'm alive, the locals are going to tie me to those deaths and then finish getting rid of me like they intended."

Lourana looked peeved. He thought maybe he might have been a little condescending. She started taking pots and pans out, thumping them onto the stove.

"If we just give them an anonymous tip, the location of the crack, won't they follow up on their own?" she asked.

Darrick shrugged. He didn't think a wacko call like that would get the FBI moving. "They would contact local authorities. If they have Marco, then it's probably no use anyway. They'll just scoop me up and arrest me for the murders. That would take care of all their problems. I'll bet those bodies are gone already." *This is nuts.* "Sounds a little paranoid," he admitted.

"Not paranoid enough." Lourana turned the oven back on and shook French fries onto a cookie pan. "We gotta work through this, and we need Marco and the evidence he has. Wish I coulda taken pictures with my camera, too, but my old phone's no good in low light."

"Isn't there someone else we can trust to get onto the Kavanagh property and document that pit? The reporter?"

"I don't know if we can trust her."

"Don't you know other cops?"

She looked at him, her brown eyes reflecting none of the terror he imagined she felt. Must feel, because he certainly did. "I don't know who can be trusted. Marco, I've known him all my life, and he put himself on the line about Dreama."

* * *

Lourana wasn't about to let him know he'd gotten under her skin. *Naive.
I'll show him naive. He don't know squat about how things work in the real
world.* She slapped hamburger steaks into the skillet and added onion
rings to the pan in the oven. She'd bought them special for him.

They ate without talking, the quiet punctuated only by the clinking
of forks and the cycling of the refrigerator.

She began to feel a little guilty about giving him the silent treatment. He
had baked for her, after all, and then cleaned up after himself, which was
the real wonder. She could feel his gray eyes appraising her, but he wasn't
going to be the first to break the silence. He was a cautious somebody.

"You made that nice dessert," she said, realizing it sounded more grudg-
ing than she meant it to be. "I'll clear away, and we'll have that while it's
still warm." Lourana started carrying dishes to the sink. She turned on
the water to get it hot, and talked over it while looking at her reflection
in the black square of the kitchen window. "I'm just flat scared, not that
I wasn't before, but if they've got Marco . . . "

"You think we'd be smart to leave."

"Not really. You think they ain't still watching? You'd be wrong. I saw
deputies on the main road and headed up to the lake. The only way would
be over one of the old county roads, dirt roads they haven't maintained
since the Depression. And now snowed under."

Darrick seemed to reflect on that. "Sometimes it's tempting, but I
can't run. And not simply because I wouldn't make it out. I have to know
why they did this, and how I ended up like this. I can't have any more
unanswered questions in my life."

She let the bubbles mount up, then shut off the water and left the dishes
to soak. She got out a couple of cereal bowls and dished up the peach
cobbler, poured a little milk over it, and carried it into the living room.

"Amanda brought me that quart of peaches this past summer. They
would have probably set there forever. This is real good."

"Thanks." Darrick ate finicky, sorting out a bite of fruit, then a bite of
crust. "So what else can we do? Is there someplace we can look for Marco?"

They both knew the answer to that. "Like I told you the first night—
people go missing around here and they don't never get found."

She thought about Dreama down in that pit. Those photos that Marco took, the dull white of skulls lit by the flash, the horrible ruck of meat and jumble of bone-ends that reminded her uncomfortably of the deer skeletons her dog used to pull in. The ribs, the backbone, had been too much like human on those discarded skeletons. The bones in the photos had looked too much like something butchered for the table.

"You've known Marco a long time."

"We grew up together, two brats with dirty feet over on Buffalo Branch. He was sorta sweet on me. Went off right out of high school to the military, planning a career, but something happened in Iraq. He come back home, took the job with the county. Still looks like a Marine, don't he? He's been a good friend through some awful rough times."

*　*　*

Darrick watched as she added their bowls to the sink and began to wash the dishes. He remembered Marco's swirl of emotion, and part of that mix had been sexual and protective—not for his wife, a distant smear in his thoughts, but focused on Lourana.

"I've hung on here, because of Dreama. Trying to find out about my little girl. You have to, right? But I don't know if I should anymore." She stood frozen, her hands in the dishwater, looking out into the night. The house seemed smaller after dark, as the cold pressed in. "I been thinking, way before all this, about going back to Charleston. Or maybe just keep going, someplace there isn't a damn chunk of coal to be found."

Something seemed to startle her, her whole body making a small jump, as though stung, and she emptied out the sink and quickly wiped the counter. She came into the living room and sat down, looking as though she was just about to ask a question, then did not. Instead, she went to her computer and clicked on some music. The familiar rhythm of "I Shot the Sheriff" came rattling out of the underpowered speaker. A half-smile ghosted across her face. "But you didn't shoot the deputy, right?"

He struggled to respond in kind, feeling the weight across his chest like a lead apron. "No, I did not do that."

They sat close together but miles apart, the darkened television screen reflecting their individual silences. Darrick kept seeing the face of the rent-a-cop Jimmy as it morphed, his eyes full of terror. A kid, really. Then he remembered that this kid had hit him over the head and thrown him in a hole to die. Still, the eyes wouldn't quit accusing him.

What am I to do with what I am?

Darrick was deep in his thoughts when he felt a touch against his palm. Instinctively, he yanked away, then realized Lourana had reached out and brushed his hand.

"Darrick? Are you OK?"

He pulled back like a snail into its shell. *How can she touch me, seeing what she's seen?*

"I'm pretty far from OK, but there's nothing to be done, is there?"

This time, there was no mistaking her intent as she reached over and firmly took his hand between hers.

"Aren't you afraid of me?"

"You haven't killed me yet. Zombie or not."

He felt something shift. The rigid emotional shell that Lourana had built to protect herself from her past, from the Kavanaghs and their creatures, the same one that had served to protect her from however he might have reacted to her feelings, was beginning to dissipate. Darrick's thoughts darted wildly. Where he could go, how he could get away from her before everything broke loose and he was overcome by the emotions pent up inside her? He started to get up, but Lourana stood with him.

"I'm not afraid." Her eyes were clear and level.

"I am." His heart was hammering, his body betraying the emotion he feared. "Lourana, please. Before something happens. I'm starting to hear your emotions."

"I know."

And with that, the great slide began, the protective shell bursting apart, her awareness surging over him.

When he had been a boy, ice jams used to build up on the river during the long winter, layers mounting like stones piled into a bulwark, until the spring rains came and then the ice would creak, explode like cannon fire, and let loose in a tumult of water and slabs of ice. No one could survive that breakup. But somehow, he was riding the release of Lourana's emotions without going under the dark water, immersed without being crushed.

He realized that he was now gripping her hands, both her hands. And she was gripping right back.

Gradually, the rush subsided. Darrick could start to identify the strands of her emotions, the barbed loneliness, guilt about Dreama, longing, a tangled braid of regret and anger. The strength of this would have been enough, coming from one of the men, to have triggered his defense mechanism. But it hadn't this time. It hadn't even as she held tight to his hands.

He became aware of the pulse beating in her thumb. How comforting it felt to be touched by another human being. The positive emotions coming from Lourana—love and compassion and loyalty—had lifted him above the darker elements, carried him along, fragile as a paper boat.

His awareness expanded. Somehow, they were still in her little house. The air was acrid with the smell of coal ashes in the grate. Music still played from her computer.

As if in agreement, their hands parted and they sat back down, exhausted.

"You're all right?"

She nodded. "Now that it's done, I'll admit I was some afraid."

"You should be." He saw Jimmy's eyes pop, saw Hovatter's mouth pooch out in surprise. "That was a reckless thing to do."

"You don't need to lecture me." Lourana sat back straight. "But there was no going forward always tiptoeing around, wondering what would happen. Truth to tell, I am just tired of trying to hold it together every blessed moment. And Darrick . . . "

"Yes?"

"I think I could feel something coming from you."

Now it was his turn to be shocked, finding himself on the other side of an emotional tug of war. "What?"

"I felt something. Not a bad something." Lourana pushed her hair behind her ears. "It was like longing. For someone. For someone you loved. Maybe your first love?"

"My first love? Honestly?" He thought of Nicole but realized how tenuous that connection actually had been. "There was this old German woman. I guess she wasn't old, but to a little boy—anyway, she was the infirmary nurse at the children's home. She had escaped from East Germany, over the wall. She used to sing to me. Read me stories."

"No, I mean love. Adult love."

That sickening twist in his memory. It never got any better.

Lourana waited.

"Her name was Nicole. We were planning on getting married. We'd talked about having a family, and how important that was to me. And to her, I thought. But she had second thoughts, though she never shared them. Then she went home to Texas, and something happened. She told me she had a good offer from a graduate program I didn't even know she'd applied to. *Poof.* Gone."

"We think we can grab onto one little corner of happiness and nail it down, keep it for ourselves, but it doesn't work that way," said Lourana. She went over to a group of family photographs, lifted one off the wall. It was her in a green dress and makeup, hair done up and earrings dangling from her ears. She was smiling and looking sexy in that way that women can just by the way they stand with one knee bent. Beside her was a lean, dark-haired man wearing a red sweater. In front of them was a girl of seven or eight, with black hair like her daddy and a face like her mommy. "You know, you love your family, your home, your town. Even when the problems are bigger than you want to admit."

"How can people let things go on like this? How can they stand it?"

"We can't, really. We cuss and gripe and lots of folks leave, always have done, but we still love these hills, more'n you can imagine. We make a home here because it is home, not because it's easy. We grow up learning to fish, hunt ramps, shake down apples. We build our homes in places that don't make economic sense. And we dig coal, because that's what we've done for generations, and there's pride in having the skill and guts to do that even when we know the cost."

She hung the picture back on its nail, where it rested crooked until she nudged it level.

"Outsiders say we're fatalistic, or backward. That we keep mining for the money, even when it's destroying our land. What they don't get is the pride part. For a man to go under the earth like his daddy and earn a good living for his family. So yeah, we know that the mines poison the rivers, tear up the roads, wreck our lungs. Nobody knows that better or feels the pain of it worse. We ain't stupid. You'd be surprised how many guys with college degrees are running the longwalls. It hurts to see the damage, but it's worse when the mines close and there's no place to work, and families slip away one at a time till there's not half a town left."

Now that she had opened herself to him, Darrick could feel the emotions that tracked her words. There was a fierceness to them, and love.

"Your husband didn't go underground but he got hurt anyway."

"It was so bad, his back. You take that pill and *bam*, the pain is gone. The doctors will write those prescriptions and Lord knows the drugstores are more'n happy to fill them."

"It's hard to get off it."

"That's a true fact. Hard as hell." The word came out of her mouth like it burned. "But Steve did and we were doing OK, until Dreama went back to Redbird. It backset him something awful."

"He started using again."

Lourana's eyes were swimming with tears. "Yes, he did. And God help me, that time, I went right along with him."

"No, Lourana." He instinctively pulled away. That hardness she could put around herself—was that an addict's shell?

"I'm clean, OK? I didn't get in too deep, not like him, and got myself straight and stayed that way."

Darrick stood up and wrapped her in his arms. She was so strong and so vulnerable. When she tipped her head back to look at him, he said to hell with being cautious and he bent to kiss her.

18

They were dozing in their chairs, talked out, when Lourana's phone rang. It was like a fire alarm going off, disorienting.

"Hello?"

She recognized Zadie's peculiar high-pitched tone, that accent you couldn't place. "Yes, what's going on?"

"I'd really like to see you."

Lourana blinked at the clock. 12:35. That would be a.m. "At the newspaper?"

"How about your house?" The weird just-chatting-with-a-friend tone continued. It was Zadie, all right, but the no-nonsense reporter was being masked by some kind of ladies-who-lunch thing.

Lourana considered that for a groggy moment. "No, let's meet at the parlor. You can park over in the church lot."

"OK, bye!"

She shook her head to drive the sleep out, then went to the bathroom, peed, splashed water on her face, brushed her hair. What was going on with Zadie? She did like to play secret agent. And Godalmighty, hadn't she let her tongue wag loose this evening. Now she wished she hadn't told Darrick the gory details.

When she came out, Darrick was shuffling around. He looked at her from the corner of his eye like a kid that's been caught doing something naughty.

"I owe you an apology," he said.

"What for?"

She could sense a simmering behind his eyes that might be any number of things.

"If you're apologizing for kissing me, then don't, because you didn't do anything I didn't go along with, right?" She sounded considerably more confident than she had felt at that moment when his lips touched hers. "I opened up to you like I don't with anybody. Anybody."

"I know that." He didn't say anything more, and Lourana thought, *It's not entirely a two-way street yet, is it?*

And then she yawned, and filled him in on the call from Zadie.

"And you're going?" He sounded doubtful.

"She wouldn't be calling if it wasn't important. But she sounded—I don't know. Off."

"Like someone was listening."

Lourana realized that was exactly it. She nodded, and broke into a yawn midway through it. She was still half-asleep, but she got her coat and fished her keys out of her purse.

Darrick held out his hand, saying she was too tired and he would drive.

"Like hell." She was more than a little peeved at the alpha-male protectiveness breaking out around her.

"Don't be so touchy. It's not safe for you to be going out alone. Maybe this reporter isn't what she seems. And if an ex-Marine could be disappeared, how do you think you'd do?"

After a moment's reflection, she dropped the keys into his hand.

They crunched out to the Subaru. It was still too cold for this time of year, but the steel-blue frigidity of the night before had softened some with the arrival of a high cloud deck. The moon was up there, finding its way between the ripples of thin clouds and making the sky glow softly.

Darrick drove slowly, cautious maybe because that was the way he was anyway or because he didn't know the road. Lourana wondered if the head injury had affected his vision or balance. It would be hard to tell, and she didn't want to ask.

As they came around a curve, a shadow swooped across the road right in front of the car. Darrick jerked the wheel toward the edge, and she put her hand out and pulled it back as he stomped on the brake. They slid to a shuddering halt, slantwise across the road.

"What the hell was that?"

"An owl. Big one," she said. "Probably a great horned."

"Scared me."

"You'd be worse than scared if you'd kept going that direction."

Darrick looked toward the edge of the road and the black drop-off without guardrail or trees, then back at her. His eyes grew wider still.

"Yeah, you forgot there ain't much leeway, is there? You oughta meet a coal truck on some of these curves, or one of those black tankers of God-knows-what for the fracking. Either way, they tend to take their share of the road out of the middle."

Darrick drove even more gingerly after that.

A sign had been wired to the post of a stop sign at the intersection with the mall road: MEMORIAL SERVICE FOR THE VICTIMS OF THE PIER, TUESDAY 10 A.M. MINERS MEMORIAL. A cross and a bouquet of red, white, and blue plastic flowers were stuck into the snow, one on each side of the sign.

"At least I never did that," Lourana said.

"What?"

"The roadside memorials. When Dreama disappeared, people came and put stuff by her apartment. Damned teddy bears and stuff, like she was a child."

"I guess it feels like something a person can do."

"Useless trash." Lourana was surprised at how angry it made her. She could still see the little heap of stuff slumping in the rain under a banner saying, WE ARE PRAYING FOR YOU, DREAMA, probably put there by people who didn't know her the least bit. "But I did try to get on TV, on that *America's Most Wanted* show. They were interested for a while, especially after they saw her picture, but there was no suspicious boyfriend or scandal or anything, so they just kinda dropped it."

The town was peaceful. Traffic lights cycled green to yellow to red, but nothing else seemed to be marked by the passage of time, of life and death, as long as you didn't look at the river and the ruined pier.

They turned left toward the sweepstakes parlor. A helicopter passed over. At first Lourana thought it might be one of the TV stations, until she saw it was a medical flight from the university hospital. Her parlor was dark, the parking lot empty, and so was the road. She unlocked and Darrick loped inside before she turned on the inside lights but not the signage, activating a computer near the back door so that it looked as though she might be reading online, crazy Lourana on her crusade, nothing out of the ordinary should anyone pass by.

* * *

Darrick found the local television website and scrolled through the headlines. Nothing about Marco. An old man had been found dead in his house, and of course someone was quoted saying that he might have been attacked by a zombie, but no one would be sure until they did an autopsy. *There won't be a stroke or heart attack for the next five years that won't be attributed to the zombie.* A demolition firm had been hired to take away the wreckage once the investigation of the pier collapse was completed. High school sports, holiday recipes, a YouTube video promoted at the top of the page. Miss Huldah.

"Dear friends," she said, stretching out her beringed fingers as though she could entwine them with the viewers'. She was seated in a bland hotel room, but was dressed like a sideshow gypsy with heavy jewelry and scarves and black mascara that made her deep-set eyes recede further into their wrinkled sockets. "Dear friends, who watch with me through this terrible night of death and destruction." She lowered her hands and sat back. "I have fasted and prayed, opening myself to the forces of the universe, to learn the truth. Know that the creature you call a zombie, this deadly invader from the other side, is no intruder but is one of your own. He is a miner who was lost underground, entombed by a disaster, and now raised from his forgotten grave."

Darrick groaned. "Are you hearing this?"

"Beware!" Her head shook and the jewelry trembled and flashed. "This may be only the first of the dead to rise and walk. He is the key to the destruction of the river, the acid rivers of hell released in the supernatural gathering of life-energy for his reanimation. Watch with me, dear friends. This creature may once have been a man, but he is now one with the dark forces. The murders of brave peace officers and the Christian souls lost at the pier—know that God has gathered all their souls to his bosom for they were praising him when it happened—prove beyond doubt that the infernal one is at work here. So I say, watch!"

The video stopped abruptly.

As though paying heed to Miss Huldah's warnings, Lourana had been peering through the gap between the edge of the door frame and the blinds. "Zadie's here," she said, as the Caprice turned into the church lot and parked back by the education wing.

"The infernal creature will now disappear." Darrick gave a stiff little bow as he left the room and closed the door behind him.

* * *

Zadie looked for a long time up the road toward town, then the other way, before trotting across and slipping inside.

"I have news for you," she said breathlessly, slipping off her coat.

"I have some as well."

"Sorry to be vague on the phone, but I'll tell you, the editor has been on my back every minute." Zadie loathed the man, from his barely disguised racism to his reek of cigarette smoke to his ostentatious brand of Christianity. "He took away the river story, *my* story, and gave it to that old fuddy-duddy Wayman who won't do a thing but rehash the DNR press releases. I'm kept busy with stories headed straight for B-8. I make time, though, when he's not looking." She leaned toward Lourana. "I file my notes under false slugs so he thinks I'm working on evergreens for over Christmas."

Lourana looked at her as though she had started speaking Greek.

"Sorry. Newsroom lingo. You have to know a lot of languages, for the composing room, for the scientists, for the kids." Zadie felt a pang, realizing the late hour, another night spent chasing a story while Zippy took on the big-sister role as she herself once had, giving her little brother a snack and tucking him into bed.

"What do you have?" Lourana asked, cutting right to the point.

"A reason for the spill, maybe."

"I've got something on that too. You first."

"I always watch for permit modifications, new permits, anything around the mines. And you know I've been digging to find out what kind of project KCL has been keeping undercover. No way they were just sitting back and letting their money stay idle. Anyway, I saw something strange, a permit application for a huge chunk of the surface right over No. 4 and the Bella Jean workings, along with the Laurel Fork strip site. It's a mammoth piece of land."

"I know they can't be stripping."

"No. Any coal that's worth taking from the surface is already gone. But the strange thing about this permit is who took it out. And what it's for." Zadie showed her the printout, an application from a company registered in the Cayman Islands, EnViro LLC, for a mixed-use landfill and remediation facility.

"A landfill?"

"I don't think it's any normal landfill. Back in the day, I was involved in fighting the big multistate proposal over in Laidley County. They were going to bring municipal waste and sewage sludge from New York and New Jersey by rail, so I know what that kind of landfill's about. This permit is something entirely different. It's hard to get the full picture, but it seems to be for highly toxic industrial materials and infectious medical waste."

Lourana shook her head. "Is there anything they won't do to poor Carbon County? People had all these grandiose plans for when the announcement came."

"I know—a four-star resort? A college? Crazy."

Lourana seemed quenched by the news, and Zadie wondered if she'd been among those hoping against hope that KCL would have some great development with the promise of lots of jobs.

"I don't know if it's connected, but here's what I found," Lourana said as she pulled up the MHSA site. "I've been following the news on the acid, too, but mostly I was looking into some new information about Dreama. I think it's all tied together, the disappearances, the spill. These are maps from when Bella Jean was still active. And I had a look at the active permit for No. 4."

Zadie was impressed. "I won't ask how."

Lourana flashed a grin. "There is a grid of boreholes, right here."

"Dumping the water." It was an old story.

"Not like you'd think. They lead from the Bella Jean into No. 4."

"You must mean the other way."

Lourana shook her head. "Nope. I had to get my head around that myself."

"That makes no sense." Zadie looked closely at the map. "It's like they wanted to blow out their own operation."

"Exactly." Lourana clicked off the website.

"That might also be connected to something else that's going on," Zadie mused. "For some reason, KCL is digging in its heels on treatment for the spill."

"Cost?"

"Could be, but it's all a write-off anyway. DNR's got its hair on fire about the extreme toxicity, as it should, and wants them setting up additional package plants like yesterday to get the needle moving on the pH, which spiked up real bad yesterday."

"So what does KCL want to do?"

"More study. Like there's any quick way to deal with this other than lime precipitation in a high-density sludge process." She could see Lourana start to tune out. "Anyway, it's baffling. KCL, bad as it is some ways, has never put up much fight about water treatment. They even do some experimental stuff, working with the university on a wetlands diversion over in Washington County."

Zadie mentally ticked off the points—land accumulated for a megasite, the blowout, the slow response, the permit for hazardous waste. "If the Kavanaghs are involved in this landfill thing through shell companies, and I'll bet dollars to doughnuts they are, then they don't want environmental issues to get in the way."

"And if the river is already lost . . . "

"Then who's going to protest?"

"People need work. It won't be a tough sell," Lourana said. "It's just shameful."

The silence settled down between them. The heating system came on and hot air hummed in the ducts.

"Zadie," Lourana began, "is there anything . . . ?"

"I wish I could tell you that I have news about Dreama, but I haven't."

Lourana appeared to take that hard. Zadie remembered how impassive she'd always been. *Something's changed.*

"Seems like everything comes to a dead end," she said at last. "But let me ask something else. Have you heard anything about Marco DeLucca?"

"Isn't he the deputy—"

"Who got fired, yeah. More dirty doing. But he's continued to help me with Dreama, even after getting fired, and on—other things. He was headed to Charleston to meet with the BCI and he's disappeared. We haven't heard word one."

"Who's we?"

Now she looked shocked, like she'd let a secret slip. Zadie felt a prickle of interest.

Lourana held up a finger, one minute. "I gotta pee," she said.

*   *   *

Darrick was standing so close behind the door that she caught him awkwardly backpedaling and had to grab the handle so he wouldn't get slammed. She gestured him to follow her back into the yoga studio.

"I think we need to bring her in," she whispered. "What do you think? Can you feel anything?"

He started to shake his head, and winced. You wouldn't think he'd ever forget about that. "I don't get anything ugly from her, though at a distance, everything is damped down. She's nervous about something."

"Who isn't?"

They looked at each other for a long minute, until he whispered, "Yes."

When Lourana emerged from the back room, she found Zadie standing near the windows, hands on her hips. "I was thinking about leaving," she said, a hint of accusation.

"Zadie, I'd like you to meet someone." Lourana felt the rest of a sentence form in her thoughts, *who's become important to me.* "This is Darrick, and he's the reason I was looking at the mine maps."

Darrick clomped forward and extended his hand. The reporter took it, reluctantly, her broad freckled face reflecting the questions that must be bubbling up.

"Because of what happened to me, Lourana may have evidence of what happened to Dreama and a lot of other people. We want you to get the word out," he said.

"What happened to . . . ," and then Zadie saw the wound. " . . . you! Good God, you still got your brains in there?"

Darrick laughed a little. "I think so. I was attacked, by the police I believe, and thrown down into a hole, where I woke up surrounded by bodies and skulls."

"Why? Where?"

"Where is right in the middle of that landfill zone you're talking about," said Lourana. "A helluva big mine crack up on No. 4 land."

Darrick said, "Why? That's what I don't know yet. I pulled myself out and found my way to this place. Lourana believed my story, despite how I looked, and smelled, when I staggered in here. She helped me." He gave her a look. "I only hope I can return the favor somehow."

* * *

Zadie watched the story edifice she had been building crash into pieces. Facts peeled away from inferences, and she started assembling a whole different scenario. This man—this story—a pit full of bones! She could feel the lede sketching itself in, even as the sight of this zombie-like figure recalled the creak of her grandmother's voice. "Duppy man! The duppy man will get you," she'd threaten whenever Zadie refused to eat her veg, while her father, an engineer at the South Charleston Technology Park and a man of good sense, did his best to hack the roots out from under superstitions carried from Belize.

She watched Lourana root around in her purse, finally pulling out a silver chain and a heart-shaped locket. "Here. He found this on one of the skeletons. Maybe it's Susan Tedesco's. I bet you can find out."

Zadie accepted the grimy locket, turning it over and back. Detectives kept records of personal items from the disappeared people, information they kept secret for investigation purposes, but she didn't need to wheedle a look at the list. She was pretty sure she'd seen that jewelry on Susan when they met a couple of weeks before her disappearance. She dropped the necklace into her purse, a painful reminder of a true believer whose energy in pursuit of the truth sometimes outpaced even her own. Yes, come to think of it, she remembered the afternoon sun striking off a silver heart in the open collar of Susan's red flannel shirt when she had arrived muddy and laced with the whip-marks of branches, eager to share notes on survey markers in some remote holler.

She dragged a stool away from the machines and sat down. "I need to hear about this, all of it, from the top." She pulled out her notebook and flipped the cover back.

Behind her, the door began to rattle violently.

"Zadie Person, I know you're in there! Open this door, or I'll have the police to get it open."

Nobody said anything. The door rattled again, the blinds crashing back and forth, and the lock scraping in its metal case.

"Who is that?" Lourana whispered.

"I'm afraid that's my editor."

"What are you doing with that Taylor woman? More about the river? I knew you had to be up to mischief. Let me in, or you'll regret it!"

Lourana raised her eyebrows. Zadie knew she'd have to face him, here or at the office. "Let him in."

Darrick staggered away to his hiding place in the back room. He did walk like the undead, the Rodeheavers not exaggerating this time.

Lourana went to the door, turned the lock, and let in Gene Earnshaw along with a blast of cold air.

Zadie always thought the editor looked like a man built out of children's blocks, square of body and head and hands, bulky but with a kind of flimsiness to him. What might have looked comical was anything but, as he marched over and got too close to her face. "You get your tail out of here, and tomorrow I expect to see your feet cutting a trail between the courthouse and your desk and not one step aside. I don't want to see another slug line in the computer that's not public safety. You capisce?"

"Mr. Earnshaw, the river . . . "

"You're off the river. Anything about the river! The spill just happened, period. An act of God."

"You can take me off that story, sir, but people have been coming in now, from outside. They'll ask the right questions and the answers are going to come out."

"So what? The old mine let loose. Why are you so interested anyway?"

"Why aren't you, Mister Editor?" Zadie pushed her notebook back in her purse and stood up, tilting her head back to eyeball the man who signed her paycheck. "Maybe the pier was an act of God too."

The editor's face narrowed and his hands balled into fists at his sides. His tone was icy. "You wanna keep those two little nappy-heads of yours? Then you'll shut your blasphemous mouth and write what you're assigned, or child welfare will find very good cause to take them away from you."

"That's not right," Lourana protested.

The editor didn't even bother to glance at her. "Right has nothing to do with it. Zadie is going to do what she's told, aren't you, Zadie?"

Zadie felt a chill knife through her that had nothing to do with the weather. Earnshaw was vindictive, and he was locked in, from the Kavanaghs all the way down to the meter maid. Zadie said nothing as she began planning how to get Zipporah and Caleb far from his reach.

Earnshaw took hold of her and turned her around like a doll, pushing her lightly toward the door. She went quietly, grabbing her coat but putting only one arm in the sleeve.

* * *

Earnshaw watched her all the way to her car, then he turned to Lourana with a look of satisfaction greasing his face.

"All you gotta do is dangle the kids and people fold up like a cheap lawn chair. Amazing. Like judo or something. Kids are a pressure point that no one can resist." He chuckled and mopped his square face with a broad hand, seeming to wink at her, or maybe she was imagining that. "Came as a surprise to you, didn't it? How quick she surrendered?"

Lourana realized that her emotional armor, maintained at such cost for so long, had also weakened for others when she let Darrick inside. She panicked, wondering how much of her feelings appeared on her face now, if she was as transparent as poor Zadie, her crushing disappointment visible to this toady.

"Never had kids myself. The good Lord didn't see fit to bless me and the missus. I figure maybe it was a sign on her, but who am I to question? Kids change a man. Like your friend Marco . . . "

Lourana tried to restore that smooth, impervious shell, but she knew by his smirk that it wasn't entirely working.

"Seems the Kavanaghs have been entertaining the former deputy at Knockaulin House, and they would like you to join him. They sent me down with their best regards, to invite you for a little visit." He grabbed her around the waist, the smell of stale cigarettes coming off his hair and clothes, along with that something that seemed to emanate from a Kavanagh creature. She tried to push away from him, shoving against his chest. Her hand got caught. She yanked and felt a chain snap, saw the flash of gold and heard a clink as something flew across the room and struck the wall.

He released her, went and picked it up. "That's no way to treat the blood sacrifice of Jesus Christ," he said, frowning as he looked at the large cross and then tucked it into his pocket. "So where were we?" He moved fast, grabbing her by the shoulder, hard, and she screamed as he bore down as though to break it. "That don't bother me. Screech away, no one's around at this hour of the morning."

She gave way, feeling her shoulder begin to separate.

"That's the way I like to see a woman." He paused, not releasing his grip, but he tilted his head so that he could see her face more clearly. "Any time you want me to stop, just say uncle."

* * *

"Uncle," said Darrick, who had come quietly from the back. "Now let her go."

The editor leaped away, pulling Lourana to her feet and shielding himself with her. "Who are you?"

The man's emotions began to surge toward him, loud and hot and violent, but Darrick found that he could restrain the pushback that had come instinctively before. He showed the wound.

"You're the zombie!" A spasm of fear crossed the man's face. He could see his free hand groping in his pocket and wondered if yet another gun would be produced.

Darrick sighed. He was getting tired of this. "I'm the innocent man they threw down a hole to die."

"I heard there was another one of those environmental busybodies that got lost up in the hills." The editor snickered, even as he edged closer to the door, towing Lourana who wasn't struggling but had a look in her eyes like she was choosing her moment for a fight. "You should've stayed lost the first time, EPA, so you don't have to get lost all over again."

"I'm not from the EPA."

"EPA, CDC, FDA, whatever. Government plates gave you away."

"I'm just an auditor who got off the highway for gas."

"A clerk!" he sneered. "All this to-do over a pencil pusher."

"A clerk, maybe, but your little cabal here is about to end." Darrick made two long strides to block the editor from the door. Now he was ready to take on the full brunt of his emotions, anticipating the familiar thrum of fear that seemed to motivate all these creatures, but what surprised him was his terror of women and a brutality entwined with that, his craving for adulation and obedience, and the seething lava of his envy of the Kavanaghs.

Now Darrick pushed back. He felt the contours of his power, how he could stop if he wished, modulate the force that met violent emotions and turned them back on their owner. He heard Lourana's thoughts momentarily but shunted them aside. The editor's face was starting to show the effects, softening and bulging, his blocky, close-cropped head swelling obscenely. Earnshaw drew his hand out of his pocket and lifted a gold cross, holding it in trembling fingers before Darrick's face.

"You're mixing up vampires with zombies. Seems to be a common problem hereabouts."

Earnshaw's eyes bulged, then sank deep in his head, as though pulled by some unimaginable vacuum. The editor's grip on Lourana relaxed, and she pulled herself free.

This time, Darrick knew that he was taking a man's life, and he did it deliberately.

19

Before taking that exit off the interstate, Darrick had never touched a dead body or even seen one close up except for that one time, a sheeted form on the sidewalk outside a brownstone where a loud domestic disturbance had ended with a stabbing. Now he was lugging the editor's cooling body like a hit man disposing of a newly deceased informer.

Lourana, on the other hand, accepted the task with equanimity. Grabbing some yellow rubber gloves from the cleaning supplies, she directed, "You take the shoulders, I'll get the feet," squatting to grasp the man's ankles.

Darrick couldn't get squeamish now. He'd made this mess and had to help clean it up. Though the gloves insulated him from direct contact, his stomach roiled when he lifted under the armpits and felt the slack thump of Earnshaw's hands against the floor. The man was not nearly as heavy as he looked; even so, this body was no easy thing to manage. He wondered about how much a skeleton might weigh without that watery bag of flesh.

The coast is clear, he thought as Lourana poked her head out and checked again for cars. They bundled Earnshaw out the door and into the back seat of his aging Cadillac. He followed in her car, down the familiar road to the fish camp. It seemed a lifetime ago, or two, when he had staggered along that same pavement with the slime of rotting corpses on his skin.

She pulled the Cadillac off into a spot beside a mint green trailer. "As good a place as any," she said as she flung open the back door.

It was another job to move the editor into the front seat. At first, they leaned him back as though he were sleeping, his head cupped by the plushy headrest, but the sight of those distorted features led them to shift his body forward and leave it slumped against the wheel. Though he had long ago abandoned the rituals of his childhood, Darrick felt a strong compulsion to say a quick "Our Father" as he leaned across the corpse to pull it forward, his face close to those staring eyes, which were somewhat jaundiced and a middling shade of blue.

Darrick couldn't shake that image as he turned the car toward home. Whatever happened when he pushed back caused something—the brain? the blood?—to squeeze into unfamiliar places, soften and reshape the features. Some of that subsided once the body had lost its living tension, but enough remained for the face to look like a clay sculpture that has been dropped. The eyes, however, did not retreat from their popped appearance. No hand could close those eyes, or coins weight the lids enough to cover them.

Three deaths. Three manslaughters, because he wouldn't call them murders, not when it was in defense of self and others, were on his hands. This time, however, he couldn't plead ignorance, or panic in the face of a threat.

For most of his life, Darrick had worried about who he was. Now he wondered what he was. Years of night sweats, waking from convoluted dreams of the parents who might have been, of the events that led to his abandonment, had eventually faded, now to be replaced with a new horror. People approached him in these dreams, smiling, and then bloated and sagged and fell. They were people he knew: coworkers, old teachers, the barista who greeted him each morning. All of them died.

He was something new. And dangerous.

He clenched his jaw and felt the sharp pull of the head wound, a moment of dizziness. At least that pain was something physical and explicable. Had all this started because of that injury, a simple physical explanation? Or had there been something else at work in that pit full of bones, something that entered a wound exposed to this violated land? There came whispers from the past, the priest's oracular mumblings, the nurse's singsong of past and future.

"Turn here."

Startled out of his circling thoughts, Darrick swung the car onto a narrow road, not much used, two icy tracks heading upward.

"Where are we going?"

"The back way."

The Subaru moved upward steadily, despite the slippery patches, and Darrick relaxed his grip on the wheel. Scruffy pine trees closed in on the road from both sides, which made him nervous. "This thing," he began, needing to release some of the pressure or he might burst himself. "I can control it now. I couldn't at first; it just happened. But I think I have it under control so I don't hurt someone who's just close by."

"Like maybe me," said Lourana. When he glanced over, she didn't look back.

"I've been terrified it would just kill anyone, anytime, but I was able to shield you completely. Right? If I get out of here, I used to think that I would have to hide myself away so that someone's anger or fear didn't trigger it. But maybe not."

They passed a couple of houses, a lonely barn. A faded sign from the last election had been nailed to a tree, remnant of the most recent round of politicians who had promised to reopen the coal mines and fix the economy and make everything better again. Adults comforting children against night terrors, not admitting that they, too, were uneasy at the shadows moving under the trees. At a fork in the road, Lourana indicated the left.

"So you're OK with this power, making that kind of decision?"

He glanced over at her, the way her jaw was set. "Do I have a choice?" He waited for an answer that wasn't coming. "I did it to protect you. You do know that?"

Lourana mumbled something that sounded like agreement.

"Now at least I know I'm not just a bomb waiting to go off. It's a terrible burden, but I have a handle on it. I am not afraid anymore of people who push you around just because they have muscles or a badge or a title. I don't have to step back while bad things happen. I don't have to grovel ever again."

* * *

Lourana looked off into the trees. Darrick's deadly gift gave her the willies, but she'd been relying on his good impulses. The kind of decent man she'd come to accept him as being. Now, listening to him blather on, she wasn't so sure. He showed that cocky attitude a man gets when he thinks he's top dog. *Just like the rest of them.*

The trees ended and they were on the ridgetop, with pasture fields falling off to each side. Last year's weeds stuck up through the snow like whiskers on a chin. She had him turn the car onto a gravel space that had been graded there for the school bus to turn around. Dawn was breaking, the sun rising into a clear southeast while the remains of the cloud bank, its edges tinged red, drifted off to the northwest. She got out and walked to the side of the road, and Darrick followed.

Down by a narrow run that wove its way through the bottom of the hollow, a simple white clapboard church sat next to an overlarge parking lot and a grassy space centered on a spire of black stone.

"What's that thing?"

"Bear Creek Miners Memorial. Back about fifty years ago, we had a big explosion in the mines. My papaw—grandfather—was one of the men who went down to try to rescue the ones who didn't make it out on their own. They got thirty-two out, all told, but a dozen of them were dead or died soon after. All the time they were bringing them up at the portal just past where you can see, at the foot of the valley, the women were gathered in that little church. And the newspapers were there for the death watch."

Lourana had seen those old photographs, time and again. The focus on worn faces and hands clasped in prayer. Men with faces blackened by coal and smoke, turned up to the light as they were lifted out of the shaft with a naked gratitude to be coming up to the sun one more day. That was then. That was also Farmington No. 9, Sago Mine, Upper Big Branch. The dates changed, but the faces didn't.

"The methane that caused the explosion, it was bad and getting worse. There was strong fear they'd lose the rescuers, too, so the decision was made to seal the mine." Lourana pointed toward the black pillar. "At least they didn't mislead people into thinking there was hope. Eleven men were left down there forever. Their names are on that stone."

"What a horrible fate."

"The mines take some all at once, some a piece at a time," Lourana said. "We had two killed in a roof fall just this summer."

Darrick thought about being trapped underground, knowing that rescuers were coming, and then that they weren't. Were any of them alive when everything went dead silent? When they were left there in the dark, the coal all around them?

"This monument has become the place for memorial services, for the miners of course but pretty much the community too. Everyone knows Kavanagh Bear Creek disaster and the Solid Rock Freewill Baptist Church. The union gathers here every October to mark the event and recognize all miners who were lost the year previous."

He turned 360 degrees to take in the forested hills, the brown patches of fields. He could smell woodsmoke and see a few curls rising from houses hidden by the trees. As he turned back toward the valley, a single deer emerged from the edge of the woods. Then another, until a small herd was moving across the bare ground behind the monument.

"Look," he breathed.

He'd seen deer enough, dead on the sides of the highway or dashing across suburban backyards where they lived somehow, threading narrow belts of trees between the neighborhoods. This was different. These moved with the ease of something living the way it was meant to live, not trapped between strip malls and beltways. Their ears flicked as they grazed, pawing through the snow under a grove of trees, and their heads lifted gracefully as they looked about and then returned to eating. A buck emerged last from the woods, carrying his antlers like a crown.

Darrick heard birds calling, but otherwise it was still. Achingly still. The sky turned bright and blue. A dog barked; the deer lifted their heads as one. Then one deer's tail flashed white and it bounded away, followed by the others, their tails semaphoring as they melted back into the trees.

"That was amazing," he said, feeling as close to the divine as he ever could recall, even when he was that altar boy trembling as the Sanctus bell rang.

"Pretty things, though we got a gracious plenty of 'em around here."

"When you're used to pigeons and squirrels, they are something special."

"Just like the signs say, *wild and wonderful*." Lourana sighed.

"Sometimes I forget about how blessed I am to live here. Even with the problems, West Virginia still has places that look like God intended. The trees grow back when they're cut. With a little effort, the strip mines will heal over."

"But not the river."

"No, I fear that will go on forever. You can treat it but you can't stop it, 'less you can halt the rain. But there's so much that's beautiful, the wild things and the woods and even the dirt that'll grow corn and tomatoes to die for. It's what keeps people here. Family and the land, both. You find a mountaineer anywhere, no matter how fancy a life he's made, and you just scratch a bit off the surface and he'll tell you, he misses it terrible."

"It's home." That word caught in his throat as he spoke it. What did that mean? How could he pretend to know? Her hand sought his and Darrick was eased by the kind touch of another human being. Standing here with her, he'd shared something deep and peaceful.

He looked toward Lourana but her eyes were clouded, concealed. He could sense the turmoil in her thoughts, but muted, and realized that she was trying hard to disguise her emotions. The shell was being rebuilt, and Darrick didn't know what that meant.

*   *   *

Back at the house, Lourana headed straight to her room, closed the door and went to bed. Worn out, she said. Darrick took his usual post in the recliner, turned on the TV but muted it. He watched the images flicker, of police, politicians, judges, teachers, analysts. Whether they wore a uniform or not, they carried authority with them always, encased in it like a second skin.

It had started early, the harassment of the bigger boys in the home, the upperclassmen in school.

Keep your head down, zaubermaus, *keep your head down.*

He had tried, but his ataxia made him a special target. Teachers made it clear they didn't think much of kids from the home and him in particular. Some at the home were harsh and unforgiving of a child's random sins. He hadn't been able to fight back then, for himself or for others. Now he could. He could put right a lot of the wrongs of the world, starting right here. That history teacher, what did he used to say? "A few well-considered deaths would make the whole world happier." He was talking about dictators, but for most people, it wasn't the distant general who made life miserable, but the bully up the block.

Darrick was drifting through a list of the terrible human beings whose departure would make the world a better place when he heard Lourana scream.

He stumbled to the door and pushed it open to find her sitting straight up in the bed, her face drained and eyes staring. Her hair was loose on the shoulders of her flannel nightgown. The terror that poured from her made him retreat a step, then two, as it threatened to take hold of him as well.

"I saw them."

"Who?" Darrick looked around. The room was crammed with furniture and shadows behind the furniture, but nothing moved. He realized how cold it was in there, shut off from the rest of the house.

"Dreama and Marco. They're together, in a black place full of bones. But they're alive, alive with the bones." Lourana shuddered.

"Down in the mine crack?"

"No." She was emphatic. "It's a room. A room that's full of bones, but I could see walls, a door." Lourana's look shifted from horror to wild hope, and then back, reflecting the shrill tremolo of her thoughts. "Dreama is alive. My little girl is alive!"

Darrick hoped that Lourana wasn't taking a vision for reality, her hopes raised only to crash again. "It's only a nightmare, Lourana. We shouldn't get our hopes up."

"You make sure not to get yours up, then, and we'll be about on the level." She had come back to herself, enough to breathe raggedly, then deeply, as the terror eased.

"If there's anything to this," he said, stopping himself again from voicing his doubts as Lourana fixed him with a look of naked need. "The editor said they have Marco. Where would they take him? The mines?"

"Mines are white inside."

He thought she was making fun of him. *Coal mines were dark, like a dungeon, all that.*

"They coat the walls with rock dust to stop explosions," she explained with a tinge of exasperation in her voice. "The tunnels are white, not black.

But this was a room, a completely black room. And Marco and Dreama were there. It has to be at Knockaulin House. Where else could it be?"

Darrick paused at the door, unsure whether to obey his impulse to go and hold her in his arms, comfort her as she had him. She looked so vulnerable in the welter of blankets, the nightgown buttoned up to her neck. The walls of her room were covered with small frames. As he looked closer, he saw that each held a piece of artwork, ragged crayon stick figures, watercolors, a certificate, school photographs that showed a little dark-haired girl growing up image by image to be a lovely young woman.

"Darrick, I'm afraid to go back to sleep. Please stay and talk with me."

He sat on the edge of the bed and put his arm loosely around her shoulders. She was shaking. When her head nestled into his shoulder, he swayed with the full orchestra of sadness and hope, fear and cautious trust.

"It was just so real. It *has* to be real," she said. "I don't know how we're getting in there, but we have to. We have to get inside. I'll tear the place apart with my bare hands if need be." He watched her fists clench as though she gripped a hammer and chisel to break through doors, walls. Maybe even through superstition.

"I might be able to help a little."

She allowed a little chuckle, but it sounded hollow. Then she brought up the conversation in the car. "I thought you sounded like you were getting cocky, earlier, and I didn't much like it."

"I knew something was wrong."

"So, are you getting cocky?"

"What are the stages: denial, bargaining, acceptance? There's no way around the fact that something has happened to me, and I can't reverse what I don't understand. So, I have to deal with it. I can claim this power for good." *Or bad*, he thought, *but why go there?* "Maybe there's a reason for it. Maybe I was meant to confront the Kavanaghs."

"What makes you think you can stand against them?"

"What makes you think I can't?" He watched her mouth turn down, her expression of disappointment. *If she thinks I'm brash, then she will just have to get over it.* "All I've seen of the Kavanaghs' power is that they have a lot of money and a lot of flunkies who'll do their dirty work for them. That, and old legends to make people afraid, but show me some evidence."

"I wouldn't be so quick to dismiss what you haven't had a chance to see. Haven't you learned that there's more kinds of power than what comes at the end of a gun?"

"Fair enough. So how do we find them? Go up to the door and ring the bell?"

"I've been inside the house. It's not, as they say, neighborly."

"There has to be some way. Maybe the sewers." His skin crawled as he said it, imagining the unmitigated darkness, dank walls, echoing vaults, foul water.

"You must think you're in New York or something. Our sewers ain't built for an army to march through."

Darrick was cut by the edge in her voice, even as her hip pressed softly against his. One part of him shrank away from her harshness, while the other part reasoned that it was just her way of coping.

They stared at a cold scarcity of options.

"You think I'm eager to use this power, curse, whatever it is."

She began to protest, but he lifted a palm to forestall her.

"I'll admit to temptation. I've never fought back in all my quiet, orderly, safe life. Maybe it seems like I'm swaggering because now I can defend myself—and remember, defend others—but I tell you that every time I close my eyes I'm haunted by the faces of those men, and I can't turn away from what I've done."

"It was justifiable."

"Maybe. I don't know. I was raised to believe that 'Thou shalt not kill.'"

"What about war?"

He nudged her shoulder with his. "Do you really want me to give you St. Augustine's precepts for a just war? This isn't war, and I've killed three people. Two of them with a degree of forethought. If I still subscribed to the faith, I would be in mortal sin."

"You're telling me this is all just to save others, no anger to it? You never been so mad you wished anyone dead? Never punched somebody's lights out?"

"Not saying that." He could feel her expectation. She had shared her stories of addiction and its degradations. He owed something back. "One time. Funny thing is, it wasn't about me. One of the bullies was tormenting a little kid, holding him down and putting dirt down his pants. I don't know what happened but I started hitting. They tell me I must have blacked out, because when they pulled me off him, I didn't remember what had happened, but the bully had to be taken to the hospital."

Lourana seemed to take that in. "So you haven't always been, what did you call it, *orderly*?"

"It scared me, that I had the capacity to hurt someone and not even know what I was doing. The administrators decided my punishment was to be shunned for one month. No one was allowed to sit with me at lunch. No activities. But I punished myself just as much, and vowed I wouldn't let it happen again."

"You were just a child, all alone."

Darrick felt the warm rush of her compassion. He focused on a painting of a house on the wall directly in front of him. A green house with a red roof on a perilous slant, and a mommy and daddy and a girl and a tree drawn beside it, all in a line. Dreama's family. A truck went by outside, and he realized it was full day, normal people going about their business, while his world was upside down and inside out. He had a sudden longing for his weekday cranberry scone, sitting with his paper at the counter and watching people hurry by on the street.

"You said once that you had a brother."

"Travis is a good bit older. Seems I was a late surprise for my folks. He went in the Navy and now he works on the West Coast for some defense contractor. He's been gone a long time and don't care to come home."

Darrick heard the hurt in those words.

"But I had all the cousins you could want, and my parents were good to me." Lourana forged ahead, putting a positive spin on things. Her ability to adapt, and to persevere, impressed him all over again. "I can't imagine how it was for you, not having parents and all. I mean, how did they know what to call you even?"

"The priest who found me would never say why he gave me that name. He was Irish, so maybe it came from his own family. Of course, he's long dead. He was an old, trembling man when I was a little boy. He was always kind to me, he and the nurse. She must have left family behind when she fled East Germany. If the priest thought I had *capability*, as he put it, she was more worried about saving me from getting hurt. Keep quiet, she would tell me, keep your head down and your mouth shut."

"Some old fears there."

He nodded. "She called me *zaubermaus*. Magic mouse. I think reality was hard for her, because she took such joy in telling me fairy stories and especially ones about knights and ladies and magical quests. I remember her whispering, 'There is another world that is not like ours.' "

Lourana turned her body into him, and lifted her face for a kiss. Which he gave.

She pulled away, and he was bereft. The cold air rushed against him, and he almost cried out for her to come back. Instead, she stood and unbuttoned the throat of that flowered flannel gown. She stripped it off over her head, morphing from a granny into a woman with a strong but soft body, her breasts lovely even as they showed her to be a mother and not a girl.

As she stretched her arms high, the ladder of her ribs shone in the morning light.

A man might climb to heaven, he thought.

He left her sleeping, gathering his clothes and her car keys quietly.

He felt light. Almost untethered. Yes, the sex had lifted him off the earth for a few moments, but it was far more than release. It was having some human connection in the world. He was otherwise free from the life he had made, or that had made him. No routine, no tasks, no calendar, no cell phone to link him to a world beyond this little house in a strange and brooding mountain community.

He would go to Knockaulin House. He would bring Marco home, and Dreama, if they were there—indeed, if they were still alive and their bodies not among those rotting in the mine crack. He felt uneasy, guilty in fact, that the days went by and nothing had been done to bring that place to light, but that was about to change.

Down the hill and into town, that much he knew, then turning away from the downtown and crossing a bridge that spanned a deep cleft thick with trees. She'd told him where the Kavanagh place was, pointing up a broad boulevard that paralleled the river. It led to a tree-crowned hill. There was no mistaking it, a gray stone manor house magicked from some British promontory and set down among the worn hills of West Virginia. The fenced grounds were wide buffers of parkland thick with trees and leathery-leaved shrubs.

Darrick parked along a side street, hidden from the view of the house by a cluster of trees with pendulous branches of bluish needles.

He considered the iron fence, at least eight feet tall and topped with spikes that were sharply pointed, not ornamental. A thin strand of wire glittered just above the row of spikes—electrified. No way over that, unless he found a convenient overhanging tree and then managed to climb it and leap inside, both unlikely. He stalked the back perimeter looking for another entrance, but there was only the great front gate on the boulevard, the one that Lourana said was always securely locked. The house was silent, might even have been a museum or a movie set, except for the sense of watchfulness from its glittering many-paned windows.

Darrick was walking toward the driveway entrance when a bent old woman came around the corner, dragging a hairless dog in a red vest. She startled back, and so did he. Then he put his head down and tried to be innocuous, but could not conceal the lurching gait that she had already seen. Her eyes were hidden behind huge geriatric sunglasses but her alarm was evident as she quickly yanked the small dog around and went the other way, half-shuffling and half-jogging. *There goes another witness to the undead.*

He stood looking at the drive that sloped down to an underground garage, barred by a tall electric gate. The place was impenetrable, short of a bomb, so he did what he had threatened, pressed the buzzer and waited.

A fit young man, African American, came out of a side door near the garage, shrugging into a navy-blue jacket.

"I'm here to see Marco DeLucca."

The man said nothing in reply, but looked him over and then spoke into an intercom. "Brodie, there's a man here at the gate, asking about the deputy."

Darrick shifted from foot to foot. *This was a crazy thing to do.* The buoyancy that had supported him this far began to evaporate. He had started to walk away when a trim man in a butler's uniform emerged from the house.

"Good morning, sir. How may I be of service?"

"I have come to see Mr. DeLucca. I understand he's a guest here." Something about the man, who moved so lightly and even looked a bit like Fred Astaire, made Darrick speak formally.

"And I may tell the Misters Kavanagh who is calling?"

"A federal agent. Darrick MacBrehon."

The butler's face remained impassive and his eyes made no comment; his training would not allow him to question that an officer of the government would be wearing clownish boots and cheap clothes that didn't fit. Darrick felt no strong emotion from him, only mild surprise. British reserve?

Or perhaps he had been expected. *This was a tactical mistake*, he thought, *or is that strategic?* But the issue had to be forced. Who knows what was happening to Marco? Was he being beaten up? Maybe having the skin torn off him, like Lourana talked about, an owner's harsh words morphed into a mountain legend? There was no one else to act, no one but him.

"If you will allow me to take your outerwear, sir."

Darrick relinquished his coat with some reluctance, as it seemed to offer a kind of protection. The butler led the way through long, paneled hallways. As he followed, Darrick heard only an even emotional rumble from the man, like soft surf rolling into a shelving beach. No strong feelings, no violence in his mind. The butler was a precise man, controlled by his ideals of service, of perfection in service. He seemed to gleam like the silver he must polish endlessly.

The doors were open to a book-lined room with a wood fire roaring in a baronial fireplace. Wing chairs flanked a heavy table before the hearth, and in one of them was a sandy-haired young man with a sensual mouth. He looked up from a slender book, his finger holding his place.

"Mr. Cormac, sir, if I may present Mr. Darrick MacBrehon from the federal government."

"Thank you, Brodie." He indicated that Darrick should sit in the opposite chair. "MacBrehon. An interesting name."

"Irish. It means son of the judge."

"Yes, I know. As you can see from this room, we Kavanaghs are quite proud of our own Irish lineage, and I have done a bit of reading in the Gaelic myself." He said that with a kind of casualness that let Darrick know he had done much more than a bit. "I thought I sensed a kinship between us."

"Mr. Kavanagh, I could be Lithuanian for all I know. I'm an orphan who was given that name by a priest." Darrick felt his words sharpen, their points and edges set against this unexpected intimacy.

"All who have power are foundlings by nature, cast up on the shores of the world," he said cryptically. He looked at Darrick with great interest, his eyes clear and the color of amber. He tilted his head just a bit, like a scientist trying to focus his view of some new specimen. "You're the one, then. The one they are calling the zombie, the walking dead."

"If you mean that I'm still alive and walking around, when I shouldn't be, then yes." Darrick gestured to his head. "Somebody didn't finish their assignment."

Cormac considered his wound with that same absorption, but whatever he thought of it, or how it got there, he wasn't saying. He stood and shelved his little book, pulled out another and opened it, leaning like Lord Byron against a wooden pilaster. "Why have you come here, Mr. MacBrehon?"

"I'm here for my friend—for Marco."

"He'll be here presently."

"And for Dreama."

His eyes flicked up from the book, then back, but he said nothing. Darrick tried to get a read on the man, but he couldn't. It wasn't like Lourana, who had built a shell of her pain, a protective wall. This man's core was concealed by something slippery, elusive, like a curtain of light obscuring something powerful.

"You must have heard the stories that circulate in these parts, that we Kavanaghs have the power of life and death."

"You have this place in an economic stranglehold, I've heard that. And seen it in action." This Kavanagh looked less like the mob boss he had imagined and more like an erudite English professor, all quotations and well-couched argument. Yet there was something, just under the surface.

"We have poured our blood and treasure into Carbon County."

"And taken more blood and treasure out." Darrick's eyes swept the expensively appointed room and returned to Cormac.

"Some people believe we are monsters. Do you?" A glimmer of a smile brightened his narrow face. "It's easy to become one, isn't it? A story starts, gets passed along. Next thing you know, there's an army of the undead rising from Carbon County's graveyards, instead of one injured stranger. People fear anything that exists beyond their daily lives. Remember that our family has been here for a very long time. Old grudges fester. We have devoted KCL to developing the county, providing livelihoods. We want this place to continue and thrive."

"Yet you deliberately poison the river."

He closed the book and reshelved it, pushing it deep between large volumes where it had not been before. *That caught him by surprise*, Darrick realized.

"We all have to accept entropy. This is an imperfect world—energy is lost, everything runs down. We've been mining here since the nineteenth century, followed every seam nearly to its end. These hills are all but worked out."

"The people are worked out," Darrick shot back, but before he could continue, a door opened behind Cormac and Marco was let in, still in his work uniform. He didn't look injured, but some change was visible in how he walked, the set of his shoulders. Darrick tried to catch his eye, but Marco kept his gaze low. Like his emotions. The tumult was tamped down—not gone, Marco was not so placid as the butler—but reduced. *The air of Knockaulin House changes people.*

Marco was followed by a man who, if it were not for his well-tailored tweed suit, looked the part of a coal miner, a tall, heavily fleshed man who walked with a deliberate tread. "Eamon Kavanagh," he said bluntly, offering neither his hand nor any other kind of courtesy. "I imagine you've had a nice literary conversation with my brother. He prides himself on being good with words."

He lowered himself in an enormous armchair and rested his hands on the wide-spreading arms. *Not subtle, this one.* A map of the kingdoms of Ireland occupied pride of place above the mantle carved with heraldic symbols. Darrick wondered where the father was, if this throne wasn't in fact meant for him. Eamon settled as though gathering an ermine of empire around him.

"I understand that you are a federal agent? From what branch, may I ask?"

"I'm an auditor. But I think you already know who I am."

Eamon stared at him without comment. Like his brother, his emotions were inaccessible, but very different. Something massive thrummed like a turbine behind an unyielding wall, not an elusive veil. This was where the Kavanagh power rested, with this brother who looked like the raw rock of a mountain crag and even sounded like one, his voice like stones breaking loose and tumbling. It was no wonder that people were afraid of him.

You don't have to crawl anymore, Darrick reminded himself.

"What is it you want?" Eamon rumbled.

"I've come to ask that you release Marco and Dreama. And that you let Lourana and me alone, you and those who answer to you."

Cormac's eyes shifted from his brother to Darrick and back. "You were mistaken for a threat."

Eamon cut him off. "Done is done."

"Understand that we bear a responsibility to this place," Cormac added, speaking as though he anticipated interruption. "Why do we stay here and not live in New York, or build palaces like the Vanderbilts? The truth is, we are as bound to this place as the miner at his drill."

"Carbon County is ours," Eamon finished.

Darrick saw Marco stand, hands loose, head hanging, and wanted to grab him by the arm and shake him back to himself. They needed to get out of this place, but he could not resist another jab: "You sound like Louis XIV."

"Wrong analogy." Eamon gestured to the antique map above his head. "The Kavanaghs were the high kings of Leinster. Their rule was sanctified through marriage to the land itself, a ceremony that united ruler and kingdom. The land gives life to the king, and he gives it to his people, and they return it to him, in an endless cycle."

"Mystical marriage?" Darrick scoffed. "If that's how you explain your actions, then I guess you'd be a wife beater. Fiction to dress up plain old all-American corporate greed."

Eamon slammed his meaty hands against the carved arms of the chair. The room went silent. The only live sound was the crackling of the flames and the small howl that fire made in the chimney. But when he spoke again, his voice was controlled.

"Have you ever noticed how weedy and passive vegetarians are?" he mused. "I would say that you are not among them, Mr. MacBrehon, judging from your assertive temperament. Plants aren't fit food for humans—we need the lively spirits of the animal to nourish us."

He looks well-fed, Darrick thought. *Must put down a quarter of beef a week.*

"Now the human soul, that is something else entirely. What is it my brother quotes, we are little lower than the angels? He is good with analogies. We are far more than creatures of the soil; rather, we are embodiments of the spirit, as you might say that coal is the embodiment of the sun."

He stood, and Darrick could sense the power gathered within him, a power he recognized too well. This was authority, wealth, position, name, everything that made him ache and shrink away. His recently gained ability began to feel inadequate.

"You want to know the secrets of Knockaulin House? This friend of yours has come to understand. His life is mine," he said, raising his hands above Marco, who immediately dropped to his knees.

Darrick tried to focus, to push out, to push back, but whatever animated Eamon wasn't like the fears of his creatures. It was a dark energy, pulsing with pride. Arrogance. Darrick struggled from the outside, unable to deflect Eamon's attack; he felt Marco's spirit dim under the terrible benediction that gave no strength to the slumping man, but instead pulled it out of him.

Eamon lifted his hands away, releasing Marco, who slid all the way to the floor. Now Darrick felt that binding energy focused on him, demanding that he cower like Marco.

I will not.

He didn't understand his own potency, much less what was hammering against him from Eamon. Nevertheless, he wouldn't fold, despite the odd sensation that his *self* was being tugged from his body. He could almost see the lines of force, a shimmering band that wove between Eamon and himself.

Suddenly, the bond snapped.

He sucked in a deep breath that seemed to rush into a new void within. Eamon turned his back to him and resumed his throne. Darrick went to Marco, helped him to his feet. The deputy clung to his arm.

"You are more than what you seem, much more, but you are not nearly as strong as you think you are. There will be time," Eamon said. The door opened and the man from the garage came in. "Take them both," and with that, he leaned back in his chair with an air of satisfaction and closed his eyes.

"Take us where?" Darrick called as they were escorted out.

"To the black room," Marco said, his voice flat.

So Lourana's dream was more than imagination. A black room full of bones. Darrick felt the terror of the mine crack. He reached out toward the young man who shepherded them through another formal room, this one lined with mirrors that flickered with their passing reflections. Darrick didn't want to harm him, but there was no way he was going to be locked into a lightless cell.

The man was taller than he, and built like an athlete. Darrick wasn't concerned about his physical strength but by the lack of any strong emotion for him to push against. Like the butler, there was no consuming passion in him, not fear or rage or envy or gluttony. Darrick tried again, probing toward the man's mind and finding only a touch of justified anger, well controlled.

The mirrors exploded with repeated reflections as Marco swung at the man, knocking him to the floor.

"I don't know what you're doing, Darrick, but if we get stuck in that room then it's game over!"

The man sprang up in a fighting crouch, and Marco hit him again, left-right-left. As he staggered back, Marco kicked him sharply in the knee and the sound of bones breaking was only partially covered by a howl of pain as he collapsed to the floor. Marco stomped on the knee again as he headed for a stairwell.

"Where is Dreama?" Darrick asked his retreating back. They clattered down to the next floor.

"I don't know. Somewhere upstairs. We have to get out while we can."

"I can't leave her here." He stopped, but Marco pulled him forward.

"They won't hurt *her*," Marco said grimly as they sprinted down service corridors, into a cavernous kitchen, a pantry, past a bank of freezers. He juked left but did not take the next set of stairs going down. *How many levels did this place have?* They burst into a laundry room, frightening a heavy-set young woman ironing sheets. She leaped back and held up the hot iron.

"Which way to the garage?"

She didn't answer, but her eyes shifted to a door behind them, which led to a corridor and then the garage, cold and dim, bulked with the shapes of big cars.

Marco slammed a red button on the wall, raising the door and the electric gate at the same time. They slipped outside into the glare of the setting sun and ran around the corner to the little brown car that Darrick was sure would be gone, disappeared into thin air.

He started the car and Marco got in, slumping against the window. *A beaten man*, Darrick thought, but somehow he had found the energy to get them out of that house. He wheeled toward the boulevard, shakily accepting the newly tested limits on his power, how close he'd come to being bested by Eamon.

Still, something in him would not knuckle under, a core of strength that he was just getting to know.

THE VOICE OF THE MOUNTAIN

Our sun, a backwater star of no great distinction, poured itself down for a billion years on this little ball of dirt, and that celestial fire was gathered, sank, solidified, its white nature exchanged for black. And there it rested, neither more nor less than any other rock, until humans struck a spark.

We created our own suns, warmed ourselves, lighted our nights, spanned the endless plains and seas by releasing the power of black rocks that remembered when they were light.

We, too, are made of sullen matter, but our spirits are fire.

Let there be light.

—CBK

Lourana woke up to find Darrick gone. She lay there listening to the hollow sounds of an empty house.

At first she was hurt. Wasn't that just like a man, to slip out of the bed without a word? She found her nightgown and shuffled to the kitchen for a cup of coffee. When she looked through the window and saw her car was gone, then she was just flat pissed.

Before she could work herself up to a proper state, her cell rang, and it was a mad search to find it, forgotten on the floor under the bed and nearly out of juice. "Hello?" she said, as she pawed around for the end of the charging cord.

"Mama?"

A shock forked through her body. Lourana turned over the phone and looked at the screen, reading an unfamiliar number, unable to make sense of it.

"Mama, is that you?"

"Dreama? Dreama?"

"It's me. I'm OK."

"Where are you? I'm coming to get you, baby. Where are . . . "

"Mama, slow down. I can't talk long. You have to quit searching for me and messing around with things that are gonna hurt you."

"Are you kidnapped?" Lourana's vision of her girl rotting to bones was replaced by one of her tied to a chair.

"I'm in love. I can't explain, but I'll be OK if you just quit."

"In love? With who?"

"Cormac Kavanagh."

"You can't love a Kavanagh!" Revulsion rippled through her and settled deep in her gut. "No one loves a Kavanagh. He's done something to you. I swear . . . "

"Mama, please listen. He's different. Cormac is a poet, he could be anyway, and we were going to leave but it's not that easy."

Lourana remembered the gold beads Dreama had taken to wearing before she disappeared. Real gold, she had said with a private smile, real gold.

Kavanagh gold.

"You know how the protestors say, *eat the rich*? The rich eat us. And they eat their own." The air went silent, a listening silence. Lourana didn't know if she should speak or if that would put her in danger. After a moment, Dreama came back. "It's true what they say about Knockaulin House. But it's not Cormac, it's Eamon. He's the one who sucks the life out of everything, who makes people do whatever he says. Cormac is a sweet man, gentle, and I know he would be a different man if we could get away from here."

Lourana's thoughts scrambled from one thing to another, from relief to terror to a sick realization that her daughter not only was willing to lie in the arms of a monster, but trying to justify him.

"Mama, I gotta go. Please. I love you. Please don't bother about me anymore."

The call ended. A few seconds of her daughter's voice after months of silence.

In love with a Kavanagh. How?

But she also thought about Darrick, and his terrible power, and that she had opened herself to him in every way a woman could.

She didn't know where he was, but she had a good idea.

Darrick felt something warm trickling on his neck. He took advantage of a straight stretch of bad road and put his hand to the wetness. It came away covered with red. The running must have opened the wound again. He felt gingerly along the side and back of his head, probing the crusted scab edges and the newly tender place where the blood welled.

"Marco." The deputy was still huddled against the window, exhausted. Shrunken. His face was averted, staring out at the landscape as they headed to Lourana's. "Marco, you said that Dreama was there. You've seen her?"

"She's with the Kavanaghs. She's theirs."

"What do you mean?"

"She's theirs," he echoed. "Body and soul." Marco gave a short laugh. "Dreama won't go home. Can't go home."

Darrick turned left, realized this street was tending down to the river rather than up, and slammed on the brakes. Everything looked different as the shadows extended. He kept looking behind, expecting to see headlights, expecting something. *Hellhounds are on my trail.*

"Which way, Marco? Come on! I need some help."

Marco seemed to rouse, then. "Take the next right." He sat up in the seat and ran his hands up and down his arms, over and over, finally gripping one hand with the other as though to stop them from moving against his will. He indicated one turn, then another, and got them back on the road after a detour along a one-lane dirt road rutted with ice, the Subaru skewing and thumping but never bogging down. There wasn't time to look too deeply into what was going on with Marco, though Darrick knew the deputy had changed. His emotions were quenched, like embers buried deep under ash.

As they wheeled into the drive, Lourana burst out of the door. "Darrick! Marco! Darrick, where did you go? And Marco, you're all right?"

They tumbled into the house and closed the door against whatever lay behind them. For a moment, they just stood, stunned, looking at each other, before the stories began to rise and tangle.

"Wait! Wait!" Lourana held up her hands. "I've talked with Dreama! She's alive . . . "

"At the Kavanaghs," Marco finished. "I know."

Lourana huffed out a little breath. "She really is OK, then?"

He didn't answer.

"She called me. Not an hour ago. She called and told me that I was supposed to leave her alone. That she was in love with Cormac Kavanagh." The name seemed to clot in her mouth.

Marco nodded. "They're together. I don't know if you'd call it love."

"How did you get out? How did you get in, anyway?"

Marco looked at Darrick, and Darrick looked at Lourana. "I went to the gate and pressed the buzzer."

"You did not." Lourana's mouth hung open in shock.

"I did. I went to the gate, and they let me in. I spoke with Cormac, who seems pretty harmless, and then with Eamon."

Marco pulled into himself and began to scrub his hands up and down his arms again. "Don't fool yourself. Neither one of them is harmless."

"Dreama," Lourana repeated. "Dreama." She was like someone hypnotized, repeating the one word that tied her to reality. Darrick realized she barely saw him, or Marco. Her eyes were focused on the image of her daughter alone, and her emotions as well, terror that twined around intense love, enough to make Darrick edge away.

"She can't come home, Lourana," Marco said.

"Is she in a black room?" Lourana asked, softly. "With bones? I had a dream, or vision, you were both inside a black room with skeletons of people laid around."

Marco stared at her. "Who needs a newspaper psychic? You saw it exactly—the black room. But she's not in there. She lives upstairs. With Cormac."

"What is this black room?" Darrick asked.

"It's like a crypt, a room filled with bones. But it's not a room. Not like a room in a normal house. It's cut into the living coal, shelves cut into the walls, with the bones arranged on them."

"More like a catacomb."

"Whatever you want to call it. It's just pitch black, soundless. One light, high up, controlled from outside."

Darrick felt a muted fear from Marco, something he was doing his best to fight. He'd been imprisoned in that room. In the dark. "Where is it?"

"Deep. The deepest. The room has two small doors. You can't force them open. I'm in it whenever I close my eyes." Marco went silent. His fear was rising through the ashes of better emotions.

"But why? What is it?" Lourana pressed.

"That's the heart of their power. They are different when they are in it. Coal is how we make a living, but coal is their life—do you understand? They draw their strength from it. In that room surrounded by the coal, they are like demons, or gods. They can—change things."

"Like the river?"

"Eamon said that they not only dumped the acid, they created the acid. Made it stronger."

Darrick wondered if Marco had been brainwashed—the dark, the bones, the Kavanaghs exerting pressure to make him see and believe what they wanted. He couldn't deny the feeling of great power he'd gotten from them, but demons? He wanted to press Marco about how Dreama was changed, and the servants, and him too, but thought he might shatter like a dropped mirror if he asked too much, too soon.

"You said there were two doors. Where does the other one go?" he asked.

Marco shook his head. "I don't know. They're locked from the outside. But that room is no place you want to get into."

* * *

"We have to get back inside Knockaulin House, if we're going to get Dreama out," Lourana said, rousing herself from the silence that followed. Marco looked at her with pity, or so it seemed. She didn't care.

She let restlessness carry her into the kitchen, where she poured coffee and shook out some cookies on a plate. Something normal, something real, your hands warming up around the curve of a coffee cup. They ate and drank, reflexively.

"The original Kavanagh mine was hand-dug, supposedly went right under the house," she mused. "The workers ran into the mine when they were laying the house foundations. That's what my papaw said, and he'd talked with the men who built it."

"Maybe that's the black room?" Darrick asked.

"It might could be," she said, putting the pieces together as she went. Flashes of old mine maps she'd pored over. The city's underside webbed with old workings. The solid squares under the bank building and the mansion—had there been a shadowy finger of a tunnel reaching into that block? The taproot of mines that took millions of tons of coal from Carbon County to be converted into the power that had lighted millions of windows.

"We need to get back into the house," Darrick repeated.

"We're not getting back in," Marco said flatly.

"We got out, didn't we?"

"How do you think we got out so easily?"

"Easily?"

"They let us go, Darrick. They were done with me, don't you understand?" His face contorted. "I told them everything." Tears began to well in his eyes and slide down his sunken, unshaven cheeks. "I told them about the mine crack. I didn't care what they did to me, but they said they would destroy my children."

Lourana put her arm around him and he leaned into her and sobbed. "I'm sorry. Lourana, I let you down."

She remembered Beth telling her about the weeks after he'd come back from deployment. The screaming in the night, how he would lash out and then cling to the children. Beth said she thought the kids were the only things keeping him together. The Kavanaghs didn't have to lean hard on that pressure point. "Your children, you'd do anything for them," the editor had bragged, and he was right. She would batter down the iron gates of Knockaulin House if that would get Dreama back.

A pall settled over them, extinguishing the excitement of the escape. They truly were hunted things now.

"Well, seems to me that we have limited choices," Lourana said. "Maybe we cut and run, try to find a way around the roadblocks."

"No. I won't leave your daughter behind," Darrick said, looking at her.

Lourana knew there was a lot more he wasn't saying. Maybe he did care about Dreama because of their brand-new connection, but she thought it was more about his stubborn need to make things add up—why he had been attacked, how he came to gain this terrible power, and behind it all, who he was.

"We contact the authorities and hide out until they show up," Marco said.

"Where's your truck?" she asked.

"Gone. With the evidence, if they found it. And my cell. All of it."

"So we got nothing. No proof, until we get at your pictures on the cloud. I say we get my girl out of there. I'll go press that buzzer myself if I have to," Lourana said, strong words she didn't feel. She remembered standing before the three, begging their help to find her daughter when all the time she was in the house somewhere. Maybe just steps away. A prisoner? She imagined her up in one of the turrets, like a princess held captive. Maybe unwilling at first, but now?

"They'll be coming to look for you, Lourana, and me. We have to go somewhere," Darrick said. "Maybe we could go back to the fish camp?"

"Too much attention, with Hovatter and all," said Marco. "I have the keys to a friend's hunting camp out at Sulphur Well."

Silence, until Lourana said, "We got precious few options any way you look at it. Let's hide in plain sight. They don't do their dirty in the daylight where they can be seen. I'll go to work at the sweepstakes parlor like I'm supposed to, and there'll be people playing the slots till midnight. We can figure it out from there."

* * *

Darrick resettled his glasses. It was clear she was thinking only of Dreama, how to get to Dreama, nothing about what would happen to her, or him. *She isn't thinking straight.* When she went into the bathroom to brush her hair, he turned to Marco and asked, "Tonight, can you go back to the Kavanagh place with me, to see if we can find some other way to get in there?"

Marco's face went stiff and fear surged from him. Darrick backed away. The tangled emotions the officer had once presented, even the rage, were flattened and there was only this now.

"I can't. I can't do it."

Darrick said nothing. What was there to say? The man was broken. He mentally retraced his steps along the perimeter of the grounds, seeing if there was some other point of entry, some weak place.

Marco shuddered convulsively. "There's an old iron gate," he said, his voice rattling in his throat as though he were choking. "The entrance to a doghole mine in Pignut Hollow, under the bridge. We used to call it the jail when we were playing cops and robbers."

"Did you ever go inside?"

"Some boys said so. I never did. But then I usually went fishing instead of playing." A harsh, hollow laugh. "Cops and robbers."

Darrick wondered if that could be the mine, the one that went under the house. The beginning of the Kavanagh fortune. He wanted to ask more, but Marco had sagged against the wall, so thoroughly quenched that even the fear had subsided. He mourned the loss of the Marco he'd come to know, but the question wouldn't quit circling: was he just broken and cast aside, or had they truly made him into one of their own? A tool. A creature. Marco's tear-streaked face reflected naked regret and shame. *He's let us down.*

Lourana finished running water in the bathroom, came out, and began gathering her things. She looked at them, impatient. "Are we going?"

"I have to see my kids," Marco said. "Can you drop me off at home? I'll join you at the sweepstakes."

"Sure, Marco," her voice becoming soft.

Darrick looked around the little house that had become, for a time, home. Lourana paused, making some kind of inventory, and apparently satisfied, reached for the switch on the table lamp.

"Leave the lights on," he said. "Please."

If there's one thing a reporter savors, it's sitting on a dynamite story she knows won't be scooped by anyone else. Zadie had not one such story, but two, and she brooded them in the back of her mind while she hummed like a good little worker bee and wrote her zombie committee story on deadline.

The morning after the night when Earnshaw had threatened her children, sending her skittering to call an aunt who would call a yet more distant relative to arrange their escape, the editor was found dead in his land yacht. She was on night cops, but the day reporter filled her in on the latest homicide.

"Just like the others," Terry said. "His head and face were deformed, but otherwise, nothing. No blood, no wounds, no ligature marks."

Terry liked to use cop lingo.

"Where did they find him?"

"Down Fish Camp Road, like the game warden. They figure the zombie, or maybe zombies, are hiding out down in there." *They* being the police and the news media, from the credulous local TV affiliate to the New York tabloid that sponsored that phony psychic. As if there were any other kind.

Earnshaw had not been well liked, liked least by the people who knew him best, but his death touched off a blazing front-page editorial by the publisher, who "picked up the fallen banner of Gene Earnshaw" to write about the zombie menace and demand action in the form of a call-up of the West Virginia National Guard. Meanwhile, the psychic had been churning out YouTube videos and lighting up Twitter with her pronouncements.

"The zombie is striking out against our brave law enforcement officers, our churches, even against the news organizations that keep us informed, all the things that hold the community together. If action is not taken, there will be chaos. Chaos in the streets," she intoned.

So before the papers could hit the morning sidewalk with that front-page screed, the harried authorities had gotten together and issued a statement: an intensive search for the killer, undead or otherwise, would be held tomorrow afternoon, with all police and reserve officers taking part in a massive sweep to clear Bailey's Fish Camp and the area around.

"If we're lucky, we'll catch him during the daylight hours, when he's vulnerable," said the sheriff. Zadie had kept her mouth shut and made notes, not raising her hand to ask if the warden hadn't been killed in the daytime.

Miss Huldah pledged to "summon all her God-given powers" to help locate the zombie.

Zadie would never have expected, back in J-school, that she would be writing in all seriousness about preparations for a zombie hunt. What would Professor Atkins have said? The screen blinked dully at her, the green cursor nagging her to finish. She glanced at the word count—still a little short to fill the assigned hole. She paged back through her notebook and found a lame-ass quote that hadn't made it on first draft, plugged it in, and dropped the story in the queue for the night editor to read.

"Sent!" she hollered.

The editor's frizzy head never turned as she kept plowing through the stories coming in right on deadline, school board, zoning appeal, and the zombie update.

Zadie washed out her mug, scrubbing at the remnants of Red Zinger crusting the bottom, and waited to be released.

She was worried for Lourana and this Darrick, what with this craziness going on. People had come loose from their moorings. Not surprising. She'd been shaken down to her core when she'd encountered the stranger, the little girl inside her screaming "duppy, duppy!" to a dead grandmother's grim satisfaction.

The night editor hit the send key. Hard. Whatever story that was, it hadn't pleased her. Must be Ken's, because he always filed and flew, wouldn't stick around to clarify a sentence or make another call. Zadie muttered under her breath, "Come on, come on," as Rhonda called up another story. Hers, she hoped. It might be late, her lower back might hurt from too much time at the keyboard, but the real work awaited her at home. An editor from *Mother Jones* was waiting on her expanded AMD story. *Mother Jones!* It couldn't be more perfect. She imagined the magazine's namesake in her black widow's dress taking the fight to the Kavanaghs. There had been no stopping Mary Harris Jones back when she organized the mine workers around here, and there would be no stopping the shit-storm that was coming when the story broke.

Lourana's access to the working permit had been the key, however she had finagled that. She spotted those wrong-way boreholes, and that had turned Zadie around 180 degrees from thinking this was just another sad story of a mine blowout. Then the permit filing, clicking like a key in a lock.

It was genius, really. KCL had been long preparing for this, while letting the stories circulate about some grand development. The coal operations, already all but tapped out, had been sold to an offshore shell company, all other mineral rights to another, and other hard assets like the loading docks and trucking company to a third. The developable real estate went to yet another LLC. The fines and penalties from the spill would go against the hollowed-out coal operation, bankrupting it, and leaving the government to foot the bill for the cleanup. KCL's new development company had its megasite poised to accept the "superdump" and incinerator to handle medical waste, biohazards, and industrial toxins too vile to be buried in any normal landfill. Breathtaking, really. Carve away the part to be sacrificed, then create the environmental nightmare, tainting the river and the land so thoroughly that the project, with its promise of tax revenue and jobs, would seem like salvation to Carbon County.

Zadie had been worrying about the closing paragraph for that article, even as she pounded out the routine news. Now, as she waited, the ending came to her. She could type those final words and then, with the house so empty of the peaceful breathing of her children in their beds, sit down with a printout and give it a last, close read.

She thought about Caleb and Zippy on the Greyhound, their school backpacks stuffed with iPads and clothes and snacks. Zippy was old enough to take care of them both, a foot taller than Zadie at age thirteen but strong, too, the way she had been. It was a long ride to Georgia, where a relay would move them to another house and then another, a friend outside the family, breaking the chain for anyone who tried to trace them. Like the Underground Railroad. It might have been paranoid, but Zadie had to put her precious ones where the Kavanaghs couldn't touch them. And where she couldn't spill no matter what they did to her, though it made her start to leak tears to think of them orphaned.

"Go home, Person," shouted Rhonda. She always shouted.

"I'm bouncing. Thanks! Hope you're nearly done," Zadie called, hitting the door and not slowing down.

* * *

On the opposite side of the parking lot, slumped down in the back of the big black Chevy, Marco couldn't stop thinking about his kids.

He didn't know how long he'd been in the black room when Eamon arrived. Hours, days. Confronted by the example of the bones he'd briefly seen and then sat among in the dark of the grave, he thought he'd been left to die and desiccate, forgotten by everyone. In the tomb he said the names of his children over and over, letting pictures of them rise and fill the emptiness. Amy. Little Michael, named for his grandfather. He remembered every harsh word, every refused request, and he cried as their sweet faces merged with the faces of Iraqi children, huddled dead in their dusty home. Then the light came on, reflecting off the rough-hewn facets of the coal that surrounded him, the door opened, and he had learned the reality of what the Kavanaghs were and how they made and used their creatures.

They ordered him to find Lourana and to get rid of the reporter, leaving her body to be found like another victim of the zombie. The town was inflamed and, as Eamon said, the problem of Darrick would be solved soon enough. But as he watched her trotting across the lot, full of energy even after what had to have been a long day, he didn't know if he could do it.

Her life or Beth's.

My honor or my children.

My soul or every person I love.

Fuck me.

She opened the door and slung her bag across the front seat, sat down heavily behind the wheel. He let her put the car into gear and leave the lot before he rose and pressed the gun to the back of her neck.

"Don't do anything that will make me have to hurt you," he said, sounding hard, hating that, hating himself. Zadie's eyes in the mirror were big, but not terrified. She looked straight back at him. "Remember your kids. Just do what I tell you," he growled.

He clicked the door lock down behind her.

"Get your phone and call Lourana. Have her meet us at the church across from the sweepstakes. Dreama is being released."

"Released?"

"Just tell her." He could tell she didn't believe him.

Zadie rustled in her bag with one hand while driving with the other. She came out with a battered old phone. When they stopped at a light, she tapped out the number quickly.

"Don't want to do anything illegal, deputy," she said dryly.

Marco made no comment, but kept the barrel of the pistol in contact with her neck.

"Lourana?" She glanced in the rearview, then back at the road. "I'm on my way over there. Meet me in the church lot. Dreama is being released."

He could hear Lourana's shriek of joy, and it arrowed into him.

He tapped her neck, whispered, "Say goodbye."

"Bye . . ." Zadie drew breath, and he snatched the phone before she could let out another word. Lourana's voice was distant, "Zadie?" He rolled down the window and tossed the cell into the river as they crossed the bridge.

They drove into the night. His nights had turned endless, a series of black rooms from which he could not emerge. It had taken a lot to get him to betray Lourana—he had never, ever quit loving her—but blood came first. His children. He was so tired. There was nothing left of him, the Marco that had been, the Marine, the deputy.

He remembered Amy looking up at him with a brief, brilliant smile as the sheriff's cruiser had pulled up to collect him earlier that evening, then she had turned back to her toys. "Daddy is going back to work," she confided to them.

The Kavanaghs had given their word. Deliver Lourana, and his family would never know anything happened. He'd get his truck back, his job back . . . he heard the echo of the bad joke about playing a country song backward. Everything would come back.

Lourana slid the phone down behind the counter and was starting for the back room when one of the machines went nuts. Yancey was dancing and whooping, snapping his fingers over his head like a Spanish dancer or something. With the place jammed, everyone had to cluster around and see how much he had hit and celebrate with him, their faces stiff with envy. By the time she had that jackpot managed, headlights sliced into the window as a car approached from town, turned into the church parking lot, and sure enough it was the Caprice. There was no time to unpack Darrick from his hidey-hole in the attic.

"I'll be right back," she yelled at Helen. She ran across the road, her thrift-store sweatshirt too thin for the night. She crossed her arms to hold in the heat as she headed for Zadie's car, pulled way to the back by the pavilion where they held revivals.

Damn, Zadie, you didn't have to park nearly in the creek.

Her heart was hammering. Whatever Zadie had done. . . . Hallelujah! Dreama was being set free. Every midnight dream was coming true, all the nightmares fading away.

The passenger door swung open, and Lourana slid in. Zadie was sitting very still.

"I can't believe it! Let's go!"

Something moved behind her, and Lourana jumped. "What the . . . "

"Lourana."

"Marco? Hey, we're going to get Dreama!"

"You'll see Dreama tonight," he answered, but there was no reassurance in his flat words. Much less in the pistol that gleamed in the light from the sweepstakes, which seemed a million miles away right now.

"Marco?"

His face contorted and for a moment, she wondered if Darrick was near, if he had followed her. How could she have run out without telling him?

"I have to do this," he grated.

"It's Darrick!" yelled Zadie, looking off to her left, and Marco's eyes flicked to verify. At that moment, she swung her purse by its strap across the back of the seat, striking the gun from his hand and then connecting with the side of his head. Lourana saw a clunky old camera fly out of the purse.

"Run!" The reporter popped out the door and was heading for the thick forest behind the church before Lourana could quite process what was happening. She was pulling the door handle when Marco's hand fastened on her arm.

"I can't let you."

She turned. His pistol now was leveled at her. "Oh, Marco." Her dreams had turned inside out.

He flinched at her tone but continued to lock a handcuff around the wrist he gripped. Lourana had the weird feeling he was putting a bracelet on her, a gift for Valentine's Day or Christmas. If he had touched her, back in the day, even once, she would have thought twice about Steve. More than twice. And now Marco was out of the car, leaning in, indicating the other wrist with a wave of his gun. She gave it. He pulled her hands over, the second handcuff closed with a metal gnashing, and she was shackled to the pull strap on the door.

"Please, Marco. I know you. This isn't you."

"You're right," he said, closing the door gently then walking around the car and into the driver's seat.

"You can't do this."

He glanced at her, his dark eyes gleaming, but not with pity.

"I know how you've felt about me. How I felt about you, how I could have felt."

"Enough. They took me apart. They'll kill Amy and Michael." He nestled the gun back in his coat pocket.

"It's just a threat." Lourana poured every bit of urgency she could into her plea. "We can go get the kids now, warn Beth, take them away. Drive to your house. We can get away."

The tires dug gravel as they pulled onto the road.

"I can't get away. You don't know what they do. They have taken parts out of me. I wish they'd taken everything, so I'd be like the others under Knockaulin House, but they left enough to make me suffer. That's what you do. You suffer."

* * *

Zadie waited until her car was out of sight, then struggled through the woods to reach the sweepstakes from the backside. She went straight past the raucous customers, around the counter, and through the door to the back room from which Darrick once emerged.

"Darrick," she called in a stage whisper. "Darrick," as she checked the bathroom, the yoga studio. "Are you here?"

She heard a muffled sound overhead.

The door to the sweepstakes opened and a grizzled man poked his head in. "What's going on? Who're you? Where's Lourana?"

"She told me to take care of things. Family emergency." Zadie started pushing things around on the supply shelves. *Try to look official.*

"Then how come her car's still outside?"

"Long story. She took mine. Now, just go out and tell everyone there's free coffee."

"All right!" He closed the door, and she could hear the muted celebration.

"Darrick?"

"I'm up here."

Following the muffled voice, she opened a narrow door to find only a closet space filled with boxes. That couldn't be where the voice came from. She started to turn away when he spoke from the ceiling.

"I'm in the attic. There's an access. She piled all the boxes back up, so you'll have to clear them out of the way."

She threw paper towels and cleaning supplies right and left, until the space was cleared enough to reveal a hatch in the ceiling. She pulled the cord and it came down, a rickety ladder unfolding, and then Darrick's feet unsteadily finding the rungs.

"It's Marco. He has Lourana."

"What? Why?" Darrick got his feet on the floor and pushed the ladder back up.

"I don't think you need to ask."

*　*　*

Darrick's heart crashed. He'd known Marco wasn't the same after they escaped, that he was scared like just about everyone here, but he really thought he had the strength not to become a creature. The core of the man was solid. Battle-tested. But as he worked to toss boxes back into the closet, he knew that he'd been deluding himself. That fear had a sound and sensation all its own.

Zadie was puffing and panting beside him, with leaves and twigs in her hair and a bleeding scratch across her chubby cheek. He wondered how she'd gotten to be such a mess, then saw his filthy hands, the grime of dust and webs. The attic was Lourana's idea, in case of a sudden raid. Another of those dark, forgotten spaces he seemed fated to visit.

"How did he get Lourana?"

"He was in my car when I came out of work. He put a gun to my head and made me call her, tell her that Dreama was being let go. She came to meet us by the church. When she got in the car I hit him with my bag and got away."

"But Lourana didn't."

She glanced up at him, and then back down.

"He drove away with her. I ran into the woods, followed the creek back around and came here from the other side."

He saw that her shoes were in fact soaking wet and her legs caked with mud. So that much was true. Maybe. Darrick didn't know if he could trust her either. Anyone. He extended his awareness, probed her emotions. Strong but clean, anxiety about her children predominating over the lower, calmer sounds. *That's how they get control,* he thought, happy he had no children.

"We've got to get to Lourana before they do to her whatever they did to Marco."

"He's really a creature now?"

"When a man sticks a Glock into your neck, he's not on your side."

Darrick felt the steely determination under her maternal exterior. She was nobody's pushover. If he had to trust anyone in this benighted place other than Lourana, he guessed it would have to be her.

And how did that work out with Marco?

He knew what he had to do, what he was not strong enough to do.

"Go out and tell the people the place is closed. Whatever you have to tell them."

Every bit of muscle and bone screamed for him to run, finally to run and save himself. But it wasn't about him now. He was in love with Lourana, he might as well admit it, daunting as that might be, and so he had to go find her. Simple enough.

He remembered the nurse's stories, especially the one about "the poor child without a name, like you" who becomes a knight. "You must remember to behave properly with the girls, and keep your head down. Too many questions will cause you problems." And then she had leaned close and whispered, "But you will know when is the right time for you to ask for an answer." Fanciful tales told by a woman lonely in a foreign land, to comfort an equally lonely child. But they had guided him, in some way, as much as the more acceptable liturgy of the Church. His life had been good enough.

Now he'd been given a power he didn't understand, and still didn't know what questions to ask. What had Cormac said? "Those who are thrust into the world," something something. He had killed, at first not knowing what he was doing, and then to protect himself and others, but it did not remove the blood from his hands. He did not have a clean soul as he went to fight the Kavanaghs and get Lourana back. He shuddered at the thought of confronting Eamon, his inadequacy before that kind of raw force.

Not so cocky now, are we?

It didn't take long for Zadie to clear the muttering customers out. With the door locked, Darrick emerged, went to one of the computers, and called up his email draft folder.

"Here it is, Zadie. My story, as much as I can tell. I'm sending it to the FBI and to you so you can write this. Somebody has to report what's happened."

"Don't talk like you're not coming back."

"I'm sure hoping to." He quelled the rush of nausea, remembering how Cormac had claimed some sort of kinship, how Eamon had lifted his hands over Marco. "But in case I don't. I've been working on this, in bits and pieces at Lourana's."

He added a couple of lines to the bottom of the account, telling how Lourana had been taken, and that Zadie was a trustworthy reporter who could fill in the gaps.

"It's not everything. I don't know what to say about the supernatural stuff. It just sounds ridiculous, so I didn't say anything. But the mine crack, what's down there, that is hard evidence." He hit *send* and let out a long sigh.

"We're going after Lourana."

"I am."

"I'm going with you." Zadie bustled to pull her coat on over her flowered dress. "This is a great story."

"You'd just be one more person they can hurt. I can't have that on me too. You have kids to take care of. Right?"

She nodded.

Darrick logged off. "Now let's locate Lourana's car keys."

*　　*　　*

Lourana watched the gate ease back soundlessly. The Caprice glided into the underground garage, and Marco parked it beside a silver Range Rover. The engine coughed twice as he shut it off.

He held the gun in Lourana's view as he released her from the handcuffs and helped her get out.

"Lourana, I don't believe they will hurt you. They haven't hurt Dreama," he said, moving her along a corridor, down a set of stairs, through a dimly lit wine cellar, and down one more stairway. "They want Darrick."

"And they think I'll be the bait?"

"Just be patient and everything will be OK."

A small wooden door, with a massive bolt on the outside. Lourana's skin prickled. She had already seen what lay beyond that door, could never stop seeing it. Marco opened it and pushed her inside, shutting the door quickly before she could make a last effort. She heard the thud of the bolt into the frame.

Lourana turned around, looked for a place to sit down. She saw bones, laid out in the shape of the bodies they once supported, white and neat as some kind of museum display on their shelves. And then she saw Dreama, huddled on the ground at the far end of the space. She raised a tear-stained face, squinting against the light. "Mama?"

The light went out.

Dreama howled in anguish. Moving on the memory of what she'd seen, Lourana made her way to her daughter and knelt beside her on the coal floor.

There in the cold and the dark, she hugged Dreama tight, her lips against her daughter's hair as she murmured, "There, there. There, there." She smelled of sweat and coal the way Lourana's father used to, mixed with the sweet aroma only her daughter had. She could see nothing, only touch, only feel tears trickling down her hand. Dreama might have been twelve years old again, awkward and sensitive, crying after a boy had said something ugly about her new dress.

Lourana rocked her daughter back and forth, comforting her, and comforting herself. She wondered what had happened to Zadie. How long would it be before Darrick found out she was gone? He was unaware of Marco's turn, would go with him, would put himself into the hands of the Kavanaghs.

"Oh, Mama, you don't know what's happened."

*　*　*

Marco stood on the other side of the door, his hand still on the switch. Mr. Kavanagh had told him to leave them in the dark. Like he had been. Let them know what the inside of the mountain was, how in the dark you could feel the coal pulsing with power waiting to be liberated. He took his hand away, and then in a moment of defiance, flipped the light back on and made his way upstairs.

He was unhappy with himself because Zadie had gotten away. That would cause problems. That would cause suffering. How fast that chubby little woman had moved! His mistake to have a moment of weakness.

Now he would have to chase her down and finish the job he'd been assigned. How far could she get without a car? Where would she go? Marco was tired, so tired. Worn to the bone.

He found the elder brother in the viewing salon, as he'd expected, watching a documentary. Marco waited until he was recognized.

"You've taken care of the women?"

"Lourana is downstairs."

"And?"

"The reporter got away. She surprised me while I was dealing with Lourana." He touched his swollen eye and bruised cheekbone.

Marco felt his muscles liquefy. He fell flat on the floor, writhing as his very self was pulled apart by Eamon's displeasure.

It might have been seconds. Or hours. Finally the pain subsided, and he was allowed to struggle to his knees.

Eamon's body had become as big as his father's, bigger. It swelled above him.

"What about Darrick?" Marco asked, wondering where he was, if he was somewhere running from the zombie hunt.

"You do not have the capacity to handle him. He is like us, akin to us, and he will come to us because he will have to."

25

The light went back on, that lone caged bulb far away in the ceiling as life-giving as the sun itself.

Lourana's face was buried in Dreama's hair, soft and long as when she was a girl. The glaring return of the light startled her. Marco had turned it off, a cruel act. Why? And why then had it been turned back on?

"Remember that necklace I used to wear all the time?" Dreama murmured against her. "The one with the coral beads that I bought at the Town Center?"

"I do."

"That's what started it all."

Lourana waited, stroking her daughter's back, shoulders to the narrow of her waist, again and again. That had always comforted her. She couldn't believe that Dreama was back in her arms, that she could feel the little shiver of her body from the cold, the rise and fall of her breathing that matched her own.

"I was helping Mr. Walsh carry files into the boardroom." Her voice was low and she seemed exhausted. "They were in these slippery binders. Some of them started to slide, and caught on the necklace and snapped it. The beads flew everywhere. I was down on the carpet, trying to collect them, when Cormac walked in."

Cormac, not "Mr. Kavanagh." She still couldn't believe her own daughter sleeping with a Kavanagh.

"He got down on his knees and helped me. When he held his hands out for me to give him the beads, and I looked him in the eyes, oh,

Mama, I don't know why, I don't know, but we fell in love right there on the carpet."

Lourana felt her stomach twist, but she said, as mildly as she could, "It was just the moment. You were attracted by the attention."

Dreama shook her head. "Then at Christmas, we had a Secret Santa thing. When I opened mine, it wasn't some little five-dollar gag gift. It was the gold beads, and a note, *for what was broken will be healed*. We were in love."

"If he loves you, darlin', then why are we sitting here?" Lourana didn't want to be hard, but Dreama had to come to her senses. "Where's Cormac to help you?"

"He's right here." Dreama pulled herself away, rocking back on her heels beside the shelves of bones. She took hold of Lourana's hand and placed her palm on the cool curve of a skull.

"What?" Lourana yanked her hand away and the skull rocked against the vertebrae, the bones arranged as they would be in life.

"This is Cormac. *Was* Cormac."

"But these bones are bare. They're old. You've been tricked, Dreama."

Dreama gave her a look that she couldn't even begin to name. The look of someone who's stared into the void at the end of the world.

"We wanted to leave. Let Eamon have everything—the company, the property, the name. Cormac wanted nothing but our freedom. But Eamon would not let him go." Dreama stroked the skull tenderly. "You can't understand what happens. I didn't either. Remember when I told you: the rich eat their own?"

Lourana nodded slowly.

"Eamon took their father. He was tired of deferring to the old man." Dreama pointed to the skeleton on a shelf closer to Lourana, which made her want to shrink away. As if there was anywhere better to go. "He *absorbed* him. Stripped the living spirit from his father and then the flesh from his bones. And Cormac—he despised Cormac because he tried to stop his plans." Her eyes were pools of misery. "He took a long time with Cormac. He made me watch."

Lourana couldn't get her head around this. How? The bones lay quiet on their benches as though they'd been there a million years. Dry bones.

Where were the bodies? She looked around and saw only coal, the raw coal that made up the roof and walls and floor, and in it the imprints of ferns dead a million years, preserved forever in the black layers.

At the creak of the bolt, Dreama flung herself back into her mother's arms. The door swung open, and Eamon stood there with Marco behind him, Eamon even bigger than Lourana remembered him. Beside him, Marco was visibly withered. He huddled into himself like a dog that has been kicked for the hundredth time.

Lourana patted Dreama's shoulder and stood up.

"Hello, Eamon. This isn't much like our last meeting."

The big man didn't react.

"What kind of a man does this? Locks up innocent people in the dark?" She saw his mouth move down a fraction. "What has Dreama ever done to deserve this?"

"You should be concerned with your own actions, not hers." Eamon motioned for Marco to shut the door. "Your little rebellion isn't going so well, is it? This Darrick you put so much faith in is now on the run."

Lourana felt a strangeness, like the air was slowly being let out of her, and she did what came naturally and bolstered the emotional barrier that had been in place for so long, sealing herself off from anyone's touch. She was not about to let him know how her heart reacted to Darrick's name. That made her feel stronger, but she knew she had nothing to back up her bravado. Looking at Marco as he leaned against the wall, his face slack and gray, she knew that bravado would only carry her so far.

"So is this what all the old stories are about? The Kavanaghs stripping a man to the bone?"

Eamon laughed, an unpleasant sound that had no joy in it. "Old stories? I'd say they are fairly current. A legend will keep people in line better than police and fences and cameras. But you must nourish it occasionally, show people that what they are afraid of is still there. Marco, for instance, can testify to our modern-day power. To what it feels like as your life is sapped away."

"Power? Parasite, more like. You're nothing but a vampire."

"As much as your friend is a zombie, yes."

"You feed on people who fall into your grasp. Leave their families

194

without an answer, while you hide the bones here, or in that mine crack."

"You mistake what this is." Eamon moved to the bones. "This is our family crypt. These are our beloved, our own. Father," and he touched the larger skeleton. "Brother. Mother. Cousins. Grandparents." His hand motioned to benches on the far end of the room. "Some of our loyal servants, too, those without families other than ours. Their willing service grants them long life, and a good life in this house. We can sip as well as drain. A little something to sustain us, year by year, until they are ready to be released into death."

He put his hand to the edge of one of the benches and broke off a piece of coal, crushed it in his fist.

"This is where it all comes from. Coal, the essence of the sun. The same seam of coal runs through all the Kavanagh mines in Carbon County, like the veins in a body." He opened his massive fist and let the black dust fall to the floor. "Marriage to damp Irish dirt made kings for generations before us—this, *this* is so much more. Our coal, our land, our people."

"Bodies dumped in the mine crack? Not a great way to take care of your people, Eamon."

His mouth turned down again, and Lourana felt his displeasure, like a wheel rolling over her. "We would appreciate if you would use our rightful name. Kavanagh. *The* Kavanagh, as we are now a single being. There is only one Kavanagh to a generation—Cormac was a mistake. Our father was too tender toward his wife, unable to remove the extraneous child. Now there is only us, the one you see as Eamon, the strongest."

"And people who blundered into your path? Are they extraneous?"

"Undesirables are not allowed to remain in Carbon County. The people who work for us . . . "

"Creatures."

He sneered at her. "The people who do our work in the world are sometimes overly aggressive in their efforts. Outsiders were wasted, thrown away in a panic, when we might have taken some of them into ourselves."

"Like Darrick."

"We're most interested in him, yes." Eamon's face became eager, acquisitive. "He does not know himself, as my brother did not understand what it was to be a Kavanagh, bonded with the coal."

Dreama, who had remained crumpled beside Cormac's bones, rose to confront him, her face flushed. "Cormac understood the coal as well as you do. Better."

Eamon waved his hand, and she cowered against the wall. "There is only one way for this to end. Darrick will surrender himself to us. He will come when he learns that you are here, Lourana."

"You think a woman is that much motivation?" Lourana glanced at her daughter, who was back on the floor. "That Darrick will come for me? If he comes, it will be for his own reasons."

"And that will be the end of the zombie, if not the legend. We've not encountered his like before, and do look forward to learning more of what exactly he is."

Lourana shuddered at his avid inward gaze, like someone preparing to carve up a turkey.

"He is so much closer to us than he knows. Son of a brehon—that name was no accident. The ancient judges held great power. They stood beside the kings, almost their equals." Eamon's hair gleamed like burning coals under the raw light. "Consider the men he has killed. Has he not taken their life force from them, and strengthened himself?"

She felt there was something wrong with that reasoning, but couldn't say what. Still, the taint of it clung.

"No matter. If our great father could not stand against us, if Cormac could not, then Darrick will not." Eamon picked up Cormac's skull, though Dreama clutched wildly after it, trying to keep it out of his hands. "Dear brother, face always buried in a book. He used to rattle on and on about names, how his middle name, Bran, was the name of a singing god, one whose head sang from a pool of water even after his death."

He held the skull close to his head, close enough that the perfect teeth seemed poised to bite his ear.

"No singing, alas." He held the skull out and turned it from side to side. "He was really never a Kavanagh. Look how the jaw and the forehead are delicate as a woman's. He was his mother's son, at the bone."

He set the skull down casually, its eye sockets to the wall.

Dreama shrieked like a mine whistle when an explosion has dropped a mountain between men and the hope of air. She leaped at Eamon, her hands clawing at his face, her mouth wide open.

She never touched him. Eamon raised one hand. It might have been a warning, but Lourana could see her daughter sag backward and struggle. She tried to move between them and snatch her little girl from that brute force, but Marco shoved her aside and put himself between Eamon and his prey.

Eamon released Dreama and turned on his creature, who twisted under the pressure, but stood.

Not for long. Marco slid down, his eyes on Lourana. His mouth moved, but whatever he was trying to say could not come out.

At first it seemed only that he shrank away from his tormentor, made himself small, but it became evident that he was wasting away. A glow enveloped him, a brightness that flowed toward Eamon, and as it did he seemed to fade. His cheeks sank and his beautiful eyes tunneled into their sockets, but Marco never looked away from her. His lips began to draw back over his teeth. His flesh was disappearing as she watched, like a time-lapse movie speeded up to madness, the flesh drawing down to the bones. Then nothing was left but skin and hair over the frame, and finally they were gone as well. The bones collapsed into the shape of a man curled in sleep.

Eamon considered the skeleton at his feet, then he kicked it apart.

He stared wordlessly at the women, opened the door, and left, taking the light as he did.

"It's no use," Darrick said.

He and Zadie had checked every possible hiding spot on the Subaru. No magnetic key box clung to the firewall or the underside of a fender. No spare key was taped to the back of a license plate. Her purse and phone remained in the store, but she must have had the keys in her pocket when she was taken.

"Looks like we're walking," Zadie said.

"Like hell." Darrick stood up from the last wheel-well examination and started to wipe his brow when he saw the road grit crusting his palms. He used the back of his hand instead. "You'll just slow me down."

Zadie let out a high-pitched whoop. "Oh, really? What John Wayne movie did you lift *that* from?"

Darrick flushed. "OK. OK. But I have to do this. You can't stand against the Kavanaghs."

"And you can."

"I can," he said, trying to make the assurance in the words fill the gut-emptiness he felt. "You need to do your job. Report this story, talk to the FBI and BCI, get some allies. That would be the best thing you could do."

"I'll get you part of the way, and then I'll head to the newspaper." And that, from the set of her mouth, was that.

In the sweepstakes parlor, Darrick took inventory. He had Lourana's battered phone, left under the counter on its charger, but it was password protected so would connect only to 911. He stuck it in his pants pocket anyway. Behind the counter, he found a small flashlight and a cheap jack-knife with one blade tip snapped off. Those went in the other pocket. Not of any use against the Kavanaghs, but maybe if he found himself cornered by the zombie hunt. The thought made him cringe, in embarrassment as much as fear. *Darrick MacBrehon, graduate of St. Bonaventure, CPA, middling chess player, civil servant, zombie.*

He grabbed one of the doughy snacks they called pepperoni rolls, a chocolate bar, and a Pepsi. The fleece jacket Lourana had bought him was gone, hung in some closet by the punctilious butler, but a ragged stretched-out sweater from the back of the door gave some warmth. It smelled of her, and with that scent her body swam into his thoughts, her breasts, her mouth when it relaxed from sarcasm, her welcoming arms. He breathed deep and refocused.

"Ready?" He tossed aside his useless hat and the matching orange gloves, now that concealment was vital. "How far is it?"

"A couple of miles," said Zadie. "It'll be getting light by the time we get there." She had buttoned her coat up to her throat, but her legs were bare between her flowered skirt and her furry boots.

The last cop car and a few oversized pickups with emergency lights on the dash had gone down the road as Darrick and Zadie skulked around, searching for a key. The zombie hunters, if they were following the sheriff's plan, would be in place well before dawn on the outskirts of the fish camp and work their way through, building by building, toward the river. The dragnet (*did they still call it that?*) must be in operation now, the sky bright in the area of the fish camp with the pulsing rosy glow of strobes or fire. He thought of pitchforks and torches, scenes of townspeople storming the mad scientist's castle or massing at the graveyard to settle the undead with a stake through the heart. Darrick imagined the men pushing through the vacant buildings, finding the trailer he broke into, the debris from his desperate hunger.

Darrick wished now that he had joined the Boy Scouts, all those years ago, done something that would have taught him the skills to negotiate this journey. The route was simple enough, but the problem was in avoiding people along the way. His ataxia, which had reawakened in the mine crack and intensified as the days went by, meant that anyone seeing him walking would immediately know who he was. He was caught between the need to go as fast as he could, Lourana's life hanging in the balance, and moving slowly enough to minimize his characteristic lurching. *The walking dead.*

He'd not had his powers tested with more than two or three people around him—what would he do if a mob came along? If they shot first, then, well, he wasn't bulletproof, but if not, would the emotional storm overwhelm him? Could he protect himself from so many?

Zadie led the way, around the back of the plaza and across some waste ground to a parallel road. That kept them off the main route, but they still had to keep a close watch for early-moving people and cars, and on that narrow two-lane, getting out of sight meant a deep ditch or brambly undergrowth. Zadie trotted along, sure of her path, her short legs taking two steps to his one.

Houses were still dark beyond the circles of their dusk-to-dawn lights. At one, a long shadow like a hanged man in a tree turned out to be a deer, its body split open. A big dog barked steadily and rattled the blinds as it threw itself against a window. A light came on and they had to get out of sight, stumbling through the snow and stepping down hard into unseen potholes.

A siren called from behind them.

The road curved into a city street, the transition visible as the houses drew closer together and stop signs appeared at intersections. He could see the big light poles along the riverside boulevard and a ragged splotch of worksite illumination around the ruined pier. Zadie turned toward the river, out of the neighborhood and into the alley behind a line of brick buildings. Trash cans filled the mouths of old garages, and across the lane, back doors let into businesses that faced the main street.

One door banged open and Zadie yanked him into a shadow. A gray animal atop a garbage can froze in the glare of fluorescent light.

"I'll brain you!" A man leaned out the door, steam following him from a kitchen, and he picked up a rock by the steps and threw it at the beast. The rock rattled against metal and the possum lumbered awkwardly along the cans and then over a chain-link fence. "Get me some goddamn traps, that's what I'll do." The door banged shut. Darrick felt that slam in his heart, *thump thump thump.*

When the door stayed closed, they hurried out of the alley and skirted the grocery store where deliveries were being unloaded from diesel trucks coughing on their own fumes, then took a well-used footpath toward the bridge. They parted ways behind a thicket.

"This path will take you to the new bridge and under it. Kids use it, bums. You get the picture. So you'll have to watch for your time to cross over to the bridge walkway. Stay low. Remember there's a curve in the bridge—you can't see what's coming from that end." She looked at him closely. "Once you get across, you'll have to duck under the bridge on that side. There's another path down to the street they cut off when they relocated the bridge entrance. That road runs right along the hollow, out of sight. Take your first street on the left and you'll come to the back corner of the grounds."

He put out his hand, but she dived straight in and gave him a hug.

"Thank you, Zadie," he said, choking up. "Be careful."

"You too. I'd say good luck, but I don't want to jinx you." And she was gone.

Alone, he had time to think about what lay ahead. The bridge, and what then? *What's your plan, smart boy?* He had none, except to find his way into that watchful house, and somehow locate Lourana. He skulked along the path, which was littered with bottles and cigarette wrappers and well concealed by overgrowth no one bothered to cut. *What's your plan? You got nothing but one lunatic idea.*

He paused, shivering, where the path came out of the weeds, crossing open space before plunging into the darkness under the bridge. The concrete structure bent away from downtown to link with the residential area where Knockaulin House loomed on its hill. A car came through the business district, headed for the bridge, moving slowly. He saw an old, old woman bent to the wheel, her face thrust toward the windshield. He thought about what Eamon Kavanagh had said, feeling the lash of his contempt but something else as well, not fear, but uncertainty. They didn't know what he is, was, any more than he did. Darrick caught at the fragments he'd discovered in his search for the meaning of his abandonment—a name that came from no one, internet pages boasting of extinct Irish glories. Judges who were among the entitled of their day, like poets and smiths allowed to move freely across boundaries. He felt none of that entitlement. He was like an escaped prisoner, always expecting the hue and cry to be raised. He watched for his moment. Finally, no cars in any direction, no one on the streets as cold dawn seeped into the sky. He hurried across the dangerous gap toward the bridge.

Just as he was stepping foot on the sidewalk, a man clambered up from the darkness under the bridge. "Heh-uh!" he exclaimed, and stumbled back. His hair was gray and wild, his face bruised. Darrick could feel the muddled panic. He was thirsty. Needy. Darrick didn't push back. He tried to move past the man, get onto the bridge, but the man blocked his way.

"No, no, no!" He flailed at Darrick, defending the only shelter he had, safe from nothing, not even from zombies.

Darrick *pushed* a little. Just enough to make the man move.

The wino began to babble and backed toward the street. Darrick let him go, hoping that was enough. But the man instead hopped and staggered into the middle of the street, his clothes flapping and arms windmilling like a crazy puppet. A newspaper delivery truck roared around the curve of the bridge and the headlights caught the wino, who jigged out of the way as the truck pulled up to the next traffic light.

"He's here! He's here!" the man screamed, running up and pounding on the side window. "The zombie's here!"

Darrick, crouched low, began to run.

The bridge had been built with waist-high concrete walls on each side of the pedestrian way, making it a rat run, the path protected from errant cars or an easy fall to the river. Darrick glanced back; the truck still at the light. How far down was the river? This bridge was high above the water, much higher than the other one that ended close to the pier.

He heard an engine and threw himself flat on the concrete as head-lights stabbed past him. He got to his feet and scuttled. The river seemed endlessly wide. Broad River, rotten with acid.

At the other end, he saw cars passing. The sky was gaining its blue, a clear, bright day ahead. He crouched, breathing hard, until he saw no cars and heard no sound, then crabbed his way around the protective wall, slid down the rubbly earth into the dankness under the bridge piers. The air was even colder here, the lightless ground exuding damp chill and the smell of urine and garbage. Broken bottles were everywhere, a gutted mattress, a lawn chair, pallets.

A chain-link fence partway down the slope barred the way to the abandoned street, but others had been here before him and a pile of ragged concrete slabs on each side of the fence gave him an easy way over. The slabs had been mined from the abandoned end of the street, and other pieces of concrete and stones were shaped into rough benches. There was a rude domesticity to it, like ancient rock shelters.

Darrick didn't take the street as Zadie had said. She didn't know about the old mine and the iron gate, and he hadn't told her. Marco had said he was kept in an underground room, carved out of the coal. One with two doors. The best bet was that Lourana would also be confined there.

What about Lourana? What if she was turned?

There was a chance, if he could find that old gate, if this was the same mine, if that mine actually led to that room, if the way hadn't been blocked.

If he could traverse that passage in the dark.

Too many *ifs*.

Darrick turned on his flashlight and probed along the slope, trying to see through vines and scrubby trees. What had she called it? A drift mine, a doghole. Marco had described the rusted iron gate in the gully not far from the mansion. It had to be here somewhere.

If he could get in, could he get them out? Worse come to worst, he could just crawl back out and try the direct approach; he wouldn't be so lucky to get away this time. He imagined what his death would be like under Eamon's hands.

The flashlight picked up a grid of rusted bars.

Darrick crashed through the thickets and shoved branches away from the gate. It was only big enough to crawl into.

Seemed he was doomed to go into the dark places. Maybe everything had been preparation, for now, for this.

27

Darrick shoved the branches and dead leaves aside. An iron frame set into concrete supported a barred gate held shut by an ancient padlock welded to its hasp by rust. He pushed and pulled at the lock; there was no give, but the shaking made hunks of rust flake off the gate. He shook harder, putting all his weight into his hands, and one iron bar broke free. Finally, the hinges gave way and he pulled the gate open on the complaining knuckle of the padlock.

He was sweating, despite the cold, and his shirt felt like a wet sheet. Darrick looked around, wondering if anyone had heard, because in the moment he hadn't thought about anything but breaking the gate. A bird chirped, a dog yipped with excitement somewhere far away and unconcerned with him, traffic hummed up on the bridge above; that was all. His sweat began to cool. He pulled out the Pepsi and chugged it down, following it with the chocolate. His heart stuttered, or maybe it was his stomach rebelling against the sweets. He breathed deep, in and out, trying to settle himself. The ragged opening to the mine exuded a smell like damp shoes left in a closet. It was small and dark, promising more dark.

His mind skittered like the rats he imagined waiting just inside that hole. He tried not to focus on that; instead, his thoughts spiraled around this whole business of brehons and kings, the accident of his name. The Kavanaghs, though, apparently didn't think it was an accident. A brehon held the power of the law, even over kings. But he was no judge, the Kavanaghs were not kings, and they were not on some rain-soaked island in the Bronze Age.

And I'm a zombie who's afraid of the dark.

Darrick forced his breathing to slow down. He got down on his hands and knees and before he could waffle any longer, crawled into the abandoned mine.

The inside was not white, as Lourana had promised. It was black, pitch black, the blackness of nothing and never. Lourana said there was rock dust on the walls of mines that turned the tunnels white, but this mine was from long ago and maybe they hadn't worried about such things back then. The cave was only a little higher than a man on his knees. A doghole.

As the pale light from the entry began to disappear, he put the flashlight in his teeth and followed the yellow beam.

The floor was almost smooth but the walls were rough. Hand-hewn timbers braced the ceiling, like in an old movie. This mine had been dug with pick and shovel. If there were animals, he didn't see them or hear them, but the light picked up a startling flurry of motion as pale insects with long antennae sprang high and far.

No sounds but the rasp of his breathing and the drag of his boots on the floor.

The flashlight beam picked up a heap of dirty rags, an old book greasy and falling apart, a pail of some kind with a lid. Names had been scrawled on one of the timbers, by kids, he supposed, maybe when Marco was one of those kids. He didn't examine any of it, fearing he would find more bones under those rags.

How far did this mine go? It seemed to trend downward, not by very much. How long could a mine be that was dug by hand? As long as the vein of coal went on, he supposed. It seemed interminable. The walls pressed closer than they actually were, felt as tight as a closet, until he swung his head from side to side to let the flashlight beam reassure him that the mine was not narrowing around him.

Right in the center of the tunnel, a heap of rock made a rough pyramid. He looked up, tracking the light, and saw where a supporting timber had cracked in two, letting the roof cave in. He had to scrabble some of the coal out of the way with his hands to make enough space to crawl through.

The flashlight was fading when he came, at last, to the end. To a wooden door.

The door was roughly carved with some kind of symbol. Maybe it was what he expected to see, or wanted to see, but Darrick was sure it was a lion, the animal he'd seen on the Kavanagh crest. And it was locked, as Marco had reported, from the outside. A large bolt was thrown into a heavy timber frame, sealing the way.

Darrick sat back on his heels. He tried to wiggle the bolt but it was rusted in place like the gate. He pushed on the door but it was deep set into its frame—no give there.

If I die in here, or wherever, no one will ever know. Just like the nurse said, the boy with no name, who would have no wife. No family, no passionate attachments to people or causes. Auditor had pretty much encompassed his life. Until now. Until Lourana. Who had to be on the other side of this door. Darrick felt his heart, or stomach, or whatever do its flip-flops again.

Then he remembered the knife, patting his pockets until he found it. He worked it into the mechanism of the bolt, chipping away at the corrosion. Slow going. He forced the broken end of the blade into the grooves and hammered it with his fist. It drove down to the wood, and he had to work it free. Again. Again. The bolt wouldn't lift, though he'd broken through the rust along the hasp.

He hunched up onto his feet to get more leverage and banged his head into the roof. An explosion of bright stars crossed his vision and he cried out as the wound reopened. He drew his head down but kept his shoulders up, using all the power he could muster to drive the knife deeper into the mechanism.

He slammed the base of his hand against the handle of the knife again, and a piece of the blade flew off and pinged against the wall.

The illumination was fading. Shaking the flashlight brought a little life back. He stabbed the truncated blade into the bolt and its track, panicked by the realization that soon he would not be able to see where to pry.

Once more, he tried to push and pull on the bolt. This time, it began to move. Slowly, wiggling it back and forth, he eased it out of the frame and then opened the door.

With the last bit of the battery's life, he probed the darkness ahead.

The fading yellow beam showed Lourana and Dreama huddled in each other's arms beside shelves of bones, their eyes enormous as they confronted whatever new horror was arriving. For a moment, there was only stunned silence. Darrick had the weird feeling that he had returned to the mine crack, a nightmare he'd never left, but this time dragging others along. And then Lourana said, "Darrick, is that you?"

"Yes."

She released Dreama and stumbled toward him, her feet scattering bones on the floor, pulling him into the room and hugging him so tight that Darrick though she'd break one of his ribs.

"Oh, my God. It is you."

"Who else would it be?"

"I couldn't tell. You're all-over black." He realized that he must look like the miners in those old photos, eyes glaring from a black face like something birthed from the coal itself. Lourana's face burrowed into his shoulder; her breath was warm against his throat. "You came for us. I knew you would." Just then, the flashlight gave out. "I'm so sorry. So sorry," she said.

"It's OK." Darrick tried to orient himself to the door he came in by. "But we need to get out of here now. Dreama? Where are you? Where's Marco?"

He felt Lourana tense against him. He heard her feet shuffle among the bones on the floor.

"Marco?" He stepped away, pulling her away from the skeleton, hearing a bone crack horribly under his feet.

"Mom?" called Dreama plaintively.

And a light flared, blinding them, as the other door swung open and Darrick squinted to see Eamon's bulk filling the entrance. He frantically pulled Lourana but she wouldn't move. She was fixed, staring at an equally frozen Dreama, and he felt the same intense pull against him that must be holding them in place.

"We said he would come to us, but we didn't expect he would find his way through our mountain," Eamon rumbled.

"The only one missing is the reporter." Eamon closed the door behind himself, barring that exit, but there was no need. The force he exerted kept them rooted. Darrick could feel Lourana's hand trembling against his. Or maybe he was the one shaking.

He could not believe how much larger Eamon was than he remembered. Not taller, but wider, a bulk that was almost too much for his legs to support. He seemed to take the air out of the room as he took the strength from Darrick's limbs, a tangible suction. Darrick could see the small door to the mine from the corner of his eye, and he wished he could be back among the familiar and unthreatening insects and broken timbers.

"We came down expecting to learn what we needed," Eamon rumbled, his eyes raking across Lourana. "Which we will."

"We? I only see you," Darrick said. He kept his back stiff and his eyes focused on Lourana, an anchor against the oppressive force that he could blunt but not push back. Eamon was not only bulkier, he was different. The emotion emanating from him was like nothing Darrick had experienced. It was not a howl of fear, like his creatures, but the source of that fear—a deep body sensation like a bass note thrumming just below the level of hearing, an amplified but silent vibration that every bone and tendon seemed to resonate with individually.

"You have grit, we'll say that. Haven't they told you, the Kavanaghs can kill with only their eyes?" Eamon widened his. "Take a body apart? We would hazard Marco did. And then got to experience it."

Darrick didn't much like the feeling he had of being a mouse that a cat has cornered for its play. "He told us about this room, about the skeletons. At least, the ones you haven't had thrown down a hole."

Eamon looked at Darrick with contempt. "This mine you so rudely broke into is sacred ground, dug by Kavanaghs with their own hands. They followed the coal seams and began the fortune that our great-grandfather used to build Knockaulin House. Domnall Kavanagh knew where his strength came from. Right here, from this coal. These are his bones, first to be interred here."

"Old Scratch is at Pleasant Grove," Lourana replied, her voice unnaturally high and strained.

"No Kavanagh goes to a dirt grave. Oh, we have a funeral, a very fine one with a closed casket weighted down with this same Pittsburgh Seam coal, and we put the coffin at the foot of that ancient Celtic cross we had brought from Ireland." Eamon rested his meaty hand against coal gleaming with the buried light of ancient suns. "But the energy that gave form to those bodies? That continues, father to son, as it has all the way back. That is our patrimony."

"You cannibalize your *own family*?" Darrick didn't even try to hide the disgust.

"That's an ugly way of stating it. Consider it conservation of energy." Eamon pushed past Darrick, the mere proximity of his massive frame enough to stagger him. He moved along the shelves of disarticulated bones. "We pass along our vital energy, generation to generation, maintaining our family's legacy. You find that horrible?"

"But it's not just your family, is it?"

"That would be a long wait between feedings. We have learned to be careful about sipping energy from our lessers. Some of the Kavanaghs have been quite abstemious. Our father was no ascetic, but for all the size he amassed from his father before him, and from those he fed upon, look what he comes down to." Eamon patted the blade of a shoulder bone. "Not much more than average. Just average at the bone."

"But there's no one to carry on your legacy."

Eamon made a dark, unpleasant sound. "The absence of evidence is not evidence of absence. We have a son at Wharton. He will take over KCL."

"And you."

He shrugged. "Of course. When my time comes. An organism is either growing or it is dying."

"Sounds like cancer."

"Robber . . . baron." Lourana's voice was tight as a guitar string wound to its breaking point, and her eyes narrowed with the strain. Darrick wondered why she kept drawing Eamon's attention. It was a dangerous thing to do, but he had no way to stop her. She had closed her emotional shield, rebuilt the wall that she'd breached for him.

"We took our father when it was time. And we took our brother." His voice was deep and textured, rough and many layered as a rock cliff. He turned away from the bones to focus on Dreama, huddled on the floor near the shelf where she said Cormac lay.

"The Kavanagh doesn't kill our own. We never really die. Your Cormac is still with us, is he not?" His tone had modulated, and Dreama cried out at the return of her lover's silky voice. "We're all here. All the Kavanaghs." The big man reached down and stroked Dreama's dark hair with the tenderness of Cormac himself, maybe, somehow. She pulled away from his touch, leaving his massive hand suspended ominously above her head.

"And you, Lourana, have been a constant irritant. But not for much longer." He swung around and stared at her. "The greater feeds on the lesser. So it has been forever, since the Kavanaghs were kings in Ireland."

"Who was not a king in Ireland?" Darrick retorted, desperate to avert his attention from Lourana. He could hear the old priest rambling about his homeland in mingled love and despair. "Every hill had its lord of a few cows and a horse or two. I imagine the Kavanaghs starved like the rest when the potatoes failed."

Eamon's anger moved against him, and he felt the lash of it, a burning, sapping pain.

"But we never forgot that we were kings. On the hill of Cnoc Ailinne, we took our place on the sacred stone and were married to the land. The king and his land and his people are one."

"Parasite." Lourana squeaked out, squeezed by a force that Darrick also felt. "Your control . . . slipping . . ."

He shrugged. "The days of coal are ending, so we must find another way. The acid was intentional, as you discovered. Each time we fed, its potency grew, well beyond what we had anticipated. No matter. It served its purpose."

Lourana's eyes showed the loathing she could not express.

Darrick thought about the people who died when the pier collapsed, eaten away by the foul orange mass. He ached with her pain as well as his own, wondered how long she would be able to shield herself. "Let the women go."

"Playing the hero, are you? A knight in shining armor?" Darrick flushed at that. "How charming, that a clerk can have lofty dreams."

"I am not a clerk," he grated. "I'm an auditor."

Eamon laughed again. "One who listens."

"I've had Latin too."

"Then you must know the phrase, *Audientes non audiunt neque intellegunt*. You do not comprehend the forces you face. You think your happenstance link to the brehon tradition is enough to save you? Like Marco relying on his gun," Eamon said with a new eagerness. He kicked the bones, and they rattled across the floor. "There's your friend—a man breathing a short while ago."

"He was a good man."

"A tool, like a hammer. To consume one of them is scarcely noticeable. Marco surprised us with what he yielded, but he was nothing compared to Cormac—and when we took in our father, that was a massive jolt, like being struck by lightning."

A great hand seemed to grip Darrick.

"Now, let's see what there is to you. We've been anticipating."

For the first time, Darrick knew the unabated power of the Kavanaghs. Eamon, or all the Kavanaghs, didn't pulse with common fear or greed or lust, emotions easily deflected. A dark furnace roared within him. Darrick felt himself being forced to his knees. He tried to lock his legs. *I will not kneel to die.*

He felt that familiar lung-emptying sensation, the air leaving him and with it something more. He tried to push back, to rebound Eamon's emotional force against him, but he could do no more than hold him off, and inch by inch he was losing.

Suddenly, Eamon relented.

Darrick whooped air into his body, shook his hands to restore the feeling to them.

"Just a taste," said Eamon, with gloating satisfaction. "Now, let us talk about your future with the Kavanaghs."

"No future." Darrick saw only darkness, and soon.

"You do have a choice. Ally your ancient powers with ours—king and judge, shoulder to shoulder as they once stood, ruler and lawgiver. It's time for the Kavanaghs to expand beyond this little plot of earth."

"You've picked the bones of Carbon County," Lourana accused. Eamon lifted his hand, and she fell against the wall, gasping.

"You'll have to do your ugly business without my help."

Eamon lifted an eyebrow. "It is a loss. We have much in common. Perhaps we'll do you the honor of laying your bones among those of our faithful retainers."

Eamon raised his hands above Darrick and then firmly set them on his shoulders.

Darrick felt something elemental in him being slowly pulled apart. Flesh from bone or mind from body. It was agonizing, pervasive yet individual, as though each cell was being set alight, burned to a cinder. Blowing away. He put his hand out to the coal wall to hold himself upright. Eamon incandesced in his sight like a demon.

Memory of a lesson. Greed, lust, anger, all the fleshly vices were secondary. It was pride that made the devil, he remembered.

Behind Eamon, he saw Lourana moving again, ignored and apparently freed from his control. He wanted her to crawl away through the mouth of the tunnel and out to the clean air and the cold sunshine, but he no longer had control of his throat and tongue. *Don't look at her. Focus on Eamon. Keep his attention.* He pushed back mentally as hard as he could, but it was like trying to hold himself from a tornado's sucking maw.

His eyesight was becoming more distorted. It seemed that Lourana was moving, not away from Eamon, but toward him.

She disappeared from his line of sight, getting away he hoped and not just hiding herself from the inevitable. Then he saw her rise, a long bone in her hand, and she swung with all the force in her body.

The femur struck Eamon in the neck, and despite his size, the blow staggered him. Darrick felt the hands lift from his shoulders and the negative pressure slacked off. He gasped for air. Oxygen burned in his lungs and his heart beat wildly, flooding his body with energy.

Eamon shook himself and turned on Lourana.

She stood with her chin raised and her ridiculous kitten sweatshirt glowing in the harsh light. Eamon bent toward her, a mountain cliff about to fall and crush her. But she stood firm, that long-hardened emotional shield protecting her.

Darrick gathered himself and whatever ability he had been given, and *pushed* as hard as he could.

Eamon grunted, and like a great beast brought to bay, swung back around to face his other enemy. Rage roared through his eyes and forced its way into Darrick's thoughts: *I will consume you, I will consume all of you, I will consume everything.*

As his hands reached for Darrick, Lourana let him have it again, first with the bone club and then with a skull that she bounced off his back.

The distraction or pain, whichever it was, gave Darrick just enough space. He pushed again, and this time he found a corner, a crack, an opening. He pushed until he felt something give. A surprised howl emerged from Eamon's thoughts, and his massive face shifted.

"It's your turn, now," Darrick said, finding himself released. "Judgment day."

The howl increased, becoming audible as well. Eamon's hands opened and closed, he reached, almost grasping Darrick, but his control had ebbed enough that Darrick could slip aside.

Darrick could see Lourana winding up for another blow, like she was aiming for the big-league fences. Just as she cracked Eamon across the middle of his back, Darrick exerted all the force he could, no longer trying to protect himself but actively seeking to hurt this man. To kill him. This man who believed he had the right to the lives of others.

"You make men fear you," he said. "Learn what that feels like."

Eamon's hands dropped to his sides, slack, and he wavered on his feet. He fell against the shelves with a great thud. His face, turned toward Darrick, morphed and settled, then morphed again.

Darrick exulted in his heart. The Kavanaghs would never prey on another person. *I can destroy them.*

Over Eamon's massive shoulder, he saw Lourana, standing with the leg bone still in a two-handed grip and an expression in her eyes that he couldn't quite read.

He had the Kavanaghs and their empire at his feet. He could destroy them. He *should* destroy them, drive a stake through their heart like any vampire. But he remembered a bloodied face. The boy he beat so savagely that one time when he lost control. He could see the wince in the boy's body whenever he came near him, for years afterward. He'd never again struck another person in anger. Now he had more power than even a fantasizing boy could imagine, power that could crush the Kavanaghs.

That's how it starts. That's how you become one of them.

He relaxed his pressure, knowing that something had broken inside the big man, something essential. Eamon's mouth went slack, and his eyes rolled back.

"He's not dead," Lourana said.

"I know."

"You can kill him." He met her unflinching gaze and slowly, ever so gently, shook his head.

She made half a smile. "You did the right thing." He could have killed Eamon willfully, vengefully. She knew that, and her knowledge made him shy.

"I don't regret it."

They watched Eamon breathing, his chest rising and falling. A thread of saliva was sliding from the corner of his mouth.

"You hitting him—that was brave."

"Sometimes a mule just needs a two-by-four to get its attention."

She bent and laid the leg bone down among the scattered skeleton, found the skull and set it back in place. "Marco did his part, at the end."

Darrick went to Dreama and helped her up. "Let's get out of this hole."

Zadie heard brakes squealing and turned, breath caught in her throat, to see a giant red four-by-four shuddering to a stop beside her.

"What the bloody hell are you doing out here?" It was George Fisher, the photographer, his owlish glasses reflecting the sun as he motioned her over.

"Heading for the office."

"Why don't you have your cell on? Where's your car? Never mind. Get in. We got bodies."

She straddled over the railing and ran to the passenger side, the truck so high off the ground that she had to make a sort of Olympic vault to get herself into the seat. The police radio was sizzling with calls.

"What's all that?" she asked.

"A bloody mess." He glanced at her, up and down, and she knew George tended not to miss a thing. "You look like you've been having a bit of a midnight ramble. How'd you manage to miss all the action out there?"

"Where?"

"Fish camp. Where the law enforcement of Carbon County mistook each other for zombies and got into a gun battle."

He filled her in as they rumbled through town. The whole thing had fallen apart as the posse moved through the camp, expecting to flush the zombies out to a "reception committee." The directions didn't stick, however, and as one of the officers got ahead of the line and emerged on the road, an overeager reservist opened fire despite the vest emblazoned with POLICE.

"We've got one in bad shape, life-flighted out to the university med center. Another one is being patched up after he took a runner into a ravine full of greenbrier," he said, slewing the truck to the left. George had a passion for British police procedurals, and the slang had infiltrated his normal western Pennsylvania "yinzer" accent with strange results.

At the scene, a pair of tall state troopers in their Smokey Bear hats were taking witness statements from those volunteers who had not melted away like spring snow as the sun rose higher. It was a sight to see, state police on the ground in Carbon County. Zadie figured they were there because this police-involved shooting had every local department embroiled, but she hoped Darrick's email had already started to do its work. The interviewees had the look of boys who had been prevented from torturing a cat, shamefaced and frustrated at the same time. George darted around getting photos of the site, the police rolling out yellow lines of tape, police photographers taking the same pictures.

One ambulance remained, and that's where she found Junior Barton having his wounds tended. "There was bullets ever'wheres. War zone." Junior, who looked like he'd been tied up inside a bag of weasels, said he had been in Vietnam. "Vietnam," he repeated, saying that he knew what incoming sounded like. "I dove for cover, right quick." Then he returned to examining a swollen wrist.

She found the lead investigator and got a minimal statement; the color for the story would have to come from participants like Junior.

"Nothing in the fish camp but cats and a raccoon we had to shoot," a Redbird patrolman said in disgust. "He might could've been rabid, or maybe just pissed off."

She borrowed George's tablet to send out tweets and post updates to the website. Unfortunately for her, the television news team that had its satellite truck parked right in the way would have the whole story for the evening broadcast. With video.

Back at the office, she was still cursing the realities of the news cycle as she pounded away at the keyboard, riffling through her notebook to find the caliber of the weapons. "Stemple was armed with a Winchester Model 70, according to authorities, while Mayes had a Ruger 9mm pistol. According to his brother, Meryldene Mayes, he had purchased the handgun just two days earlier to defend his family against reported zombies."

The phone on her desk started ringing, and she ignored it—*not now*—but it wouldn't quit, so she answered in her best "leave me alone" voice.

"Person speaking," she growled.

"It's Lourana. You need to come to Knockaulin House."

She flung herself back in her chair, which squealed at the weight, and tried to figure out who was really on the line, Lourana or a creature? It wasn't something you could tell over the phone.

"What's the story?" she asked cautiously.

"It's over. Eamon is out of commission. Darrick defeated him. We have to figure this out. Please come."

Zadie slammed down the phone. "Filing!" she called out to the city editor. "It's a little rough. I need a car—can I take yours?"

"What? Where are you going?"

Zadie held out her hand. "To get a better story. Hold the top of page one for me."

"Better?" He tossed her the keys. "I don't know what you did to your car, but take it easy with mine, OK?"

On the way to Knockaulin House, Zadie tried to scope out all the angles. After Marco, anything was possible. Lourana as a creature. Lourana not changed, but under duress as she had been. Someone pretending to be Lourana. What she couldn't imagine was what she found.

The manor house was dark behind its fences, but then, it seldom showed much light to the public street. The iron lanterns mounted beside the doors glowed amber. She pulled around to the side entrance and was alarmed when the gate silently rolled back to allow her in, until she saw Darrick standing just inside, operating the controls. He was covered with coal dust and his pale eyes stared from that mask, but he was waving her in. She had a bad feeling about being trapped behind those spiked fences and decided to leave the borrowed car on the street and walk into the house. *My babies, I'm gonna be alive to bring you home, I promise.*

"Good seeing you," she said, telling half the truth. Darrick seemed to have aged years since she parted ways with him at the bridge.

"Good to be seen."

Darrick sketched in what had happened, the struggle with Eamon, downplaying his role she was sure. Something terrible had happened in this place, deep under the house. He and Lourana had faced off against the Kavanaghs in a hidden room lined with bones, and somehow, they had won.

They went down many sets of stairs until they came to a heavy wooden door, standing open, and inside she could see black walls and skeletons arrayed on shelves of coal, as he had described them. Eamon Kavanagh lay sprawled on his back, felled like a great tree. His head was in the lap of a whip-slender man in formal dress.

"Is he dead?" Zadie asked.

"No." Lourana had been kneeling in the corner, beside Dreama—alive but haggard—and now she came to Zadie and gave her a hug. "He's in there, somewhere."

The talk must have roused him, because Eamon's eyes came partway open, the blown-out pupils quivering back and forth in formless panic.

"He'll need my care, now," the butler said, stroking the brick-red curls from Eamon's forehead.

Lourana exploded. "Don't you know he was feeding off you?"

"They always took care of us."

"You know that you were going to end up here, like this?" She waved at the skeletons. "Eaten alive?"

"Who do you think tended this place?" The butler looked calmly from Darrick to Lourana. "Tell me that you don't trade the hours of your life for a paycheck. I don't regret it. I've had a very long life, thanks to the Kavanaghs, and a good life, better than a lad without family or prospects had any right to."

Zadie saw Lourana's eyes flick toward Darrick. *Something going on there.*

Darrick, however, was focused on the immediate problem. "There is a hell of a story here, Zadie."

"No doubt." She could see in their faces, drained as they were by a struggle she couldn't imagine, that they knew how this news was presented would decide the course of their lives. They wanted her to tell that story, trusting her, even as they were apprehensive she would spill too much about Darrick. *Oh, duppy, duppy man.* "And I can write the hell out of it."

"Have you called for the emergency car?" pleaded the butler.

"Right now," said Lourana, as she led the way upstairs.

They found a black phone in the kitchen, an implement that seemed to be of a piece with the antique fixtures there. As they waited for the sound of sirens, for police and EMS to converge on the house, they made their plan.

30

"Police are refusing to make additional comments while the investigation progresses, but this much we know: the skeletal remains of seventeen individuals have been removed from a basement crypt here in the Kavanagh mansion. The remains have been transferred to the state crime lab for DNA and dental analysis."

Lourana thought the local TV reporter, though she still had a death grip on the microphone, had started to gain some confidence. She looked directly into the camera with her face set on solemn.

"Meanwhile, authorities are investigating a second location on the Kavanagh mine properties that may link this prominent family with a series of mysterious deaths and disappearances in Carbon County, including that of an environmental activist. Police remain tight-lipped about what they have found in an excavation of the site. For Channel 8 news, Tiffany Smith, reporting."

"Nothing. She didn't advance my story any," Zadie said with satisfaction.

They sat in the living room of Zadie's apartment, a cheerful place with bright drapes and an upriver view of the polluted Broad, less orange that it had been. She'd laid out celebratory cookies and tea, which Lourana drank though she despised tea. There was reason to celebrate: Zadie had been able to break the full story, the biggest of her career, and she'd kept her promise, threading the needle by keeping Darrick's participation to a minimum.

The front page of the *Gazette* was all hers this morning, with exclusive interviews with Lourana and Darrick. But that was almost a sidebar to the bigger story, the one she'd pieced together over weeks: the plot by KCL to destroy the river and bring in a toxic waste dump, and the effort to silence opposition by "disappearing" people, including Darrick, who had given a brief but compelling account of waking in the mine crack. And that was just the start. *Mother Jones* was offering a job; the *Washington Post* and others were calling.

"So does this put the zombie legend to bed?" Darrick asked.

"The psychic has a new video out saying the 'influences were perturbed' but not backing down on her predictions. Someone told her about the Old Scratch legend, stripping the flesh off people, and she's grabbing onto that." Zadie reached for another cookie and held out the plate to Lourana.

"Kavanaghs as zombies?" he responded.

"One more part of the legend. Stories tend to stick around," Lourana said, waving the cookie away. "I figure the Carbon County Zombie is going to enter the state's lore like the Moth Man and the Flatwoods Monster."

The TV news turned to sports, and their conversation drifted for a while before Zadie announced that she had an appointment to keep.

"You've got stories to keep you busy for weeks." Lourana carried her half-full cup to the sink, where she quietly ran it full of water and emptied it before setting it on the counter.

"That's for sure, but this appointment is with my children. They're coming into the bus station in an hour."

Lourana was truly happy for Zadie, but there was no joyous reunion ahead at her house. Dreama was in deep mourning for Cormac; the girl who'd been so proud of her brand-new boots was not the one who had shuffled out of the crypt of Knockaulin House.

Darrick came up behind her, startling her a bit. With a new set of clothes that fit him right, a doctor's visit, and some rest, she supposed he must look more like the man who took that turn off the interstate to Redbird. As she once told him, "That wasn't an exit, that was a new life." It was only a little bit in jest. His gray eyes were clear but shadowed. Not all the damage would heal—she could see that in the lines creased in his face, and hers.

None of us will ever be the same.

Maybe he was reading minds, but Darrick put his arms around her and held her deep and long and with intention.

|||||||||||||| **ACKNOWLEDGMENTS** ||||||||||||||

The author gratefully acknowledges support provided by grants from the North Carolina Arts Council and ArtsGreensboro, and the gift of time and space offered by residencies at the Weymouth Center for the Arts and Humanities.